Beyond Her Calling

THE CHRONICLES OF ALICE AND IVY, BOOK 4

Beyond
Her Calling

by

KELLYN ROTH

Published by Kellyn Roth, Author
Wild Blue Wonder Press

ISBN: 978-1-7341685-4-9

Scripture quotations are taken from the King James Version (KJV).

Cover design by Carpe Librum Book Design
Edited by Andrea Cox

Kellyn Roth, Author
Wild Blue Wonder Press
3680 Browns Creek Road
The Dalles, OR, 97058

contact@kellynrothauthor.com

www.kellynrothauthor.com

For the Jordy to my Tris, the Bingley to my Darcy, the Tigger to my Eeyore, the Finnick to my Katniss—also known as Miss Bailey Ray.

If it makes you feel any better, I didn't ever plan to write the book this way. It just happened. I'm sorry. Kinda.

Love you loads!

Your best friend,
Kell

CHARACTER LIST

Ivy Knight — a young lady with little to do and much to think about.

Alice Strauss — Ivy's now-married twin sister.

Peter Strauss — Alice's new husband, an American reporter.

Mr. Philip and Mrs. Claire Knight — Ivy's parents. Owners of Pearlbelle Park, an estate near the village of Creling in Kent.

Ned, Caleb, Jackie, and Rebecca Knight — Ivy's younger siblings.

Nettie, Tom, Malcolm, Ella, and Deborah Jameson — Ivy's former nanny and her family, who live at the gatehouse.

Kirk Manning — the estate's stable manager, a former stable boy, and a dear friend of Alice before her marriage.

Violet Angel — a dear friend of Ivy's from her time at McCale House, a home in Scotland for mentally challenged young people.

Mr. Rupert and Mrs. Dorothea Angel — Violet's parents.

Mrs. Daphne Wright (Aunt Daphne) — Violet's maternal aunt, a widow.

Agnes and Duncan Graham — Aunt Daphne's maid and her illegitimate young son.

Dr. Callum and Mrs. Emma McCale — the founders of McCale House.

Dr. Jordy McAllen — Dr. McCale's young ward, now a doctor himself.

Mr. Albert and Mrs. Annis McAllen — Jordy's parents, residents of the village of Keefmore in Scotland.

Edith, Benjamin, Michael "Mick," William, and Thomas McAllen — Jordy's siblings.

Tristan "Tris" Kendrick — Jordy's best friend and his sister Edith's sweetheart.

Ena Owen — a young half-Irish widow from the village of Keefmore who is currently being ignored.

Bridget Owen — Ena's only living child.

Mairi Blakely — Bridget's best friend.

SCOTS TRANSLATION GUIDE

Ach = "oh" or "ah;" sometimes used to express frustration or disagreement, as in "ugh"

Are no' = are not

A'right = all right

Aye = yes

Bairn = child

Blether = babble, talk nonsense

Bonnie = pretty

Braw = fine, good, nice-looking

Burn = stream, brook

Canna = cannot

Canny = clever; can also mean pleasant or nice

Changeling = a fairy or other inhuman creature who was swapped at birth with a human child

Chitter = chatter; to shiver

Clipin' = tattling

Coos = cows

Couldna = could not

Crabbit = crabby

Da = dad, father

Dafty = silly, foolish

Didna = did not

Dinna = do not/don't

Doesna = does not

Dreich = dull or gloomy, often referring to bad weather

Drookit = extremely wet, absolutely drenched

Eve = evening

Fash = to fret, get upset, or be angry

Faye = fairy, fairies

Flichterin' = fluttering

Glaikit = foolish, thoughtless

Gowk = from "gawk," meaning to stare vacantly; a fool

Hasna = hasn't
Havena = haven't
Havering = to talk foolishly, to chatter
Intae = into
Isna = isn't
Is't = is it
Ken = know
Ken't = knew
Lad/Laddie = boy, young boy
Lass/Lassie = girl, young girl
Loch = lake
Me = my
Minna = minute
Morn = morning
Nae = no
Needna = need not
No' = not
Noo = now
O' = of
Ontae = onto
Oot = out
Shouldna = shouldn't, should not
Tae = to, too
Tha' = that
'Til = until
'Twill = it will
'Twould = it would
Up tae high doh = to be in a state of nervous excitement
Verra = very
Wasna = was not/wasn't
Wean = literally "wee one;" a young child or baby
Wee = small/little
Wee Folk = small, imaginary beings; elves, fairies, or leprechauns
Weel = well
Werena = were not/weren't
Wha' = what
Wi' = with
Wi'oot = without
Willna = will not/won't

Wouldna = wouldn't
Ye = you
Ye'd = you would; you had
Yer = your
Ye're = you're
Yers = yours
Yerself = yourself

"For I know the thoughts that I think toward you, saith the Lord, thoughts of peace, and not of evil, to give you an expected end."

~Jeremiah 29:11~

CHAPTER ONE

September 1881
Pearlbelle Park
Kent, England

Ivy Knight hummed a soft tune as she paused at the crest of the hill. Below her, a gently rolling landscape swept down to her father's estate house. To the right, a small glade of trees filled a crease in the hill, and a lake sat between the house and the sunny rise where she stood. It was a beautiful view, with the trees' green leaves interrupted, in small increments, by yellow and orange.

"Come now, Ivy." Behind Ivy, her twin sister Alice set the picnic basket down and rubbed her hands together to remove any threat of blisters. "This is as good a place as any to have our lunch."

They were hatless, since Alice hated hats and she said this was her last day to be a girl—though Ivy thought her twin sister had probably started being a woman long ago. Maybe even before she needed to. Their hair was intricately braided and twisted in buns, and they wore pale-green sprigged muslin dresses. Matching was important. It was the last day. Things had to be perfect.

Ivy offered a tremulous smile. "I'm glad it's not raining."

Alice glanced up from the basket she had just opened. "Yes, darling. I'm glad, too. Would have put an awful damper on our picnic, now, wouldn't it?"

Ivy nodded. "Though you would have made us go anyway." There was nothing Alice hated more than weakness.

Alice chuckled. "I suppose I would have. I think it's important that we spend some time together before I leave. I care about you very much, and I'd hate to waste a moment. Here, help me, won't you?"

They unfolded the old tablecloth they'd stolen from the kitchen and placed it flat on the ground.

"Just so!" Ivy patted down the edges and raised her eyes to Alice, forcing her lips to turn upward. Since the smile couldn't be maintained for long, she dropped to her knees. "Mrs. Bennett put her ginger biscuits in! Those are my favorite."

"That's grand."

Ivy leaned back and brought her knees up to her chest while Alice set out their picnic. Alice was quite intent upon doing things for herself lately.

"Are you excited to leave?" Ivy forced the words past the sudden lump in her throat. She hated herself the moment they left her lips. She shouldn't have darkened their beautiful day with reminders of the dreaded tomorrow. Today was the present; afterwards followed the future and nothing more. She couldn't hop back and forth between them, or she'd cry again.

Even the music in her head stopped when she thought about Alice leaving. It had always been her twin's job to take care of her, although they were the same age, due to Ivy's problems.

Alice glanced toward the manor, eyes darkening, then back at Ivy. Her lips were also trembling. "Yes, I am excited. I'm a little afraid, too. It didn't seem real until we bought the tickets and started packing." She paused for a minute and twisted her hands in her lap. "God would never ask me to carry more than I can. Still, it's frightening!" She shuddered, then smiled. "Will you be all right?"

Ivy bobbed her head up and down emphatically so Alice wouldn't think she was selfish. "Yes. I'll be perfectly all right. I have so much to do here! Why, I can play my piano or walk on the estate, and Ned promised to teach me a game."

Alice raised her eyebrows. "What game?"

16

"I don't know—some game he plays," Ivy said. Ned was becoming an increasingly active little boy, as was Caleb, and they had so many occupations that Ivy couldn't keep track of them all.

Alice's brow furrowed. "Tennis? That's his most recent obsession."

"That's the one! It doesn't sound too hard."

Alice cocked her head to the side. "It's not, I suppose. Just don't let him make you do it unless you want to, darling. I don't want you overtiring yourself." She squeezed Ivy's arm before returning her eyes to the basket.

"I won't." It was an easy promise to make; there wasn't much risk of exhaustion when her entire life was so void of activity.

"Good." Alice passed Ivy a sandwich. "We haven't gotten to talk much in these last few months." She sucked her bottom lip into her mouth and worried it between her teeth. "I wish I'd spent more time with you. I've just been so busy."

Ivy understood. Though Alice hadn't really been doing anything much since she became engaged to Peter Strauss almost a year ago, she had seemed busy. They were always together. Ivy felt just a little bit left out. But she supposed it was the way things were supposed to be. Girls grew up, they got married, and they forgot about their sisters.

Still, it ached.

"But we have today," Alice continued. "Today is about us."

"We can write to each other," Ivy said. "You'll remember, won't you?"

"How could I *not* remember—you remind me every fifteen minutes." Alice's eyes sparkled. "But, yes, we will write to each other."

"Almost every day?" Ivy suggested.

"Yes, almost every day."

Ivy nodded, content, and took a bite of her sandwich. Alice could sometimes forget things like letter-writing, and Ivy wasn't taking any chances of being forgotten. After all, Alice didn't have any excuses. Even a hatred of writing wasn't a justification when it came to one's sister. Alice had to write; Ivy needed her to. That was all there was to it.

"What will you do while I'm gone? Besides learn tennis and write letters, I mean."

Ivy blinked. "I don't know."

"Mm. I'm sure something will come to you. You have your music and our family and ... other things." Alice handed Ivy a glass of lemonade. "Careful—this ground isn't level enough to set it on. Perhaps you can concentrate more on your music now that I'm not here to bother you."

Ivy nodded, though she wasn't too excited about the prospect. Alice had never really "bothered" her, especially now that Peter seemed to take so much of her time, and Ivy already devoted at least half the day to her music. Yes, she loved it, but it would be nice to do something else. Sometimes even doing the thing she loved most could get boring.

Ivy had to try several times before the next sentence got out. "What will you do in America?" She didn't want to make Alice sad. She was glad for her. Really, she was. It was just so hard to give up her sister.

"At first we'll stay with Peter's family. Then we'll get our own house. Probably a small place—maybe an apartment. But I hope—" A slight smile flickered across her lips. "I hope we'll need more room. I want to start a family."

"That's nice." It was also nearly all Alice talked about, actually, and though Ivy did like children, she was sure there was some other conversation topic they could pursue.

"Indeed, it will be. A girl, of course, and a great many boys. Odd to be nineteen and thinking about children already, isn't it? I don't feel as old as I am."

Ivy knew that statement was much truer of her than of Alice, although her "thinking of children" was more wishful dreams than reality. She wanted children of her own, and of course a husband, but that seemed unlikely. No man would marry someone like Ivy.

Alice interrupted her dour thoughts. "Ivy, I feel as if I should have this ginger biscuit before I finish my lunch. Would that be terribly wicked of me?"

Ivy blinked, snapping back into reality at this outrageous suggestion. "Yes, it would be! You're always supposed to finish the main course before dessert."

"Who says so?"

"Mother."

Alice smirked. "Guess what?"

"What?"

"Mother isn't here right now." Alice took a biscuit from the tin and bit down. "Delicious. Have one?"

"*Alice,*" Ivy hissed.

"What? I'm not getting in trouble, Ivy." She grinned. "I'm grown now. If you think having a biscuit is going to keep me from eating my lunch, then you're wrong."

Ivy scowled. "I can't let you do it alone. Pass me one," she said, resigned.

Alice laughed. "Now I feel dreadful, tempting my sister on the path to destruction and bad eating habits." She handed Ivy the tin. "Just let the flavor of evilness envelop you."

Ivy glared. "You're going to ruin the taste."

"Only if you let it be ruined. Go on. I dare you!"

Ivy took a bite. It was delicious—even more so because she wasn't already full. She couldn't keep her smile back.

"See? Isn't it sinfully tasty?"

Ivy almost choked with laughter. "I wouldn't put it that way."

Alice dropped onto her back and stared up at the few wispy clouds painting the sky. "It's a beautiful day," she murmured. "I don't want it to end."

Feeling the exact same way but having no words to express it, Ivy nodded. Somewhere in the back of her mind, the words pounded: *last day, last day, last day.* But she ignored them. Better to focus on the present and smile back at the past than to worry about a future so unsure. A future *without* Alice.

"We'll come visit, eventually," Alice said.

Ivy would have glared at her twin if her eyes were open. Hadn't she just resolved not to think about the future?

"And there will be children. You'll be an aunt. Won't that be strange?"

"Yes. It will be strange." Because if Alice was old enough to be a mother, so was Ivy, and that couldn't be true. But, of course, though they were only a few minutes apart in age, Alice was years ahead of her mentally. Ivy was just *less*.

Alice sighed. "But a good strange. A wondrous strange. I've never wanted anything more than this, Ivy. I can't explain it. It's just the feeling of all my life's goals coming together as one and everything being perfect. This is my calling."

Ivy jerked upright, trying to shake the melancholy melody in her heart. Glad that Alice was so happy, she wouldn't let the ugly envy invade. Their relationship was too precious. *Alice* was too precious. What mattered was that Ivy loved her and, even if a distance of thousands of miles separated them, they were still sisters. Still best of friends.

But it was so hard to be *Ivy* when her sister was so very *Alice*. Hard to be content when her sister fell in love, married, and began a brand-new life—one Ivy could never have. If only she was worthy of Alice's life.

"Alice?" Ivy said after a long moment of silence.

"Yes?"

"Do you ... do you think I have a calling?"

Alice opened her eyes and pushed herself up on her elbow. "Why do you ask?"

"I just wondered."

There was a long beat of rest before Alice answered. "God has a plan for everyone's life. He has a plan for me. I'm sure now that plan is following Peter to America as his wife and being the mother to his children. As for you ..." Alice noticeably swallowed. "I can't say what

God wants for your life. It's between you and Him. But we can serve God best through our daily life. Loving our family, being a help to them as best we can—that sort of thing."

Ivy waited, but Alice didn't continue. She just sipped her lemonade and looked out over Pearlbelle Park's grounds.

"Is that all I can do?" Ivy asked at last. "Do you think ... do you think I don't have a calling?"

"No, darling, no. Of course not! Calling is about coming to Christ —and how we serve Him. But our manner of serving depends on the individual. Some people are equipped to go out into the world and be missionaries. To help people. To do great things. But some of us—it says in the Bible, 'Whatsoever ye do, do it heartily, as to the Lord, and not unto men.' No matter what you do in your life, you must do it to the glory of God."

Ivy nodded. "But what is it I'm supposed to do?"

Alice literally squirmed, and Ivy knew whatever she was going to say next wasn't going to be pleasant. "I don't know, but perhaps what you're doing now ... That might be it. Be content with what you have. God has given you more than enough."

Ivy waited for Alice to offer further explanation, but she didn't, and Ivy realized that what her twin was saying was that she shouldn't want more than she had. That what she had now might be all she'd ever get. All God planned to give her. Bowing her head, Ivy understood the truth. She was not enough of a person to truly live life —not the way she wanted, at least.

All around her, bells clanged in alarm, and she fell silent for the rest of the day, overwhelmed by the cacophony.

CHAPTER TWO

Creling, Kent

Ivy wrapped Peter in the tightest hug she could muster and held on. He returned it gladly, almost picking her up off the ground, then released her. She stepped back, pulling her coat tighter as a sudden draft of cold air hit. Summer was turning to autumn, slowly but steadily, and the early morning breeze confirmed it.

"You take care of yourself, all right, little sister?"

Ivy smiled, warmth filling all the hollow places in her soul, if only for an instant. Peter was the dearest man, always kind and caring no matter how early in the morning—though Ivy knew Peter woke up with much grumbling and begging for coffee, so being kind was sometimes a challenge even for him. But he took care of Alice, which was not something her sister let many men do.

"We'll come visit as soon as we can." He winced. "Granted, it might not be for a few years, but we'll write and tell each other everything." He squeezed her shoulder with a gentle smile. "It will be just like we're here. I promise."

Ivy jumped as she remembered, nearly falling into the wall of the ticket booth at her side. "Oh, will you remind Alice to write? Every day? She promised she would, but sometimes she gets wrapped up in things and forgets."

Peter chuckled, eyes crinkling at the edges. "Yes, Ivy, I'll remind her. Though I'm sure she won't forget. Believe it or not, she really does want to write to you. Don't worry."

Ivy smiled as bravely as anyone in her circumstances could manage. Her breath was catching in her throat, though, and she wasn't sure how long she could keep the tears at bay. "I'll try not to. It's hard sometimes. I'll miss Alice so much."

Peter took her hand and pressed it. "I know. I understand. It's hard to leave someone you love. Why, I got upset when I went to college and had to leave my family. A bit homesick anyway."

Ivy's breath evened out at his words. That was what she loved about Peter. He was never ashamed to admit his emotions, even the ones most men would call weak—like grief, disappointment, or missing someone until it hurt. Admitting them didn't make him weak. It made him stronger, which, in turn, made her feel braver.

"You'll take care of Alice, won't you?" Ivy furrowed her brow. "I know she doesn't act like it, but sometimes she needs someone to love her, too. She has all kinds of emotions, but she never shows them to anyone."

Peter chuckled, though Ivy didn't see anything amusing about what she'd said. "Yes, I'll take care of Alice. She'll always have me."

Ivy flung her arms around his neck and gave him another quick hug. "You're the best man in the world!" She stepped back and straightened her hat. "I think Alice is lucky to have you."

Peter grinned. "Thank you, Ivy. I think I'm lucky to have her—but, either way, I'm glad she's mine." He took a deep breath. "We'll do fine, I'm sure. It might take some getting used to, as Alice has to learn to live in a completely different world, but we'll do fine."

The train whistle blew again, and Alice disentangled herself from her younger siblings and Nettie, a dear family friend. "We need to board."

Peter shrugged. "I'm sure we have another few minutes."

Alice's face tightened in frustration—Ivy knew her sister wasn't exactly the best example of patience. "What else have we to do? We've said good-bye six times to everyone." Alice tugged gently at his arm.

Peter placed his hand over his wife's and smiled. "There's no rush. Let's take our time with these good-byes."

The whistle practically shrieked this time. Alice insisted they find a compartment, and Peter complied. He kissed Ivy's cheek, said one last farewell to their little siblings, and walked toward the train with Mr. and Mrs. Knight, who would be accompanying them to London and to the docks. They would be the ones to say the last good-byes to their eldest daughter.

Alice lingered, eager as she had been to leave earlier. She held Ivy close and dropped her lips close to her ear. "I love you, Ivy. I promise to write. Just remember that it will take a month or so for the first letter to arrive—or longer, perhaps. It doesn't mean I've abandoned you."

"Oh, I know." Ivy held Alice even closer. "I'll miss you so much."

"I'll miss you, too." Alice pulled away and darted off to catch up with Peter and her parents. In moments, the train started to move, chug-chugging its way to London in a thrumming, accented beat.

Alice was gone.

As Anna, the children's nanny, rounded up Ivy's younger siblings and got them into the carriage, Ivy watched the smoke from the steam engine disappear into the distance. Her brain had registered the loss, but her emotions lagged far behind. It couldn't be. Not see Alice for years? What would she do? How would she survive? There were too many questions and too few answers, and Ivy felt her throat tighten again.

She chose to take a seat in the second carriage, separate from the little ones. Much as she loved them, they were noisy and rambunctious, and she needed time to herself. She needed peace and quiet—and a private place to cry.

The first few days were difficult, but Ivy could ignore the pain. It took a significant amount of prayer and about as much music, but she could do it.

In a week Mother and Papa arrived home. With her parents there, Ivy was sure to find something to do. Perhaps she could be a comfort to them now that they'd bidden farewell to their eldest. Perhaps Ivy was who they wanted, *needed*, couldn't do without.

On their first day back, she went to find her mother, hoping she'd want to sit down and talk. Perhaps they'd be able to have one of their discussions, like they used to, about the Bible and God. She felt that if she could refocus—redirect her attention to Him and cast off her fears and worries—everything would be all right.

Mrs. Knight was speaking with the housekeeper about the menus. When Ivy tried to talk to her, she shooed her off.

"Later, perhaps?" she asked. "I need to make a few changes, dearest." Then she returned to the housekeeper, her back to Ivy as if she didn't exist.

Her father's reaction was similar. He was buried "up to his ears" in correspondence, as he so vividly described, and "could they talk about this later?"

Heartbroken, Ivy walked slowly out of his office and into the garden. Thankfully, it was a warm day for September, sunny once again, and she didn't need to run upstairs and get her coat. Not that she would have, regardless; she wasn't in the mood to delay.

From the garden, she circled around the house, trying to think of some way to entertain herself. She'd heard that "the devil makes work for idle hands," and she would hate for that to happen.

Most of the flowers had faded already, and the leaves had started to turn brown and fall. She scuffed a pile of them up with her foot and watched them twirl back to the ground, a few getting caught up in the light breeze and flurrying along the path.

At last she came to the stables. Ivy disliked horses as much as she had as a child. She'd never ridden one. Open carriages frightened her, as did walking across a street—or even along the pavement, if it was too narrow. But she went in anyway, knowing that the horses that weren't out to pasture were safely in their stalls, unable to trample her.

As she walked along the aisle, a few horses stuck their heads out to greet her; many had either been shut up behind the top portion of their Dutch-door stalls or simply didn't care about the young woman walking outside their domiciles. She had expected to find the stables empty at this time of day, except perhaps for a stray stable boy—most of the staff would be in the training paddock—so she was surprised to see a man leaning against one of the stall doors.

At her light footstep, he turned and smiled. "Miss Ivy." He removed his cap, which had slumped down over his bright-green eyes. "Miss Knight, I suppose I should say."

Ivy cocked her head to the side. "Mr. Manning?"

"Right." Mr. Kirk Manning, the manager of the Knights' stables, returned his eyes to the stall. "Just checking on one of the mares. I wanted to make sure she was taken care of."

Weren't there younger staff for that? "That's not your job anymore."

Mr. Manning laughed. "I think I have horse blood flowing in my veins. I still feel like the stable boy I used to be, only then I was doing it to support my family. Now I could get a job elsewhere, I suppose, but I'm here because this is my sustenance."

Ivy narrowed her eyes as she tried to categorize this unfamiliar word in her mind. She thought she had a rough definition—but, no, that didn't make sense. "Sustenance?"

Mr. Manning hesitated. "I don't know if I can explain it. It's what makes you get up in the morning—that indescribable gift from God that directs your future and your calling." He sighed. "I suppose it's not much, but I love horses, even though these beauties aren't my own."

A slow smile took over Ivy's face. "I understand. I thought for a moment that you meant you ate them."

Mr. Manning burst out laughing. When he recovered, he shook his head. "Never! That would be such a waste."

Ivy didn't know why it would be a waste—if he ate horses, then he wouldn't be squandering them—but she nodded.

He let himself into the stall and patted the horse's side. "What have you been doing lately? I can hear the piano playing sometimes when I'm in your father's office. Sounds lovely."

Ivy beamed at the praise, but she almost wished she didn't play often enough that Mr. Manning felt obligated to comment on it. After all, there should be more to her life than music, shouldn't there?

"I love playing. I suppose you could say it's my sustenance. Or at least it used to be." She still loved music—it cleared her head and helped her gain mental and spiritual balance. But lately, it hadn't been enough. Chords clashed raucously in her mind at night and played in minor keys during the day. That probably meant it wasn't a useful source of calling, as Mr. Manning described, right?

"Oh?" Mr. Manning gave her a sympathetic look. "I suppose if you do anything continually—even something that you love with a passion—you're likely to get tired of it eventually. It's human nature, I suspect, fickle as it may be."

Ivy cocked her head. "Do you ever get tired of horses?"

Mr. Manning crossed the aisle, opened the stall door opposite, and stepped in with a dainty bay mare. "Sometimes I get tired of ... of life. I don't want to do anything. But I force myself to live until I learn what it was I was living for in the first place." He paused. "Sometimes you need to look at your life and think, 'Is this the best way I can honor God?'"

Ivy wished he'd go on, eager for even the slightest information on what God might want her to do.

But, instead, he turned away from her and pinched the back of the horse's foreleg. The mare shifted her weight and let Mr. Manning examine the underside of her hoof. "She stepped on a rock, and Miss Parker didn't notice. That girl is going to grind every horse we own into the dirt. She doesn't pay attention. She's insensitive to the horse's needs." He grunted in annoyance.

Ivy understood. She loved Posy, her cousin who visited occasionally with Uncle Charlie and Aunt Lois, but she could be unfeeling, especially when she wanted something.

"The mare's healing well. Easy, girl—that's a good girl."

Ivy didn't know what to say to that, so silence reigned until Mr. Manning spoke again.

"I've always wondered—what was Scotland like?" Mr. Manning said as he examined the mare's knee with his hands.

Ivy wrinkled her nose. "Scotland?" That didn't seem like a natural progression of the conversation. She supposed he was trying to prevent silence. She'd never understood why everyone felt such a need to fill the day with words. The sound of silence was the most beautiful in the world, and that was saying something.

Ivy loved good sounds—birds chirping, the sea, the wind. Her mother's laughter. Her sister's voice. The click-click of Nettie's knitting needles. But most sounds weren't beautiful. Screams, trains, and most animal noises frightened her. She could hear God best in the silence.

"Yes, Scotland." Mr. Manning's voice shook her out of her reveries. "You did go to Scotland and stay at an, er, school, didn't you? Mc ...?"

"McCale House," Ivy supplied. "Though I suppose you know it wasn't exactly a school, Mr. Manning. It was a place for people like me, who can't think right. That was six years ago now. I've only visited once since then."

She'd forgotten about how she missed McCale House and the people who lived there. Abrupt but caring Dr. McCale, gentle and serious Mrs. McCale, Violet—her dear, confused friend. Jordy McAllen, a young man whom Dr. McCale had been schooling to become a doctor, would probably still be in London. Last she'd heard, he was working at a hospital there. She hadn't seen him since she was thirteen, but she still missed his jokes and silliness—and the caring boy who listened well behind the wide grin and boisterous attitude.

"I see." Mr. Manning moved to examine the other hoof. "I believe you think all right, though. I've never seen any evidence to the contrary. Maybe you just think a little different, and maybe you get confused or frightened from time to time. But I think we all do."

It was kind of Mr. Manning to say that, but she shook her head. "I wish that were true. I wish it was all right for me to think a little different, and I wish I didn't get any more confused and frightened than anyone else. But, you see, no one wants me." She took a big gulp of hay-scented air, which helped somewhat with the growing tightness in her throat. Being different was hard.

Mr. Manning rose from his knees and patted the horse's side. "She'll be all right." He stepped out of the stall and fastened the door. "It's a matter of perspective, I suppose. But I believe you're something special, Miss Ivy. So did your sister, I think. Even sisters who are only a few minutes older like Alice tend to smother with their love a bit." He winked. "I'd best get on with my day. I hope to see you again sometime. I admit I don't talk to people as much as I used to." He shrugged. "That's my own fault."

"I hope to see you again soon, too," Ivy said, but her mind was too focused on other thoughts to say more. She drifted away without another word, her mind on Scotland and people who thought differently.

CHAPTER THREE

That night, Ivy couldn't sleep. This wasn't an unusual occurrence; she tended to toss and turn in bed. However, tonight was worse. She was wide awake, not even the slightest bit sleepy. At last, she stood and pulled on her dressing gown and slippers.

She made her way down the hall to the upper floors. As she knew the house well, she wasn't afraid of the dark. Something about growing up had taught her that, in her own home, nothing could hurt her. She felt safe here and could walk about in the pitch black without hesitance.

Outside of Pearlbelle Park was another matter, of course. Her emotions took over her mind away from home. Here, at least, there was peace.

In the small music room, distant enough from the rest of the house to not bother anyone when she chose to play the piano late at night, she found a lamp and matches. A soft glow soon filled the room. She set the lamp atop her piano and lowered herself onto the bench.

There was no fire in the hearth, and the room was chilly, but she hardly noticed. Placing her hands on the keys, she began to play a soft, melancholy tune, influenced heavily by Beethoven's *Moonlight Sonata* but not note for note. It was a wistful, gentle version, with all the agony and loneliness—and none of the monotony. Unless called upon to do so when performing for family or friends, she rarely followed sheet music. She imitated, never copied.

As she played, she allowed her mind to wander away, to Scotland with its castles and crags, to McCale House, gray against the green fields in the spring.

"I want to go there."

Her hands slid off the keys for a moment, then she returned them. The music grew louder, wracked with sorrow.

"I won't," she whispered. "I can't. I need to stay here. I can't run off to McCale House and think all my problems will be solved like they were last time. That's not how it works. I need to let God be my Guide. I need to stop looking for other people to heal me. I am ... I am what I am. Only God can change that."

She kept playing, trying to exorcise the inner demons that made her feel so helpless, so worthless. So deprived. Almost angry.

I'm not angry. I'm never angry.

But the emotion that tightened her chest felt like anger. Anger that she was born into this useless state. Anger that her family didn't believe she could ever be more than a child. Anger that she was not like Alice, like her other siblings, like any other woman in the world.

"Oh, God," she murmured, "I don't want to be like this. I don't want to be bitter! But how can I help it? I know I can't handle life. I know I can't handle people. I know I lose control and am afraid. I'm so afraid of ... of everything, God. I know I should trust in You to take away that fear, but it seems to be such a huge part of me. I am my fear. I am ... I am less, I suppose. I don't think the same way. I don't act the same way.

"Lord, I've heard what they say about me. I'm an idiot. A fool. I'm not *enough*. There's nothing that I can do in this world besides keep out of the way and try not to shame my family. But I want more, Lord. Perhaps what I'm asking is for You to make me content. Make me ... make me want what I have already. Make me want to simply be the best daughter and sister I can be. Make the aching go away."

She sat there silently for a minute, eyes closed, trying to hold the tears back. She thought she'd come to peace with herself, but, at this moment, she doubted she would. She knew the old demons would always be there, ready to haunt her when she most needed them to stay away.

"You are what I made you to be."

Frustrated, Ivy banged on the piano keys, wincing at the discord. *You didn't make me enough,* she protested. *You made me an idiot. Why? Why me? I don't understand. I don't see why I'm the one who You chose to suffer so. Why this way? Why in a way that attacks me from the inside? I could bear a physical ailment. I could bear it if I couldn't walk as well as other women or something like that. But why my mind?*

"You are enough for your purpose."

I have no purpose.

"You have a purpose which I gave you."

Exhausted, Ivy slid off the bench and curled up on the floor, held her knees up to her chest, tried not to sob.

"I made you beautiful. I made you lovely, inside and out. I made you smart and capable of whatever you set your mind to. I made you sweet, loving, kind. I made you to take your place in the world, the place I'd designed for you since before time began."

Ivy wanted to believe it. She really did. But her heart wasn't so easily persuaded. After all, everyone she'd loved told her it wasn't true. She wasn't really enough. It couldn't be true. Yes, God loved her. Yes, He had made her as she needed to be to survive in this life. But she didn't have a purpose—a calling. She was just meant to be Ivy. Useless, meaningless Ivy.

She turned toward the piano again, picking herself up and sitting on the bench. Only this time she didn't play—she prayed.

In words muddled and incoherent, she begged her Lord to direct her path, to show her what she needed to do to serve Him. She admitted her fears, her weaknesses, her doubts. She asked for contentment, then settled back, waiting for it to come.

Yet, instead of the rush of peace and joy Ivy anticipated, she grew uneasy and paced up and down the room, wringing her hands. She played some worried Mozart and then Bach. Next she moved to the more modern Chopin, but even the prettiest little tune came out stressed.

Frustrated, she went out onto the balcony, not noticing the bitter cold. A few deep breaths, and the battle was won. She opened her heart, and it came to her in a rush.

"I need you in Scotland."

Scotland? Ivy's brow wrinkled in confusion. What did He want with her there? But, even through the lack of understanding, her purpose remained clear. Had it been written in the bright stars twinkling overhead, it couldn't have been more intelligible.

But what then?

The next morning, Ivy arose and made her way down to the breakfast room. This was the only meal of the day where everyone was sure to be there, and, in truth, she treasured it.

She slid onto her seat between Rebecca and Ned and absently thanked the footman who had helped her—even though she'd been told time and time again that she wasn't supposed to notice servants.

On the other side of the table, there were two empty chairs—one for Alice and one for Peter. It almost shook Ivy out of her good mood, but not quite. She had something to do now, even if it wasn't much.

As the conversation about the table rattled on, Ivy didn't listen. She concentrated on her plans. But they were dreadfully vague. How would she get to Scotland? What would she do there? She couldn't visit McCale House more than a week before she'd start to become a burden. Then what?

But God's instructions were clear as ever: *"Go."*

"Ivy, did you hear me?"

Ivy's head jerked up, and she felt her face grow warm as everyone at the table looked at her expectantly.

"What ... what did you say?" she asked.

"I wondered why you seem so preoccupied." Mother smiled. "You haven't said a word since you came down."

"It's unlike you," Papa said. "Usually you at least say good morning."

Ivy cleared her throat. "I'm making a plan."

"Oh?" Papa's lips quirked up in a smile; he must find her amusing. "A plan for what, Ivy?"

"A plan for my future," Ivy said with as much dignity as she could muster with her father's condescending smile trained on her.

"Ah, I see." There was no amusement on Mother's face, to Ivy's great relief. "What do your plans include, dearest?" She was focused on helping Rebecca butter a muffin, and Ivy felt slightly safer with her mother's eyes off of her.

"I'm going to Scotland," said Ivy.

Again, all eyes were on her.

"Perhaps to McCale House at first," she continued, forcing herself not to be embarrassed. This was what God wanted from her. She wasn't ashamed of it, even if her family was going to be shocked at first. "It's what God wants. I know it."

"Oh." Mother glanced at her younger children, then returned her gaze to Ivy. "Dearest, can we talk about this after breakfast? I'd like to sit down with you and have a serious conversation. This is quite the claim you're making, you realize."

"We can talk," Ivy said, "but it won't change anything. I ... I know this is what He wants. He told me."

Thankfully, Mother didn't seem to think she was insane, although she obviously wasn't quite convinced. "We'll see."

In the sitting room after breakfast, Mother closed the door and came to sit on the lounge next to Ivy. Papa took a seat on a chair opposite. At least her father hadn't called her into his office and sat her down across from him at the desk. She wasn't in trouble. She was an adult now—if she told herself that often enough, she could almost believe it—and she was having an adult conversation with her parents.

Ivy wasn't exactly the average young lady. If she had been, she would have experienced the social season in London, been courted and called upon, danced and gone to operas—and married—like Alice. However, that wasn't to be.

The few times when she'd made an appearance in the drawing room with her mother and sister, she'd inevitably ended up making a fool of herself. Besides, she could hear the whispers, see the cutting glances. The world thought her insane and seemed to think madness was catching. They also seemed to think that insanity and deafness were more closely linked than in reality.

Mother was the first to speak. "So you think God wants you in Scotland?"

"I don't think, Mother. I know."

Her eyebrows raised. "Very well. What makes you *know* that?"

"I'm ... I'm not sure I can explain," Ivy said. "Last night, I was playing the piano and asked God to give me peace. Then I knew it. It was something that *was*, not something I could question. I am to go to Scotland."

Mother was quiet for a long moment, her eyes focused on a point above Ivy's head. "Philip," she said at last, "I know it's strange, but I feel as if ... What does it hurt?"

"I thought you were the one who said that Ivy needed to stay close to home." Papa gave her a curious look.

Mother sighed. "I didn't take into account one thing." She smiled to herself. "True, Ivy wasn't safe in London, and I wouldn't let her go there. But what does it hurt for her to go to Scotland? To McCale House, for a time? Just a few weeks. Then perhaps she'll be ready to come home. If God really does want her in Scotland, she'll find her purpose there quickly. If not, she can come home—and, in the meantime, she's safe with the McCales. I trust them. She does have an open invitation—Dr. McCale told me many of his past students visit."

Ivy was growing frustrated with being spoken of as if she weren't in the room. Of course, she was accustomed to it, but lately, it'd started to wear on her. "I'll go, then?"

"Yes," Papa said slowly. "You'll go, as long as Dr. McCale agrees that this is a good time for you to visit. I'll write him and ask."

Ivy's heart leaped in her chest, and she pushed to her feet. "I'll start packing."

Papa laughed. "Wait a minute, young lady. Don't get ahead of yourself. We don't have Dr. McCale's assent yet. We have to wait."

"Oh, it will happen." Ivy smiled. "God wants it."

Ivy's optimism waned during the weeks that followed, but, at last, they received a reply from Dr. McCale.

Dear Mr. and Mrs. Knight,

I was happy to receive your letter. We would be delighted to have Ivy come stay with us. We all remember her well, and we had hoped she would come see us again soon—the sooner the better.

As a matter of fact, we have two of our own in London at present—a former student, Violet Angel, who you no doubt remember, and Jordy McAllen—now Dr. McAllen—my former ward. Jordy will be traveling to Scotland, and since Violet is also returning to us for the time being, I asked him to escort her.

However, if Ivy would like to, she could travel with them. I'm sure Jordy would be willing, and though I trust both him and Violet entirely, I admit to being concerned about the appearance of them traveling alone, even as doctor and patient.

They'll be traveling from London by train to Edinburgh, and then we'll have our carriage waiting for them at the station. I believe Jordy was planning on leaving by September 20, if not earlier, but I'll write him and ask him to get in contact with you.

Regardless, Ivy is welcome here at any time.

Sincerely,

Dr. Callum McCale

Not far upon its tail came a letter from Jordy McAllen. During Ivy's stay at McCale House, he had been a dear friend whom she'd often turned to for advice. He'd known Violet Angel better than Ivy did, too—at least at the beginning—and as drawn as Ivy was to Violet, he'd proven invaluable in helping her develop the relationship.

Of course, that had been back when Ivy was twelve, back when she thought she could change someone. She couldn't, of course, but she liked to believe God had used her in little ways to help Violet.

Jordy was, as always, direct.

Dear Knights,

Dr. McCale suggested your daughter Miss Ivy could join Violet and me on our trip back to McCale House. I think that's an excellent plan. I saw Violet yesterday, and she threatened me with physical harm, but Ivy has a way with her.

I would keep them both safe. We'd only be on the train about a day and a half, so if we leave Tuesday next, we can arrive by Wednesday afternoon.

I hope you're all doing well. I think it'd be nice to see your family again, Miss Ivy included. Violet, who writes Miss Ivy more often than I remember to, told me you have a little girl now along with the boys —thank goodness!

God bless,
Jordy McAllen

CHAPTER FOUR

London, England

The Knights' carriage stopped outside the Angel home at half past four as promised. Ivy's eager feet hit the pavement before a servant could arrive to see her safely down, her mother's quiet protest barely registering.

She hurried up the steps and was admitted into the house. Moments later, she entered the elegant parlor and folded Violet in a firm embrace, despite her friend's vague attempt to escape.

Violet had only gotten taller and slimmer as she aged, and the dark circles under her eyes had never quite dissipated, but she seemed otherwise well. As Ivy stumbled over the first several words of acknowledgement and excitement, she took Violet in, reading as much into the outside of the woman as she could.

She wasn't at ease here, Ivy felt, but then whenever she visited Violet while she was at her parents' house, this proved true. The only place Violet seemed relaxed was at McCale House, and being there wasn't always possible, though Violet still stayed there more often than not, more of a perennial visitor than a patient or student.

Ivy had overheard Dr. McCale refer to Violet as the only one of his children who was potentially insane, but she didn't believe him. Kind and gentle as the man was, he could be overly brusque, and he couldn't mean it. Not really.

There was insanity in this world, but she was determined not to find it in her friend. Not where there was hope; not where there was Violet. Ivy could be moody, too, though perhaps not to the same level; she could lose herself to fear as easily as Violet could to anger—and Violet's anger seemed to come as much from her anxieties as from actual sources for her wrath.

Ivy didn't know. She honestly didn't. Violet could be confusing at times, and as Ivy grew older, she had only developed more questions, and the answers she had arrived at when she was twelve didn't make as much sense now that she was nineteen and had lived a little longer.

In the end, she determined as she finally released Violet from her arms, love was about all she could offer—and, if that wasn't enough, nothing really could be.

"So here you are," Violet commented. She kept her expression neutral, as always, but Ivy could sense the struggle not to smile, which made her beam.

"Here I am! And my parents are behind me." She glanced over her shoulder, but they hadn't quite made it past the formality of the butler yet. "Will Jordy be here soon?"

"No." Violet rolled her eyes. "You know him. If you say four, he'll be here at five thirty. I've started saying an hour or two before I want him, just to get him here at somewhat of a decent hour, but he's caught on to me. He'll come when he comes, probably when I've despaired of him entirely." She flipped her hand in a dramatic arc. "I can't imagine how anyone bears the man."

Ivy laughed, delighted. Jordy always marched to the beat of a different drummer—or, perhaps, it was more accurate to say he marched slightly off-beat. "We'll see him when we see him, then. I've never actually met with Jordy since I left the McCale House that first time. I always mean to, as we're often in London at the same time, but he rarely remembers to return my letters, and though he's talked about it, I don't think it was ever a priority for him." Which saddened her, in some ways, but she did understand that he was busy. That much he had always managed to make clear to her.

Then her parents arrived, and Mr. and Mrs. Angel appeared. Violet immediately lost what little talkativeness she'd possessed before and fell into grouchy silence, but Ivy stayed near her, held her hand, and tried to keep her included in the conversation.

Mrs. Angel was all talk about her younger daughter, Dory, who had managed to secure a promising match. During the entirety of the conversation, Mother's eyes were glazed over, but she nodded at all the appropriate times. Mother was so very good at being proper, one area in which Ivy eternally failed to excel.

Tea was brought in, and the adults kept chatting, while Ivy and Violet communicated primarily with an occasional glance or eyebrow raise. Or, rather, Ivy murmured responses in reply to Violet's expressions—she, herself, wasn't able to communicate a paragraph with a flick of her eye.

"Violet wants to visit my sister Daphne while she's in Scotland."

Ivy's eyes snapped from Violet to Mrs. Angel. The woman's tone was obviously scornful, and Ivy had learned to pay attention to scorn. It was sometimes—oftentimes, even—pointed in her direction, and if it wasn't, Ivy felt a need to offer her emotional support.

"She lives in a tiny village ... at Violet's suggestion, no less." Mrs. Angel's voice droned on. Not that she had a deep or slow voice, but somehow it still droned, though perhaps Ivy only felt so because she disliked Mrs. Angel, despite her best efforts at judging the woman fairly.

Violet cleared her throat. "I wish you wouldn't hold on to that, Mother—all I did is mention to Aunt Daphne that, if she were looking for a place to build a house, I'd heard there were several lovely locations in Scotland, including Keefmore, and she might want to—"

"To leave England behind for the wilds of a practically foreign land? Oh, I know, Violet—no harm done, I'm sure." So even Mrs. Angel wasn't above rolling her eyes, apparently. Like mother, like daughter. "But I suppose Daphne must be excused—she has always been a bit odd."

Violet cast Ivy a helpless look and raised one hand in surrender. Apparently, she didn't think so negatively of her aunt.

Mother seamlessly guided the conversation in another, slightly less conflicting direction, while Ivy slid closer to Violet and took her hand. Though Violet flinched away, as always, she still allowed it.

"You never told me about an Aunt Daphne," Ivy whispered.

"I don't tell you everything, Trifle," she replied, the old nickname slipping easily from her lips. "She's my mother's sister, Mrs. Daphne Wright. I suppose she's never come up—she's lived on the Continent since I was a baby, and of course I never got a chance to see her when she visited. But lately she's taken an interest in me—she's lost her husband, you see, and is childless, so I suppose I'm as good a pet project as any." She let out a heavy sigh, but the flash in her eyes suggested that the attention wasn't entirely unwanted.

"What is she doing in Scotland?" Ivy asked.

"She said she wanted to find some 'small borough' on the isles and hide herself away from society—and I was only joking when I suggested Keefmore! That's Jordy's village, you know, in the north." Violet shook her head with a small smile. "But Aunt Daphne is nothing if not efficient. She traveled there at once, and she's had a house built, and she's living there and 'consorting with the locals,' as she puts it. Heaven knows what she's doing. Such an odd duck."

Ivy couldn't help but laugh. "Have you thought that your aunt frustrates your mother because she's a little like you?"

Violet didn't do Ivy the favor of replying, but Ivy guessed that the thought had occurred to Violet—and perhaps that was why she wanted to visit her aunt while in Scotland.

"Dr. George McAllen" might seem like a fine way of addressing a man to some, but to Jordy, it was distant. He could be Dr. George McAllen, if they wanted, but as soon as he left the hospital halls behind, he would far rather be *Just Jordy*.

That's the thought he concentrated on as he ducked through the London mist and drizzle outside of the hansom cab he'd hired. He'd left his flat approximately fifteen minutes after Violet had asked him to arrive at her house, and though a doctor could not see fit to engage in such behavior, *Just Jordy* felt comfortable doing just that.

The Angels' British house rose from the British street with British stiffness and a fair share of British formality. Jordy hurried up the steps and rapped on the door. Their disapproving butler glared at him as he tossed his cap in the crisply uniformed man's general direction with a half-shouted greeting. He then jogged up the stairs to the parlor, where the Angels took their tea. Same routine as always.

However, something was different today. Perhaps only because Jordy was a bit of a romantic, or because he was *glaikit*, but he loved the idea of a new beginning, a moment that changed the world. A quick glance was all that was needed to alter the course of his life.

Aye, he'd known Ivy Knight would be a beauty. He'd known, hadn't he? But he hadn't cared because she'd been a child, and he'd had other things on his mind, and he hadn't known womanhood was so close. Hadn't he seen her only five or six years ago? That wasn't that long, and yet here Ivy was.

She was a beautiful woman, really. Dark-blonde hair that somehow managed to glint like gold, big blue eyes, an angelic face— somewhere between stunningly gorgeous and refreshingly innocent. He caught his breath and took a step back, confused. Weren't angels supposed to keep to Heaven or at least avoid sitting in mere mortals' parlors?

"There's our prodigal." Violet's harsh voice broke through his thoughts. "I said four thirty, if you remember."

Jordy turned to face her, affecting an at-ease posture. "Right."

"How is it, then, that you didn't manage to arrive until five?" She rambled on, something about how he never failed to disappoint her.

Jordy nodded along and scarcely heard. Yes, Ivy was certainly a great beauty. She rose and walked toward him.

"Jordy!" she said. "I can't believe it's you. They told you I was coming, didn't they? You seem surprised. But ... it's a good surprise, isn't it?" She hesitated, standing an arm's length away from him. "Is everything all right?"

He forced himself to pay attention to what she was saying, to put on a gentle smile. "Ivy! Is tha' really me wee friend? I'd heard ye were comin', aye, but I didna realize ye'd be so ... so grown up."

Ivy beamed. "Why, thank you, Jordy. I'm glad you're glad that I came." She paused for a moment, confusion shadowing her face. Then she brightened. "I missed you. I've met Violet, but not you since the last time we were both at McCale House."

Jordy swallowed hard. Biggest mistake of his life, apparently. "Tha's right."

Ivy smiled charmingly. "We'll have to catch up soon." She turned away from him and returned to her seat, and Jordy breathed again. He'd never have imagined that awkward little girl—too small for her age, long-legged, looking more ten than thirteen—could grow up so fine. His thoughts went around and around in circles.

Then he realized he was being a complete and utter idiot and flushed. He shouldn't think on this. Why, not only was it unprofessional, but it wasn't right. Here he was attracted to a woman whom he had no intention of marrying.

He took a moment to focus his thoughts, then settled on a chair to join the conversation—they were talking about the arrangements for the trip to Scotland. That's right—his little adventure with his little friends. How did that suddenly sound far more complicated than it had originally?

He found himself continually glancing at Ivy. He hoped she hadn't noticed his lapse in discretion. He didn't think she had, especially if she was anything like the Ivy he'd known. Of course, that could no longer be counted on. He wasn't really sure of anything about Ivy anymore.

A quick glance around the table confirmed that the parents were oblivious ... but Violet knew. Of course she did—somehow, Violet always knew what he was thinking before he thought it. He hated it because it put him at a constant disadvantage in their battle of wits.

Not that it was a battle he wanted to win, but that, with Violet at least, he'd like to have an even playing field. Something had told him not to trust Violet too deeply from the earliest days that he'd known her, and though in some ways they were close, he'd heeded that internal warning in all the ways that counted.

It wouldn't hurt if Violet knew he found Ivy pretty. As long as Jordy kept it there, it wouldn't hurt a thing—he believed he had the necessary control to keep it there, a harmless attraction that would never morph into something more sinister.

Because he was not a suitor for Ivy Knight romantically, and he never would be. At this point in this life, he wasn't ready to court any woman—and with Ivy, it applied even more so. He could never try to persuade a sweet thing like her to spend her life with a man like him.

Not that she would even if he opened the option between them for a deeper relationship. No, it would be all right. He just had to be watchful of his thoughts and feelings—and have a good time taking his friends to Scotland for a visit.

That was all there was to it.

"How have you been, Jordy?" Ivy had a soft, melodic voice, of course.

Did Jordy have a chance of resisting? Aye, he did. He was a man of God, after all. It was almost blasphemous to say he had no control. The words devalued God's influence in his life, and though Jordy struggled, he wasn't a complete heathen.

"I've been weel," he replied. "An' ye?"

"Oh, perfect! My sister got married last month, and now I'm going to Scotland to see the McCales, and it will be quite lovely. Violet has invited me to visit her aunt, so if she travels there, I'll come, too."

Jordy chuckled. Of course Violet had managed to get Ivy involved. She'd been practically harassing him about it for a week. "Do ye want tae visit her Aunt Daphne, Ivy? She's way up in th' wilds o' Scotland—no' quite th' Highlands, but verra near, depending on wha' ye call th' Highlands. An' ye dinna have tae go along. I'm no' quite convinced I shall take Vi there meself."

Violet snorted. "Of course you will. You want to visit your parents, don't you? And if Ivy comes, you haven't any more excuses for not taking me with you."

That was true. He'd been telling Violet, over and over again, that it wasn't right for an unmarried man and woman to travel together through so much open countryside. They might be more open-minded in Scotland, and she might technically count as a student or patient of his, if one squinted hard enough. However, it just wasn't right, and Jordy didn't want to risk it. Especially since Violet knew about his past. Though maybe that eliminated some of the risk. He wasn't sure.

"It's ... true tha' me greatest concern was needin' a chaperone ..." All the same, he wasn't sure he wanted to commit to getting Violet and Ivy both to and from Keefmore safely. He wasn't all that decided on his plans for the next several months—or years—and he'd rather keep it that way. "I dinna ken how things will ... develop. Let's wait an' see."

Violet sighed. "Very well."

"What are your plans, Jordy?"

Of course Ivy would ask that. All the more reason to remember that they were not suited for anything more than a casual friendship. Much as he liked her, now that they were adults, he doubted he'd be able to offer her even companionship. A woman like Ivy needed stability. Jordy couldn't give her that.

"'Tis a bit hard tae say." He cast a sideways glance at the Knights, who were preoccupied with the jabbering Mrs. Angel. At least he wouldn't have to explain it to anyone but Ivy. Not that he minded being questioned but that it was always irritating, regardless of his not giving most people a mind, when people judged him harshly. Especially since he so rarely did anyone else the disservice. "I want tae discuss me plans with Dr. McCale an' then perhaps me parents. I suppose I'm lookin' for God's next step for me, whatever tha' might be ... but who's tae say?"

"Ah." To his surprise, rather than reacting in confusion, Ivy nodded, expression serious, eyes downcast. "I can understand that. I feel as if God wants me to travel to Scotland, but I don't know what else He wants from me. I'm hoping the McCales might have some thoughts, too."

"Oh." He'd have thought Ivy's life was fairly structured by the regiments of society. She'd grown up so fine that he'd assumed ... Perhaps that wasn't right of him. Assumptions seldom did anyone any favors. "I see. Wha' do yer parents say?"

Her eyes flicked across the table to her mother, and she lowered her voice slightly. "That I should be happy where I am. But I'm not. Perhaps that's just a call from God to find contentment, but, Jordy, I can't help but want to find *something* to do. I know I won't ever be normal like Alice, but—"

"Stop right there!" he protested. "Normal is relative. Have I taught ye nothin'? Ask Vi. *We* believe in ye, even if no one else does."

Ivy flushed and dropped her eyes, a slight nod her only response, but Jordy truly hoped it had sunk in. He wanted her to know it and believe it and realize that she stood on equal footing to her sister or to anyone else on this earth. He knew it, and he'd known it since almost the first day he met her.

Jordy wasn't a big believer in classes of people, really. Everyone had the same abilities to strive and survive in this life, but perhaps their paths to reach those purposes would be different and more aided by others. But that didn't make Ivy unworthy or whatever other nonsense her family was feeding her, directly or indirectly.

"Vi, tell Ivy ye feel th' same," he demanded. Nothing like a little positive peer pressure.

She hesitated. "I believe Ivy can do whatever she wants, yes."

He'd already had this discussion within the last few weeks about Violet's own respective worth and the length and breadth of her ability to control the elements of her life, so he let her uncertainty slide, deciding to circle back to another Bible-laced lecture later this week.

Not that she would listen to him. He'd be very grateful indeed for Ivy's presence on this trip.

CHAPTER FIVE

The rumbling of the train was comforting to Ivy, a rhythm that reassured her with its repetitiveness. There was a music in the clack of train tracks, a music to the way the people seemed lulled by it.

Her party sat in a private car her parents had funded. Since it would only take them a day, they would be arriving in Edinburgh in the evening. At first, she'd tried to engage Violet in conversation, but her friend had been grumpy since they met up this morning, and Ivy had, at last, given up.

Jordy chatted with Ivy almost continually, and they caught up on the last several years. Honestly, Ivy felt like they'd never parted. There was such an easy feeling about being with Jordy that made her feel wonderful in his presence. He filled the air with a kind of warm comfort that allowed her to relax and focus on the conversation rather than how she was perceived.

Perhaps it was because Jordy clearly didn't care about how he was perceived, with his coat tossed on the seat beside him and the top two buttons of his shirt undone, cravat having disappeared somewhere when they first boarded. He fidgeted while they talked, playing with his clothes and ruffling his hair and drumming his fingers on everything—and then eventually twirling a pen between his fingers in a constant rhythm.

"Wha' do ye think God has for ye in Scotland?" he asked once.

Ivy hated that question. Everyone asked her again and again, as if the frequency of the question would allow her to come to a conclusion. The problem was, she didn't know. She'd had a long talk —several of them, really—with her mother which had clarified some of her thoughts on calling and purpose. Her mother separated the two, referred her to Bible verses in which *calling* seemed to refer more to salvation than some specific missionary-esque occupation. Then she gently but firmly told Ivy that the more she gave in to discontent, the less likely she'd be to find whatever it was she was looking for.

But it didn't ring true. She understood what her mother meant, and she agreed with the sentiment. However, in this case, her direction from God was clear. Sadly, He'd only given her the first step of obedience ... none of the following ones. Even when He did give her the next step, she had a feeling that the destination would be too far away to peek around the bend.

Yet, in this moment, she had to think of an answer for Jordy. She forced herself to meet his tawny eyes rather than stare absently out at the countryside rolling by and the wispy clouds on the horizon. "I wish I had even an idea, but, really, I don't."

"Mm ... scary." He slouched back in his seat. "Ye must be strugglin' with tha'."

"Oh, yes. But I trust God." At least, she tried to, and she wasn't so much afraid of the waiting as what might be just around the riverbend —or down this stretch of train tracks, rather. She wasn't Alice; she was Ivy, and she could be patient. Not that the current moment was requiring patience; it was full of unknowns even as she navigated her current state of being. Even at her most stagnant, Ivy seldom found that she had nothing to do. There was always another breath to take, after all.

"Tha's th' point o' it all, isna it? Tae trust God?" Jordy grinned. "No' tha' I always do, ye ken. I'm stubborn as they come. I canna count th' times I've said tae God, 'Ach, but why dinna we do it th' way *I* want?'"

A fairly common problem in humanity, as far as she could tell. "No one can be perfect all the time."

"Aye, but it takes a special talent tae be perfect none o' th' time." He winked and straightened. "Hmm. Three o' clock now. Only a few more hours, Ivy, an' we'll be home."

Ivy smiled, for though it wasn't her home in the same way it was Jordy's, she nonetheless felt the arrival as significant. *Oh, Lord, guide my steps.*

Mrs. McCale pulled Ivy into a firm, tight embrace as soon as she reached her, and Ivy laughed at her exuberance. She was a small, plump woman, self-controlled but endlessly loving to those she cared for.

"Ach, Ivy, how you've grown! What a lovely young lady you are." Mrs. McCale placed her hands on Ivy's arms and held her back. "Callum, look at her. I always ken't she'd be a beauty, and of course she is. You take after your mother, don't you?"

People said so, and Ivy considered it to be the greatest compliment she could receive. "Everyone thinks so."

"And so do I." Dr. McCale approached her and placed a hand on her shoulder lightly before drawing back, but he smiled through his ever-bushy beard.

They were ushered into the parlor where new students and their parents were greeted, one Ivy had seldom had cause to enter during her stay here. Walking through those doors and taking a seat on the plain, serviceable furniture was very different as an adult than it had been as a child. She shuddered at the memory—how frightened she'd been! But how could she have known that McCale House would be such a wondrous place for her?

She pulled Violet down onto a settee with her and squeezed her hand. Violet rolled her eyes; she must know that Ivy was in the grip of nostalgia and disapproved. Regardless of her friend's opinion, though, Ivy couldn't keep herself from feeling happy-sad at the memories.

"Oh, Ivy, we were so glad to hear you were coming with Violet and Jordy. We've had both of them here often, but you only once since you left us the first time, and how we've been missing you!" Mrs. McCale was beaming from ear to ear. She, too, much understood the benefits of nostalgia. It dawned upon Ivy that, now that she was no longer a child, Mrs. McCale might prove somewhat of a kindred spirit.

Was that Your point in bringing me here, Lord?

"But," Mrs. McCale said, "your letter was vague, Ivy. What do you intend to do here? We welcome a visit, for as long as you like, but I admit to curiosity."

Ivy let go of the nervous chuckle that always bubbled up from somewhere in her whenever the subject was raised. "I don't really know. I wish I did! I just felt God shoving me toward Scotland, and I thought, 'I'd better go.' I'm glad my parents allowed me—I don't know what I'd have done if they weren't favorable to me traveling here."

"I see." Mrs. McCale glanced at Dr. McCale briefly. "I can promise that God will show you the way—but I can't tell you what that is. Wait on the Lord, Ivy—you can be here as long as you need until then. Perhaps you can even help us. Callum, could we—?"

"I think we'd best let all three of our adventurers rest before we make any decisions," Dr. McCale said. "Jordy, did you see to ...?" The men turned to discuss luggage.

It was already late, and after a light dinner, they retired for the night. Ivy soon drifted off to sleep, curled up in her bed.

She was awakened by an unearthly wail. For a moment, she lay still, confused, then understood and leaped to her feet. She pulled on her dressing gown and hurried out the door.

Outside of her room, Ivy made her way to the stairway at the end of the hall and followed the old, familiar route to the third floor and Violet's room.

She reached the door at the same time as Dr. McCale. He stepped back, allowing Ivy to enter the room first.

"Be careful," he murmured as she stepped across the threshold.

Violet lay in her bed, weeping and moaning softly, quite a contrast from the wild screams of a moment ago. She was shuddering as if afraid, her eyes flicking about even as tears streamed from them.

"Violet?" Ivy murmured, approaching the bed. "What is it, Vi? Are you all right? Are you in pain?"

When she saw Ivy, Violet jerked back and cried out as if Ivy were more frightening than whatever her nightmare had been earlier. "No!" she exclaimed, pushing herself up. "No. Not you. It's ... it's not fair. I've waited too long, and I can't let you." She dropped back onto the bed. "It's not *fair*."

"Violet," Ivy crooned, lowering herself onto the bed next to her. "How can I help you?"

"Stay away," Violet panted, scrambling to a sitting position. "Stay away from me. Not ... not you. Oh, God, anyone but her. I can't bear it." She began weeping again.

Ivy turned to face Dr. McCale in confusion. She saw Jordy behind him and lifted a hand. He inclined his head toward her before focusing his attention back on Violet.

"What can't you bear?" Ivy asked, reaching over to rub Violet's back. "Can you tell me about it?"

Violet shook her head, rolling over, away from Ivy. "No. I can't tell anyone, Trifle. I can't. If they knew, they would think I'm a fool. I *am* a fool. A stupid fool to ever think—" She buried her face in the pillow to smother a sob.

Ivy glanced up at Jordy and Dr. McCale. "Do you think we could have some time alone?" she asked. "I know she won't hurt me. I understand. I can help."

Jordy and Dr. McCale glanced at each other and shuffled out of the room, leaving Ivy and Violet alone save for the glow of the candle Dr. McCale had brought in, which now stood in its holder on the nearby bureau.

Ivy shivered. "I'm going to add to the fire. It's chilly in here, and you've nothing but coals left. I'll only be a moment."

She hopped off the bed and threw some kindling onto the fire, applying the poker liberally, and soon a blaze sparked back up again. Beaming at her success, she returned to Violet's side. She had calmed now, and her breaths were slow and even, though she continued to weep openly.

"Violet, can you tell me?" Ivy asked. "What was it? A nightmare?"

Violet hesitated. "Yes." Her voice rasped against Ivy's ears like a rock against pavement. "I suppose you could call it a nightmare."

"So you woke up ... disoriented?" Ivy suggested after searching for the right word for a moment.

Violet shrugged. "I woke up insane."

Ivy shook her head. "You're not insane, Violet. Please don't say so. Yes, you're troubled. I see that your spells can be difficult. But I don't truly believe you're insane."

Violet smirked. "Always optimistic, aren't we, Trifle? It's a quality you and he share."

"He?"

"*Jordy.*"

"Oh. Well, we both are optimistic," Ivy agreed. "Though I'm more optimistic for other people than for myself," she admitted.

"Only natural. One half of the world thinks they're a god; the other half hates themselves. There seem to be very few in-betweens. Humankind, as a whole, is unhealthy."

Though Ivy didn't quite understand Violet's statements—or agree with what she did understand—she was pleased to see Violet returning to normal. She smoothed a hand over her hair. "What was your dream about, Vi? It might help to tell me."

Violet shrugged. "Nonsense, really. What I can remember of it. It was ... You were there, Trifle. You were walking away from me. Leaving me. I called out, but you didn't come back. Jordy ... was with you."

"Ah," said Ivy. "Well, that will never happen. We won't leave you. Jordy's here to take care of you, and I'm your friend, Violet."

"I want to believe that," Violet whispered. "I really do. But it's so hard, Ivy. It's so hard to believe when everyone I've ever loved has left me before. Or rather, sent me away from them." She sat up. "I don't really remember a time when I lived with my parents in London. I was too small. But I do remember trusting. Loving. I remember betrayal. Being left." She took a deep breath. "You don't forget the emotions even if you forget the people. Which makes it all that much worse."

Ivy managed to coax Violet to let her slip an arm around her waist and pull her close. "There, there, dearest. It will be all right. I'll never leave you. Not really. Sometimes ... sometimes we won't always be together, but I'll write, as I always have, and tell you all I think, and we'll encourage each other. I won't really leave you. Not in my heart."

Violet snorted. "Don't give me that. The moment you grow up— which you will someday, Trifle, though you may deny it to yourself and others with all the vehemence you can possess—you'll forget. You have no reason to remember me. I'm ... I'm what I am, and what I am is practically useless. So please don't try to pretend you would be here right now if pity didn't drive you."

"Of course I would!" Ivy exclaimed. "I love you, Violet."

Violet didn't reply for a long moment, then she spoke. "Ivy?"

"Yes?"

Violet glanced at Ivy's face. "Do you really?"

Did it mean more tonight than it had the hundred other times Ivy had insisted upon it? Yet, all the same, it was true, even if Violet seldom seemed to hear her. "Yes. You're like a sister to me."

Violet's body relaxed. It was a moment of vulnerability, then. "Do you sometimes wonder if I would be alive today if not for you?"

Ivy pulled her friend's head on her lap, determined to use this moment of actual Violet for all it was worth. "No. I don't think about that. I know that God would have taken care of you in some other way if I hadn't been there. He loves you, too. So very much more than I ever could! Even if something were to happen to me, you can trust God."

"God," Violet murmured, starting to drift off to sleep. "I believe He exists, Ivy, but sometimes I worry ..."

"I think we all worry." Ivy certainly had worried more than her usual amount lately. "It's hard not to. But He's there, and He's planned your every breath."

"Mm. I know." Violet sighed. "I lay up all night thinking about it. Wanting so desperately to have the faith you and many others around me do. Aching for it. But no matter how hard I try, I still have fears. Doubts."

"I do, too," Ivy said.

Violet shook her head. "Not like mine, my dear Trifle. I doubt that He exists sometimes. I doubt that He would die for me. That He knows I exist. That He cares about me. That He hasn't sent demons to persecute me day in and day out."

Nonsense. "But you know what's true. You have to believe."

"I know. I know I do," Violet said. "I can't stop myself from thinking about it. I sleep very little, I suppose, compared to most, so I think a lot. About all the things that I don't understand. About all the things I want to believe in but can't. About all the people that have hurt me ... and all the people that might. I'm afraid."

"I know, Vi. I know. But you're precious. To God, to the McCales, and to me. You're precious to *me*." Ivy pressed a kiss into Violet's hair. "You're my first friend except for my family. You're especially the first friend I ever made my age. I didn't really get to know Jordy for a while, so you're the first."

Violet smiled. "I'm glad."

Ivy squeezed Violet's shoulder. "I'm glad as well. Now, go to sleep. We can talk more in the morning when you're feeling better."

After seeing that Ivy was going to be able to manage Violet, Dr. McCale and Jordy left them alone and proceeded down the hall. As neither man felt able to sleep, they decided to adjourn to Dr. McCale's study for a time. Jordy wanted to ask a few questions about Violet's place at McCale House, and Dr. McCale agreed that Jordy should be informed.

"She's not really supposed to be here." Dr. McCale lowered himself onto a chair opposite Jordy. "In fact, I'm keeping her here despite the instructions of the board, of the colleges we're indebted to, research institutions ... against the policy and purpose of McCale House. Yet she comes back, Jordy, for she must."

"But why?" Jordy asked. Dr. McCale was a stubborn, set-in-his-ways man, and he rarely followed the beaten path—he was downright eccentric in many ways—but Jordy had never known him to disobey an absolute rule, especially one of his own making.

"Because I don't ken where to put her." Dr. McCale sighed and ran a hand through his hair. "As you can see, she's a troubled lass. You've seen her in London with her parents?"

Jordy nodded. "Aye, it's bad—but she canna just adjust ...?"

Dr. McCale shook his head. "I'm afraid not. She seems to become worse in their presence. I even see her become more tense and then manic while at McCale House when they're under the roof. It's not the situation or the location, though those contribute. It's her own parents. She can't be near them. Not for any length of time."

Jordy's brow furrowed. "Why would tha' be?"

"You ken the story. Abandoned before she can remember what they look like but remembering the hurt and betrayal. She barely tolerates anyone's presence—let alone that of two people she considers her worst enemies. Perhaps she even blames them for her problems, feels it's their fault for bringing her into the world. It could be. Before she came to McCale House, her parents were told difficulties during her mother's pregnancy accounted for Violet's problems, and she may've heard some of the rot. But, no matter the reason, she reacts violently to them."

Jordy cocked his head. "So her Aunt Daphne ...?"

"That's why she wants to go to her, I think. She believes she may find respite there; she's no fool, Jordy. She kens what a problem she's been for us, and I believe there's enough kindness in Violet to not wish us to struggle with her."

"I see." That made sense. "So if she canna go tae her aunt, then we have nae choice but tae keep her here, aye? We canna send her out intae th' world. She wouldna last long."

Dr. McCale shook his head. "No. She wouldn't." He rubbed his forehead. "I can't send her to an asylum. If she leaves here and isn't able to settle elsewhere, she will end up in one. I know they're not all terrible, but for the most part ... And a bonnie lass like Violet—" He grunted. "She's a beauty in a way, more so than most, and no one would mind what happened. You ken what I mean, Jordy."

Jordy straightened his posture. He knew. Besides the abuse—physical and mental—which worsened the problems of the people kept there, the terrible living conditions, and being treated like an animal, an attractive lass like Violet could be subject to other horrors. Ones Jordy wouldn't feel comfortable speaking of with a lady present. He didn't even want to think about them.

"Aye. She wouldna last long. Shorter than some, I'd think. We've already seen her suicidal tendencies. If anythin' o' tha' sort happened ..."

Dr. McCale sighed. "Can you imagine what that would do to her? To a sane woman, it scars more than almost anything I can think of. It's a violation of the body and soul. But Violet? She'd be lost. Forever, perhaps. She has nothing to comfort her—no real faith." He stood and walked to the window, staring out at the blackness for a few moments. "I don't ken what to do, Jordy," he said at last. "I really don't. I've had children I couldn't save, children I couldn't help. Children who wouldn't *let* me help them. But this is different. Violet is ... Violet has come to mean something tae me. I haven't helped her become that much better, but she still makes me love her through her bitterness, her caustic attitude, her inability to rise beyond her own demons."

It was rare that Dr. McCale talked this much. Jordy knew to keep silent and let him speak. The rarity made it precious.

"If you're going to Keefmore, take her with you. Though I suppose there is a problem with taking her alone." He grunted. "Hardly an ideal situation for either of you."

"Right. But ... I think Violet was sayin' Ivy might come wi' her. Then they could both stay with her aunt for a time." In Keefmore. His home village. What was he getting himself into? He didn't want Violet there, let alone Ivy. It was a world he had separated from McCale House, left behind, moved beyond, and he had no desire to combine the two different narratives. He had half a mind to accuse Violet of deliberately pointing her aunt in that direction to bother him, but that seemed like a bit much, even for her.

"But were you planning to go home?"

"No' ... no' for long. But, aye, for a few weeks." Just to visit, to see his family, and to remind himself of his roots—and why he wanted to move beyond those roots. It wasn't his loving family or his disdain for the rougher aspects of being a Scottish farmer—he loved that part of his heritage. However, the memories, the past Jordy—they had to be abandoned. He wanted to be more than that.

"Perhaps you could stay on longer." Dr. McCale brought his hand up to stroke his beard, an action that never failed to unnerve Jordy. "At least until Violet's settled. Ach, and if they need to leave, someone will have to take them back. And—"

Jordy held up his hands. "I ken. If I commit, I have tae stay—I canna just abandon them an' run off."

"Exactly. So would you commit to that?" Dr. McCale, sure of himself and structured within an inch of his life, would never understand Jordy's hesitance.

"Give me time tae think it over." He'd need at least a few days to make the decision. Nothing like a potential commitment to make him procrastinate.

"Very well. But, Jordy?"

"Hmm?"

"Don't take too long, or you'll never decide." As always, he seemed to know what Jordy would do before he was quite sure of it himself. And Jordy was grateful for that—he needed someone like Dr. McCale in his life to offer him some structure, some steadiness. He'd never let his parents do so.

Perhaps that was the problem, really. Jordy saw his family as loving but naïve ghosts in his life, ones who could never have access to his true thoughts and feelings. But that wasn't fair in the least.

No, he had to let his family into his life again. Perhaps this trip to Keefmore would facilitate that. All the same, he would take time to mull it over before committing to caring for Violet and Ivy on the trip to Keefmore.

Right now, the fluidity of his life was comforting, and he didn't want to trap himself to any one thing until he was absolutely sure it would reap the most benefits.

CHAPTER SIX

The next morning, Jordy overslept even though he'd promised himself he'd wake up at least an hour early. He barely took time to comb down his reddish-brown hair before leaving his bedchamber and making a familiar mad dash to the dining room. He had, by far, the darkest hair in his family—they were all carrot tops of the more orange-ish variety—and it tended to lie down more than his brothers'. However, his hair insisted on sticking up in eleven places this morning. *Of course.*

At the top of the stairs, he barely restrained himself from sliding down the banister to save time. He had to be dignified—in front of people, anyway. He'd wait until no one would see him to take a slide down that railing, he thought; some lazy afternoon when everyone was in a classroom or occupied elsewhere.

He didn't imagine anyone had thought to dust the banister in that particular way in his absence.

Jordy made it down to the dining room as Dr. McCale was going from amused-annoyed to angry-annoyed.

"Some things never change," he heard Mrs. McCale murmur as he slid onto his seat.

He grinned at her in spite of himself. "I'm sorry. I truly am. I overslept."

Dr. McCale gave a begrudging nod in his direction before beginning the prayer. While the doctor spoke to God, Jordy uttered his own private prayer—a prayer that some things *had* changed. His past was as left behind as he believed it. Whatever came next would prove Jordy McAllen a man of God.

And, of course, that one beauty sitting down the table from him, hands neatly folded and head bent, looking as angelic as ever, would not be the victim of any fall he did experience.

Jordy spent that morning helping Dr. McCale. Since he wasn't foolish enough to believe that the students would trust him right off, he wasn't worried when they didn't respond to him immediately like most everyone else did. He'd never met a stranger, even if sometimes it took time for the other person to realize that.

Most of the children gave in to him shortly. He loved spending time with these little folks. So much untapped potential, and not very many people would take the time to help while they were still young, before they were permanently damaged by rough treatment and a lack of loving, focused care.

That was why he loved McCale House. It helped the simple and confused in a way that no place else in the world could.

Though not a lover of routine in general—variety was, after all, the spice of life—there was something nice and familiar about following the old schedule like he used to as a young man. He enjoyed making ticks on Dr. McCale's clipboard and continually reminding him what was happening next and exchanging amused glances with the other staff at the doctor's domineering attitude.

That afternoon, a servant arrived from Edinburgh with the mail. Jordy was surprised to receive a letter; he'd hardly told anyone that he was coming home to Scotland. His father's simple, blocky script decorated the envelope.

It was surprising that his father had received his last letter, in which he'd mentioned visiting McCale House—even more surprising that he'd spend the money to post this return letter. Jordy hoped everything was all right. He took the letter into one of the sitting rooms and opened it.

Dear Jordy,

Received yer letter yesterday and are glad to hear that yere coming home. We have missed you. Especially your mother. Hoping you can cum visit soon, even if its only for a bit, though we would like you to stay longer.

Edith is getting married to Tristan in December. I dinna ken if yer mother told ye, but I have never seen a lass so stubborn. But it won out, for she has him under her claws now, and there is no escaping. She has him tied in nots. But, come to think, she does the same to her brothers. If ye cum, dont spoil her as you always do.

For all shes a smart girl, Edith wants a big wedding with a pretty frock and the hole village there. Always putting on airs, that lass. But I suppose I dinna mind. She's me only daughter, and I ken a woman wanting to have a nice wedding.

Jordy smiled to himself. It really was a stretch for his father to spend any amount of money on anything as pointless as a wedding. He was surprised that his father had even considered it—in Jordy's experience, Mr. McAllen was much more likely to insist that Tristan and Edith sign the marriage register, announce it to the village, and buy a farm.

It was a little odd to think about Tristan, his friend, marrying his younger sister. Yet, it had been written in the stars for so long. Tristan just hadn't been willing to admit it.

Then Edith had finally given Tristan an ultimatum—which he apparently responded well to. Jordy hadn't been there, but from what Edith said in her last letter, "some men need a wee nudge." The little manipulator. She hadn't changed. She was still the same girl who could have the world twisted around her little finger if she so desired.

Jordy returned his attention to the letter he still held.

Were getting the harvest in fast this year. Everything is going as it always goes. I am proud of yer brothers. Ben and Mick are almost men, and William reaches my shoulder now.

Edith is the saem as always, steady as a rock, my rite hand. Tom is no help. Hes only seven. We dinna need him to grow up faster than he has to.

Jordy lingered between annoyance and amusement. Ever since the youngest McAllen had been born, his parents had spoiled little Tom rotten. He supposed that was the way of the youngest. And, having lost a babe between William and Tom, it was only natural that his mother should cling to the son who must have, emotionally, replaced the little girl she'd never met.

Now, Jordy, I have got a favor to ask ye. More like a request. And I know its a hard thing for me to be asking for.

Over the sumer, a bad fever struck Keefmore. We told ye about it before. Many died, mostly weans but a few adults too. It was bad. Sumone sick in all the cottages. By Gods grace, we were spared.

Many folks say a good doctor could have helped. I dinna ken if thats true, but we dinna ken how to treat it. The midwife, Mrs. Dunmore, tried, but failed.

Then it passed. Some medicin was brought to the town which might have helped. We dinna ken for sure. I admit Im ignorant of all yer doctoring ways.

So the town is wanting a doctor. I told them I could ask ye if ye ken of someone. Or perhaps, ye could come yerself?

*If thats a fool idea or something yer not wanting
to do, then forget ye received this letter. But wed
love to have ye home, lad.*
  Your father, Albert McAllen

Jordy set the letter down and leaned back. He blinked. *Well.* That wasn't something he'd been expecting at all.

It took him a few seconds to gain his mental equilibrium. Work at Keefmore?

Aye, he was looking to work in a small town—to be the well-respected, much-liked country doctor one heard about but rarely saw. He wanted to be looked up to. But the possibility of that happening in his hometown, where people knew him, had known him all his life ... It would be an uphill hike, to be sure.

He'd have to build his way up not from the ground but from a cave at the bottom of the earth. They no doubt respected his medical prowess—his ability to get out into the world and learn things—but respect *him*? He was almost, but not quite, the village idiot. Or he had been as a boy. Who knew what they thought of him.

But Jordy was never one to shrink from a challenge. Anything but —he welcomed them. And, if he could prove himself responsible to the townspeople of Keefmore, he could prove himself anywhere. After all, it was where this journey had begun. There was a kind of poetry to ending it there.

He would have liked to work in a new place. To have new experiences. To travel. To enjoy life. He didn't expect to stay in one place forever. That would be as boring as all those medical textbooks he'd spent years reading in his school days. He wanted to see the world. However, perhaps that could wait until he had the necessary funds. This would be a new sort of adventure.

He could do it. He *would* do it.

Stuffing the letter into his pocket, he rose and marched out of the room, only to march back in again when he remembered that a desk with stationery stood in the corner. He took a seat and began penning an epistle to his father.

Violet's enthusiasm for the trip to Keefmore was unmatched by anything in Ivy's recent memory, which was why she felt so obligated to join her friend. Ivy also suspected that her presence would put Violet more at ease in the new situation with an aunt she barely knew, but neither of them talked about how nervous, or even how at ease, Violet was with the thought.

As for Ivy, nerves had skittered about her chest from the first time Violet had suggested they all go to Keefmore together. It skittered to the point that she doubted God could want her to do it. After all, she had her own problems—could she really drop everything and travel with Violet and Jordy to some unknown locale?

But she felt nothing from God, not exactly. Her nerves continued playing an intense staccato beat, but whenever she brought it forward in prayer, whenever she listened ... the beat stilled. Though it wasn't as direct as the call before, it was still clear enough for Ivy. So, despite her fears, she'd written her mother a week ago requesting permission to travel with Jordy and Violet to visit Mrs. Daphne Wright for an undetermined amount of time.

Today three letters had arrived—one from her mother and two from Alice, forwarded from Pearlbelle Park. The staccatos had started again, and Ivy slipped into her room, intent to read these in private.

Her courage abandoned her, and she chose to read the letters from her sister first.

> Dear Ivy,
>
> I miss you, darling! How are things in England? How are Mother and Papa and our little brothers and sister? And of course you must tell me about Nettie, Malcolm, Ella, and Debby—and the Parkers

and Aunt Christina and Uncle Charles, if you hear anything of them and their families.

As for me, I am quite well. A bit out of sorts sometimes, though, and nervous about what's to come. Wishing I were there, of course, and that I could talk some things over with Mother and Nettie, but that's to be expected. I'm sure soon it'll feel quite natural to be away from home.

My mother-in-law, Lilli, has made this transition easier than you can imagine. You always hear horrors about overbearing mothers-in-law who ruin a new bride's happiness through their difficult manners, but Lilli is nothing like that. She's been a blessing. You may be shocked to hear me call her "Lilli." Mrs. Strauss is the correct form, I believe, and perhaps "Mother" if we should become close. However, she insisted, and who am I to go against her wishes on this matter? Besides, it is so nice and familiar. I feel as if we are old friends. We get on well together.

Peter's sisters are lovely, of course. Caroline is close to my age—she's married with a son, and we've been best of friends whenever she comes to visit. Meanwhile, our little Dahlia is quite a funny little girl, but I love her. It's wonderful to have two new sisters. I feel Caroline especially will be a wealth of knowledge when the time comes.

A kettle drum promptly decided to roll into Ivy's stomach, and she felt for a moment that she was going to be ill, but the feeling subsided, and she read on.

Peter's brother Andrew is more of the "tall, silent" type, although he's not very tall—an inch or so above Peter at most. We haven't spoken much. You remember him from the wedding. I suppose you remember them all from the wedding, really, but I still feel as if I ought to explain who I'm with.

Chris—Peter's father—is nice. He seems to be a clever man, and he loves his family very much. I think we're going to be close someday, too, though he's quiet and rarely speaks except to tease his wife. Our family doesn't rip each other apart like the Strausses do, but it's so sweet, honestly. I just have to get used to it.

Of course, I'm still fighting with Mr. Farjon, Peter's friend. I doubt we shall ever be close, and I admit sometimes it's harder still to get along with his wife. She wants me to become more involved in our new church. I suppose I ought to tell you all about that, and about the other people I've met, and about the differences between England and America, but that will have to wait for another letter.

Peter enjoyed getting back to work at his newspaper office. His editor—"Teeb," Peter calls him, though his true name is Thaddeus B. Goodington, Jr.—isn't quite the pleasant sort. He's like a petulant child, if you ask me, and he has a filthy mouth. But Peter seems to love him. Of course, Peter loves everyone, so that's nothing new.

Tonight Peter is coming home early to make up for not getting to spend any time with me last night— we had dinner at the Farjons' house and got home rather late, so we didn't talk. Anyway, he'll write you fifty letters as soon as he's settled, of course. Peter's good at that.

By the way, Peter wants me to read over any letters he sends you. We both know you're like a sister to him, but he's bashful about writing to women who aren't blood relations now that we're married. He says he wants to make sure I'm comfortable with it. I am—with you and with the greater half of the others. He still asks me to read them, and I can't refuse.

So here I am reading almost twenty correspondences a week. Why is it that Peter must advise every woman he knows? And why must I read over them? It's kind, but I do trust him. With those women, anyway. There are others I would not be so forgiving of, but those I can keep an eye on without reading dozens of letters.

A word of sisterly advice: marry a man who either can't write, doesn't want to write, or isn't the advice-giving sort. I married a man who every man, woman, and child in the world wants as a confidant, and it's exhausting when I have to play proofreader.

As of yet, though, it's all been very dull—"Mother won't let me buy a new parasol, and I hate her." "My new beau hasn't called on me in a day; do you suppose he's alive?" "My canary died, and now I am miserable." How do even women bear women?

But his letters are the sweetest, most innocent thing in the world. Except when he's debating Calvinism (have you ever talked to him about divine election? Heavens!) or some such, in which case the pages are practically crackling with the fires of theology. I love those ones. That's what Peter and I talk about.

I suppose I ought to be jealous, but I can't be. Peter is a master at friendship; I can see that romance has never been in the cards with any of these girls. Peter doesn't go about breaking hearts;

it's not in him to do so.

Next week Peter and I are traveling to a place called 'Buffalo,' which is a name he couldn't explain except to say that there might have been buffalo there once. He'll be gone for almost a week on an assignment—the president has finally died of his wounds, or did as of last month, if you didn't hear, and there are many threads to explore—and we wanted to get away and have time to ourselves after these last few weeks. So we'll stay in this 'Buffalo'— which is to the north—after he gets back, and I'll have a break from living in such a loud house.

Naturally, I don't mind the noise, but the Strausses have kept us both active since we arrived. I suppose we're looking to prolong the honeymoon stage. We really ought to get our own house soon, especially as hopefully—

Here the letter cut off. Alice had scribbled out a few words and replaced them with, "circumstances will have changed" in a smaller script in the margin.

I'll leave you now, my darling. May your day be lovely or your evening be pleasant or your night be full of sweet dreams, depending on when you read this.

Next time I write, if it's far enough out, I shall have something more interesting to tell you, but that will do for now.

Sincerely,
Alice Strauss

Ivy sighed and opened the second letter from Alice. It was dated only a week later, and Alice's handwriting was rushed, almost sliding off the page in its hurry to leave her pen.

> *Ivy,*
>
> *I thought I had something to tell you, as I mentioned in my last letter, but I don't. Forget I said anything, and please don't tell Mummy or anyone. I haven't even told Peter; I don't want him to be disappointed. I was so sure, Ivy—so sure. I thought I would tell you last week, and tell Peter that same day, and then I almost told him again before he left, but something held me back, and now I'm glad.*

Ivy didn't quite know what Alice was rambling on about, but it seemed her sister had been sad when she wrote this letter—and the use of 'Mummy' was very telling. She said a quick prayer and hoped Alice was much better now.

> *I had my heart set on it. I suppose it was the traveling that did it. Though I'll never know.*
>
> *I don't know when I'll write again to you. I'll try to get something off to Mummy so she won't worry. Tell her I talked about twin things in this letter. That will be true, as it is just between us. I know you will understand.*
>
>

Your sister,
Alice Knight

Ivy blinked. Had Alice signed with her maiden name? Odd. Alice took great pride in writing "Alice Strauss" in big, curling letters. It wasn't like her to forget. She didn't want to pry, but there was something decidedly *Der Ring des Nibelungen* about the letter's entire tone.

She'd just have to keep Alice in her prayers. That was all she could do. Shaking her head, Ivy set both of Alice's letters aside and reached for her mother's.

Dear Ivy,

I was quite hesitant when we first received a letter from Dr. McCale, as well as one from you, requesting permission for you to travel to Keefmore with George McAllen and Violet Angel. My instinct was to reply, "No." Of course not!

However, your father convinced me to wait until the morning, and sometime during the night, I knew it was the right choice for you. I admit to skepticism at the beginning, but I believe this is what God wants for you. If not, no harm done; you can simply return home.

I trust you to be an adult woman who can handle herself with decorum and maturity, and if Dr. McCale trusts Dr. McAllen, I must assume he will care for you with the utmost kindness and respect. I also know you to have a heart for Violet Angel, and I believe you can help her. Your empathy will aid you in that.

In short, yes, you may go. Please be careful of yourself, though, my dearest girl! I love you so, more than you can possibly comprehend, and it would break my heart if anything happened. Keep God foremost, stay close to Dr. McAllen and Violet, and try to be aware of your surroundings. You should be fine.

I miss you, and so do your father and siblings. We'll keep you constantly in our prayers. I needn't remind you, of course, but we appreciate your letters and will treasure each one.

God keep you.

Your mother,

Claire M. Knight

She could go.

She wasn't sure if the prospect more relieved or frightened her, but she could go to Keefmore with Jordy and Violet, and perhaps, just perhaps, God would provide her with an opportunity to do something worthwhile.

Maybe she'd even find a calling.

CHAPTER SEVEN

Mid-October 1881
Outside Keefmore, Scotland

Ivy awoke, jarring her head against the side of the coach, when the conveyance went over a bump. She pushed upright, steadied herself by clinging to the edge of the window, and rubbed the sleep from her eyes.

Violet sat to her right, sitting at the edge of her seat with her eyes staring straight ahead. She seemed to be in a world of her own, not even glancing at Ivy despite her sudden movements.

Through the dim light, she could vaguely make out Jordy's smile across from her. "We're almost there," he said. "A few more miles at th' most." He drew the curtain aside. "A bit dark tae see much, but I can tell by all th' wee hills an' burns."

Ivy smiled and leaned forward to see better. "I can't wait to see it in the morning."

"I canna, either," Jordy admitted. "I've no' visited these last ... ach, for a long time. When I have, me visits were short." He seemed depressed by this statement.

"You were in London learning to be a fine doctor. You were busy," Ivy reminded him. She understood the guilt of things beyond her control—the way her music insisted that every new bar was another potential mistake, *Da Capo al Fine* again and again—and she hoped some encouragement might perk Jordy up at least a bit.

Jordy nodded. "Aye. But tha' doesna give me an excuse tae abandon me family."

"Well. You're coming home now. And it's the present that matters—not what you did in the past. Not once you're sorry, anyway," Ivy added, "and I know you are."

"I hope they ken why I needed tae," Jordy said. "Did I sacrifice them for a dream—or did I simply make a way for meself in th' world in th' only way I could?"

"I don't know," Ivy admitted.

Violet turned her eyes toward her companions. "They're your family. They would have left you if they'd been given the choice."

Jordy sighed. "Vi, me family would never have left me. They're steady as th' sun, an' they love me. So dinna ye go thinking tha' because ye believe everyone's out tae get ye tha' everyone else believes th' same."

Ivy placed a hand on Violet's shoulder. "Violet, really. Not everyone wants to hurt you."

Violet rolled her eyes. "Everyone's naturally bad. Sin nature and all that."

"Yes, but that doesn't mean you can't trust anyone," Ivy said. "If you shut yourself away from everyone, then you lose so much. Love, family, comfort ..." Her voice trailed off. "You have to trust God to protect you. You can't protect yourself. And, if you get hurt, you must trust Him to do the healing, too."

Violet shrugged noncommittally.

"We've reached th' outskirts!" Jordy's voice was as enthusiastic as the sun at the height of summer. "You can see a building more often than every few miles."

Ivy turned to Jordy, determined not to let Violet spoil their arrival. "Yes, I see," she said. "It looks quite lovely. Really, it does. I know I'm going to love it here."

His honey-gold eyes twinkled as he smiled. "At least ye havena called it rustic yet."

"Rustic? Why not?" Ivy asked.

"Because 'rustic' is generally used as an insult, Vee, if ye havena noticed," he said, winking.

Ivy shook her head. "I'd never insult Keefmore, Jordy. Why, you're from Keefmore, so it must be a wonderful place." She felt her cheeks grow warm when she realized what she'd said and let her words trip on, *accelerando*. "Why ... why ... I mean, what did you call me, Jordy?"

"Vee."

"What?"

"We-ell," Jordy explained, "yer name is 'Ay-vee,' but tha's rather cumbersome."

"It's two syllables," Violet muttered. "That's hardly a mouthful."

Jordy grinned. "Ye're right, there; it's not tha' long. But I still like tae be able tae address me friends by one syllable. It's so much quicker. Tris is me friend—his name is Tristan, really. An' I call Violet Vi ... an' so, takin' th' second syllable o' yer name, I got Vee. An' then," he finished with a grin, "I can call ye Vee an' Vi. So much simpler."

"And confusing," Violet said. Ivy noted that this had, for whatever reason, made her friend more prickly; her clenched teeth and stiff posture reminded Ivy of a cat with its back arched and fur standing on end.

"We-ell"—this time the word could only be described as *adagio*—"I suppose it could be. But only if ye make it so." He winked at Ivy, which she supposed was his way of saying he was dragging on this conversation to cheer up Violet. She smiled in return. How sweet he was.

"No, it's confusing no matter how you say it," Violet protested. "And why would Ivy need a simpler name? And how will anyone know who you're talking to when you use it? And—"

"I think ye're over-complicatin' this."

"No, I'm not. And you're deliberately making yourself sound like a *rustic*, common man to prove a point."

"I am not," Jordy said, some of his brogue leaving him in a falsified British accent. His eyes danced, and Ivy couldn't help but giggle.

"Aye, ye are," Violet responded, as game as he was. Despite her best efforts, the corner of her lips twitched, and her eyes laughed. She enjoyed his teasing as much as Ivy enjoyed watching. Violet wasn't all the way hidden behind her bitter exterior, and for that, Ivy thanked the Lord. There was a part of Violet that she still left open to her closest friends—and more importantly, to God. For that reason, Ivy truly believed that there was hope for her friend. That someday—somehow—she would accept God's grace and love fully, not just when it was easier to do so.

The coach came to a stop in front of a large building—"Th' inn an' tavern," Jordy said—and the three passengers stepped out.

"Just stay here for a minna while I get our things unloaded," Jordy whispered, guiding Ivy and Violet to stand to the side. Violet wasn't wrong; his brogue had thickened the farther north they got, and now even Ivy, accustomed to him as she was, was struggling to keep up. However, she knew she'd adjust, too.

"Is that my niece?" A cheerful, proper voice that reminded Ivy of Mrs. Angel's in tone but not in inflection, came from behind them.

Violet and Ivy turned to face a tall, middle-aged woman with graying dark hair and a firm, upright posture. She wore a simple, navy-blue day dress and had a knitted shawl tossed over her shoulders.

"Aunt Daphne. Good evening." Violet stumbled slightly over the words but collected herself. "Thank you for ... letting us come. This is Ivy Knight, my friend—Jordy is gathering our things."

A loud crash from behind them indicated that Jordy had managed to get the last trunk down from the top of the coach. The horses whinnied nervously, and the driver urged him to "give a mind."

Ivy winced.

"Indeed." Aunt Daphne's eyes flicked to the coach, then back to Violet's face. "Well, I'm glad you could come—and I am most pleased to meet your friends. I had Agnes, my maid, prepare your rooms, and

I have hot tea waiting in my parlor."

The next sound they heard was Jordy's feet meeting the hard-packed dirt of the road. "Tha's th' last o' it." He drew alongside them and doffed his cap. "Mrs. Wright, is it?"

"Yes. Dr. McAllen ...?"

"Jordy is fine, ma'am, if ye weel. I'll follow behind wi' a man or two from th' pub, here, an' get all th' luggage taken tae yer house, if tha' will suit."

"Yes, it will, quite. But I imagine we can carry a thing or two." Aunt Daphne darted forward, snatched up two bags that lay at Violet's and Ivy's feet, and started off at a brisk clip. "Come on, ladies—an English rose might smell nice, but it's no good if it can't carry half its weight. Which is where the analogy always fails me, but suffice to say, I'll be having none of that useless, spineless behavior in my house."

Violet let out an incredulous little laugh, plainly both delighted and nervous, but, nonetheless, picked up a bag and gestured for Ivy to do the same.

They trailed after Aunt Daphne along the road between a few small shops. The older woman took a sharp turn down an alley, and they followed, soon emerging into the open night air to an empty field —in the midst of which sat a large, impressive house.

"I have grand intentions to start a garden in this space," Aunt Daphne practically shouted over her shoulder, "but I never have gotten to it. It's only been a year, I know, but I'll be saying that for the next five—watch me."

Unused to carrying bags and scrambling over somewhat rough terrain after Violet's crazy aunt, Ivy didn't manage a reply—only a soft huff. Violet laughed, but it was breathless, and Ivy knew she wasn't the only one unaccustomed to physical labor.

They arrived at the front door, and Aunt Daphne managed to get it open with a foot before proceeding in.

"Agnes! Agnes!" she called. "I have my niece and her friend, Miss Ivy Knight, with me. And that McAllen boy, too, who you said was so charming—so far all I've seen him do is toss a few trunks off a coach, which left no impression upon me whatsoever."

A young lady appeared out of the side door. "I've their tea in th' parlor, ma'am."

"Of course, of course." Aunt Daphne set the bags at the bottom of the stairway that curled up from the foyer.

Ivy glanced around her, taking in her dim surroundings as best she could. It appeared to be an elegant London townhouse that had somehow gotten transported to this wild moor. Though she'd not seen much of Keefmore yet, she could already tell how out of place this home was.

And she wasn't sure how she felt about that at all. She supposed it interested her ... and, as she thought about the house and all it said about Aunt Daphne's sense of what was proper, the more delighted she became.

Violet and Ivy also set their heavy bags down and rubbed their arms.

"I suppose I ought to introduce you," Aunt Daphne said. "This is Agnes Graham. She takes care of me—and of this house. If you need anything, she's the one to turn to. She has a dear little boy, too, Duncan—though he's asleep in Agnes's room behind the kitchen."

"Thankfully." The woman smiled and gestured into the parlor. "Would ye like—?"

"Oh yes." Aunt Daphne bustled forward. She didn't at all seem like the type of woman who would bustle, willowy as she was, but she did, with as much efficiency as any woman Ivy had ever met.

Violet and Ivy followed Aunt Daphne into the parlor, where a small table was set for four.

"It's just tea and a few cakes, though they're mostly for me," Aunt Daphne said, taking one of the seats. "I can't imagine you'll be too hungry right now."

"No, I'm not," said Violet, and Ivy echoed the sentiment. They'd packed a dinner at the last inn and eaten it in the coach.

Actually, Ivy didn't even really want tea—she just wanted to take off her shoes, lie down in a warm bed, and fall asleep. But she politely perched on the edge of a chair and sipped.

Agnes disappeared, and Ivy soon heard her showing the men where to put everything. Ivy was glad she didn't have to help move all their things up the stairs. The trip was of an undetermined length, and both Ivy and Violet had packed as if it would be at least a few months.

Jordy appeared in the parlor after that. "We've gotten everythin' placed, Mrs. Wright."

"'Aunt Daphne' might be more suitable. That is, if I'm to shelter you for the night. Which I would very much like to do." Aunt Daphne rose, leaving a half-finished tea cake on her plate. "You saw I prepared a room for you? I know you have family in the area, but I thought, since it's so late—"

"Tha' would be greatly appreciated." Jordy nodded. "I suppose ye wouldna mind if we went up sooner than later, Aunt Daphne? It's been a long journey."

Ivy cast Jordy a thankful glance as she stood. "That would be lovely."

"Of course, of course." Aunt Daphne urged them away with fluttering gestures. "I wouldn't keep you a minute more than you want. Sleep, and sleep as long as you want, and we'll have breakfast when you're ready."

"An' then I had hoped tae take these two ladies tae meet me family," Jordy said. "I've ken't them both so long, an' talked about them in me letters, an' I imagine they'd all love tae meet th' real Vee and Vi."

"Naturally. Perhaps you can start out after breakfast! We'll all get acquainted some other time." Aunt Daphne glanced at Ivy and Violet. "You heard him. Run on upstairs! There's warm water for washing, and you can settle in as soon as you like. Agnes, will you show them where everything is?"

Agnes, standing behind Jordy, gestured behind her. "Aye, I will."

Gratefully, Ivy and Violet left the parlor behind, bidding the energetic Aunt Daphne good night, and slipped up the stairs.

CHAPTER EIGHT

The next morning, Violet woke Ivy at dawn, and they prepared for the day quietly. Surprisingly enough, Jordy was already down at the breakfast table when they arrived.

"Me brothers will come tae town an' get us with th' wagon first thing, an' I didna want tae keep them waitin'," he explained.

"Oh! Should we eat quickly?" Ivy asked, sliding onto a seat at the same small table in the parlor. Apparently, Aunt Daphne was in a habit of eating here—another delightful little eccentricity. Ivy felt there was something so formal and cold about dining rooms, but this was wonderfully comfortable.

"Nae, ye needna. I'm sure they willna be here for another half hour. What possessed ye tae get up so early, though, Vee?" His eyes twinkled as he used his recent shortening of her name.

"Violet woke me. She said we wouldn't want to keep you waiting."

Violet glanced at Ivy and then turned the glare to Jordy. "That wasn't exactly what I said," she grouched.

Jordy grinned. "Ach, Vi, are ye goin' soft for me, then?"

She rolled her eyes and didn't reply.

Ivy indulged a knowing glance at Jordy, and he smirked back at her. Violet had been *thoughtful.* Would Jordy ever be able to let her forget that?

They were soon outside of the house, bidding Aunt Daphne good-bye over their shoulders and heading toward the main street. Almost as soon as they emerged from the alleyway—how had Aunt

Daphne gotten this bit of property behind the town, anyway?—they heard a deep voice with a hint of a crack to it.

"Jordy!"

Jordy whirled around, but not before Ivy saw the huge grin on his face. "Mick! Ben!"

Two young men dashed forward. Both had orange tops—brighter than Jordy's dark auburn-brown hair—and big, broad-shouldered bodies. Ivy lingered somewhere between intimidated and curious, her neverending *leitmotif* since agreeing to come to Keefmore.

Jordy embraced both of his brothers, pounding them on the back and teasing them about their growth over the last several years, then turned back to Ivy and Violet.

"Ivy, Violet, these are two o' me brothers—Benjamin an' Michael McAllen. But ye can call them Ben an' Mick. Tha' is"—he glanced at his brothers—"if ye havena started usin' yer Christian names in full?"

"Nae," Mick said, and Ben shrugged.

"Ben's six years younger than me," Jordy said, his mouth hopping and twitching as he attempted to restrain his enthusiasm and act condescending. "Mick's seven years younger."

"An' ye willna ever let us forget it, will ye?" Mick said, laughing.

Jordy smirked but didn't reply to his brother's question. "Ben, Mick, this is Miss Violet Angel an' Miss Ivy Knight. They'll be stayin' in Keefmore for a while."

Ivy closed her eyes for a minute and took a deep breath, as Dr. McCale had suggested, uttering a quick prayer for calmness, and then opened them and smiled at Jordy's brothers.

"Pleased tae meet ye," Mick said, shaking her hand enthusiastically. "So, ye"—he nodded to Violet—"must be Lady Wright's niece. She keeps tellin' us she's no' a lady, ken, but she *acts* like one. She's an odd duck, but we all like her anyway." He had a gentle, boyish face. His hair was slightly darker and shorter than Ben's.

Ben hopped back in the wagon without so much of a word of greeting.

"Ben's no' a great talker," Jordy said. "He doesna feel it necessary."

"I understand that," Ivy said softly.

"Well, I dinna." Jordy's face displayed disapproval. "What would we do if we couldna speak tae each other? How would we have friends or companions o' any sort?"

Ivy didn't know what to say to this; she preferred silence but knew it would be hard to get along with life without any talking.

Jordy led Ivy and Violet after his brothers. They came to the side of a small wagon pulled by a pair of mismatched horses—one chestnut, one gray.

"We'll ride in the back?" Violet guessed, her expression skeptical. Violet would have a bit of a hard time adjusting to Scotland, perhaps more so than Ivy, if only because she'd complain. Ivy wouldn't dare to.

"Aye, lass," Mick said cheerfully. "Left a space for ye an' Miss Ivy both. Jordy will be behind, too. If tha's a'right with ye, tha' is."

Violet hesitated, glancing at Jordy, then nodded. Jordy cupped his hands around her waist, lifted her up, and all but passed her to Mick. Violet shrieked, causing Mick and Jordy to laugh.

As Violet settled in, Jordy apologized for startling her, saying he hadn't thought about anything but getting home as soon as possible. Violet deliberately drew her lips down in a scowl, but Ivy could tell she was amused. Jordy was always so ... so *Jordy!*

"Can I help ye, Ivy?" Jordy asked, thoroughly chastened.

"Yes."

He scooped her up, and, with Mick's help, she was soon settled in the wagon bed next to Violet.

The air was cold, and Jordy passed them a heavy blanket that Ivy and Violet snuggled up under, Ivy resting her head on Violet's shoulder. The road wasn't as smooth as she was used to, but, tired already from her early morning, Ivy soon found herself drifting off as they jounced toward Jordy's home.

She awoke only when Jordy gently shook her shoulders, and she found herself lying on the bottom of the wagon bed. Violet was already on the ground at the wagon's end, peering up at her with the lazy expression of one half awake. She was clutching her arms around her against the cold. Her breath came out in frozen puffs.

"Come on, sleepyhead," Jordy said. "We're home."

Ivy accepted Jordy's hand, and he helped her to stand and climb out of the wagon. On her feet, she looked quickly around her at a large barnyard and a quaint cottage, gray stone with a brown roof and white-framed windows. There were several other outbuildings, and when she turned, she caught sight of craggy hills surrounding them, a mix of green grass and harsh, sharp rocks. The strong smell of a farm whispered in the air, but it was distant from her at the moment, and the sunlight streaming down, catching the rising mist, was much more worth noting. She beamed up at Jordy.

"Wha' is it?" he asked.

"This is a lovely place!" she exclaimed.

He chuckled. "I'm sure we're all verra glad ye think so. Let's go inside."

They stepped through the door of the cottage, and Ivy was immediately greeted with a rush of warmth and the scent of freshly baked bread. Directly in front of her was a round table with quite a few mismatched chairs sitting about it, set for breakfast. The kitchen appeared to be beyond that, and a common room to her right had more chairs and another smaller table.

"We havena had our breakfast yet," Mick proclaimed, jostling past Jordy, Violet, and Ivy. "We had tae get ye instead."

"Shut it, Mick." Ben followed Mick into the room and jostled him with his arm. "Dinna complain."

"Ach, I wasna complainin'! Just explainin'. We're goin' tae eat soon, I hope, and tha's because—"

Mick didn't finish his explanations, however, as an older woman appeared from the kitchen and dashed across the room and into Jordy's arms.

"Me lad, me grown lad! There ye are." She embraced him

enthusiastically and then stepped back. "Let me look at ye! Ach, Jordy, ye're braw an' big, like yer father. How is't tha' ye've been away so long?" And here she placed her hands on her hips, but they quickly dropped. "Ach, I canna be mad—ye're home. An' these lassies must be—?"

"Violet Angel an' Ivy Knight," Jordy supplied, touching each of their arms lightly as he said their names. "I thought they'd break their fast with us, Mum—I saw they hardly picked at wha' they were given at Violet's aunt's house."

It was true; Ivy hadn't eaten much. But she'd been so recently awakened. During the ride, and now smelling all sorts of lovely scents wafting out from the kitchen, she'd regained an appetite, however.

"Aye, tha' would be just right." Mrs. McAllen smiled at each of the girls in turn, giving them a slight nod. "I love nothin' more than tae share wha' th' Good Lord has seen fit tae give us. An' I always make more than we'll need, what with these lads scarfin' down all they can fit in their bellies. Come out o' th' doorway! Jordy, yer da is out gettin' th' chores done—an' should be here any minna."

At her words, the door opened behind them, and Ivy stepped out of the way to let three more men into the room—well, a man and two boys.

The man was older, his hair turning a shade of blond as the auburn grayed. His eyes lit up upon seeing Jordy, but he didn't rush to him like Mrs. McAllen. Instead, he crossed the room and took a firm grip on Jordy's arm.

"At last, ye're home, lad," he said, softly but earnestly. "I'm glad."

"We're all glad!" Mrs. McAllen called over her shoulder as she returned to the kitchen. "Time tae eat. Wash up, lads."

The two younger boys peeked at Jordy shyly. Ivy guessed the older one was somewhere between ten and twelve, and the younger six or seven. Jordy greeted them both with more hugs and teasing and then introduced them as William—sometimes called Liam by the McAllens, who apparently favored nicknames above all else—and Thomas, who went by Tom.

Just then, there was a loud banging sound from the kitchen. Ivy took a second to recover before realizing that there was probably another door from the back that opened into the kitchen, and someone had opened it rather loudly.

"Is tha' our Edith?" Jordy called.

"Aye, it's me," a woman's voice replied, but without getting any closer to them, indicating to Ivy that she was staying in the kitchen for now. "Was out collectin' th' eggs. Wha's th' idea o' leavin' me alone tae manage these lads for so long? Where've ye been?"

"London an' Edinburgh an' thereabouts." Jordy grinned and gestured to the table, indicating that Ivy and Violet should take a seat. "An' who put ye in charge here, Edi? Why canna ye just let them run wild? It's nae skin off yer back."

A half-incredulous laugh. "I imagine th' Lord wouldna give me brothers tae let them grow up like wolves on the moors. Nae, someone has tae keep them in order, Jordy, an' if it wasna tae be ye, it would be me."

"It'll be good for her tae have her own home," Mr. McAllen said in a conspiratorial whisper. "She's up tae high doh, as yer mum never could be."

Jordy smirked but kept his eyes in the direction of the kitchen. "Come out an' see me at least."

"In good time, if I please tae."

Ivy wasn't sure, based on this exchange, if she liked Edith at all. She sounded controlling and worried and grouchy, and those three seldom made a good combination. That was why she steered clear of Alice at her grouchiest; she wasn't about to willingly submit herself to more well-meaning management. But Ivy had learned of late, at Peter's encouragement, that she was, in fact, an adult, and could do what she pleased, no matter what Alice said. It was freeing.

Edith did appear shortly after, a woman close to Jordy's height and slim, with auburn hair tied in a loose braid over one shoulder. She *allowed* Jordy to embrace her rather than participating, but she was smiling as she looked him up and down. "Tris is up in th' hills noo, with th' sheep, but he'll be glad tae see ye," she commented placidly.

"Mm-hmm. I've heard all about Tris." Jordy wiggled his eyebrows, and Ivy stifled a giggle behind her hand.

Edith rolled her eyes. "Ach, dinna ye start, tae."

"I've no' even begun yet, Edi! I canna believe—"

"Leave it 'til he's here, at least."

Jordy held up his hands. "Verra well. If ye canna take th' teasin' alone, I can always wait 'til Tris is here tae take his share. But ye ken it is comin'."

"Ach, aye, as if I could stop ye!"

In no time at all, the food was ready, and they were all seated around the table.

"Now, what're th' plans for th' day?" Mrs. McAllen asked. "I ken Jordy mentioned somewhat about gettin' an office ready? He was offered tha' empty buildin' in th' village, wasna he?"

"Aye," Mr. McAllen said. "With yer permission, Annis, I'd like for Edith and William and Tom tae go with him tae Keefmore tomorrow tae clean out th' office. Today Jordy'll just look at th' inside an' see what needs be done, willna ye, Jordy? But like as no', it's a big job, an' he could get it done in half a day wi' th' right help, an' start tae work right after. Jordy brought all sorts o' medical supplies an' such—"

"No' a great many, Da." Jordy talked around a bite of food. "But enough tae get me started, aye." He'd told Ivy that was what was in his trunks—he'd only a few changes of clothes.

"Anyway," Mr. McAllen continued, "he'd like tae get started right away, ye see."

Mrs. McAllen nodded. "I see. I believe ye've come up with th' best plan, Bert, though I'm no' sure why ye're willing tae give up William and Edith both in th' middle o' harvest. Still, I'm proud tae see ye takin' an interest in Jordy's work." She tipped her glass to him and then returned her mind to her eating.

Jordy leaned over to whisper in Ivy's ear. "Did ye sleep well? We didna talk much this morn, did we?"

She jumped, surprised to find him so close. "No, we didn't. Yes, I did. Thank you, Jordy. Did you?"

"Aye, I did! Th' Scots air is better, Vee, an' nae mistakin' it—though maybe ye'll be thinkin' I'm dafty, it's true. Th' air this time o' th' year makes ye chitter, an' th' rain'll have ye drookit, but there's days tha' are no' dreich, and I expect all o' us will have our health improved by them. But I've been haverin', havena I?"

Ivy smiled. There was nothing more amusing than Jordy's ever-thickening brogue. She could feel her cheeks reddening, and she glanced down, but not before Jordy caught the expression, apparently.

"*Ay-vee*," he said, dragging out her name in a teasing manner, "what is it?"

Ivy simply smiled again and shook her head. It was too difficult to explain—and embarrassing that she'd noticed.

"*Ay-vee*, ye can tell me. Please?"

"Have you heard yourself this morning?" Ivy asked, examining her hands folded on her lap. She started twisting them about nervously; perhaps she shouldn't have commented on it.

"I've better things tae do than listen tae meself talk," Jordy said. "But, aye, I suppose I've been hearin' meself talk all morn. Why?"

"Your brogue—it's been thicker since we came here and saw your family. And the words you use—I've never even heard them before! I was thinking about that and enjoying it."

"Enjoyin' it?" he asked, raising his eyebrows. "Whatever do ye mean by tha'?"

Ivy was sure she blushed even redder at that. "Nothing," she replied all too quickly. "I thought ... I love the way it sounds," she said, barely above her breath.

Jordy laughed aloud. "Ach, for heaven's sake, Vee, if tha's all!"

"What are you two whispering about?" Violet said. Ivy looked up to see her brow furrowed, irritation lining her face.

"Nothin'. Vee here was just commentin' on me funny accent." Jordy winked in her direction.

Edith nodded at Ivy and smiled. "Ye'll get used tae it, same way as we'll get used tae yer speech. Ye can ask me if this gowk"—she gestured to Jordy—"willna tell ye straight wha' somethin' means. I will."

"Nae, Edi—she'll be catchin' on fast!" Jordy protested. "She's a canny lass. Which, by th' way, Vee, is a compliment. Clever, ken?"

Ivy blushed again but nodded. Jordy squeezed her hand under the table and returned to the multitude of well-buttered, thick slices of bread he'd stacked up on his plate.

After they ate, Jordy took Ivy and Violet back into the village, where they could start getting acquainted with Aunt Daphne.

Slightly nervous, Ivy was grateful that Jordy again took her hand as he dropped her off. "Enjoy yerself," he told her. "Nae use in th' worryin', Vee. Ye're such a charmin' lass—I canna imagine Aunt Daphne willna love ye. I'll see ye tomorrow, a'right? We'll take a look at tha' office space together."

Flushing again—she hoped for the last time today, for her cheeks felt tired of it—she nodded and slipped into the house to face Violet's aunt.

CHAPTER NINE

T here you young ladies are!" Aunt Daphne materialized in the foyer almost as soon as Violet and Ivy stepped into the house. "Why don't you both go find a shawl? The wind is nippy, but we're going back outside with Duncan to play in the garden."

Agnes appeared behind with her baby on her hip. Ivy's heart instantly squeezed—he was a sweet little thing with rosy cheeks and bright-blue eyes and a fluff of dark hair atop his head. "I've been wantin' tae clean oot th' pantry, an' I thought if ye took him, I might get a chance," she commented.

"I didn't mean you'd have to work while we watched him," Aunt Daphne said, brow furrowing. "I'd hoped you'd be able to stay and relax in the garden, too."

"Ach, nae! I'd rather have time tae meself. Besides, it looks like rain, so ye willna be oot long." Agnes transferred the little fellow into Aunt Daphne's arms. "I'll make meself a cup o' tea while I work."

"Very well." Aunt Daphne awkwardly maneuvered the boy onto her hip. Ivy longed to rush forward and take him, but she'd better not —yet, at least.

So Violet, Ivy, and Aunt Daphne walked back out of the house with wee Duncan, and the three settled in the patch of weeds and long grass and randomly piled rocks, which would someday, supposedly, be a garden.

Aunt Daphne placed Duncan on the ground and threw herself head first into the largest patch of long grass, beginning to pull it out with a vengeance. "I'll work on this if the two of you will just talk and mind the baby," she said over her shoulder. "Might as well try to get some of this out."

Ivy didn't see the point of doing a lot of weeding in this patch of land before spring came, but if Aunt Daphne was determined, Ivy was starting to realize there would be no stopping her. For her part, she was content to kneel next to Duncan and meet his dear little eyes.

"Hello, baby," Ivy whispered. "What pretty eyes you have!"

"'The better to see you with, my dear,'" Violet quoted in a slightly distorted voice.

"Oh, shush." Even Violet's wolf impersonations couldn't ruin Ivy's enjoyment of this perfect darling. "He must have gotten them from his father." Agnes's eyes were darker.

"He did, I've heard." Aunt Daphne leaned back on her heels and placed mud-caked hands on her lap, thereby completing the ruination of her light-blue skirt. It appeared practicality was not her strong point. "Of course, I've never met the man. He was one of those restless types, drifting from village to village—it's been about a year and a half since he was here, and Agnes has heard nothing from him." She sighed. "A sad story, but not an uncommon one. Agnes's own parents haven't spoken to her."

"So he's illegitimate?" Violet said bluntly. Of course she would say such a thing aloud, when, to Ivy, naïve though she was, it was a perfectly logical and obvious conclusion.

"Yes, he is. But none the less human for it, I hope." Aunt Daphne smiled, though it was tinged with sadness. "I dislike the attitude that the circumstances surrounding our birth somehow give us our worth. Especially since the Bible has made it very clear indeed that our worth comes from other sources—which, in my opinion, are much more reliable."

Violet nodded. "I wasn't judging. Only observing."

"How old is he?" Ivy asked. Time to move the conversation away from this rather uncomfortable path and back to the realm of safety—to all the sweet, lovely things there were to discuss about a baby.

"About ten months now, I think."

Duncan screeched aloud to confirm this statement and, having decided Ivy was not a very frightening person, for indeed she wasn't, lunged forward and caught at the collar of her dress, not quite taking a step but very near to it.

Ivy gladly accepted him into her arms. "Hello, dear boy."

He managed to pull himself up with both hands on her shoulders and patted her cheeks with more happy squeals and gurgles. Ivy gladly entertained his babbles, for there was nothing more precious than this.

"I've always had a heart for the out-of-the-way people." Aunt Daphne resumed her somewhat hectic weeding, if her disorganized 'pull everything in sight out of the ground' method could be called weeding. "People like Agnes and Duncan, who have no one—and who have been returned cruelty for their brokenness. Agnes has suffered enough from her family and the village to be as repentant as one can be, and she entered the entire affair with a great deal of innocence."

Ivy nodded as if she had an idea what Aunt Daphne meant by that. Of course, she understood the general gist of it—it wasn't as if she hadn't lived in the world, and she'd heard a lot and in general observed a great deal more than most people thought. But she tried not to dwell on the more dramatic aspects of life—not even to cluck her tongue and shake her head. She had little time for such moral posturing.

"That's why it's so important to stay moral, and Agnes should have thought twice." It would seem Aunt Daphne couldn't decide between honesty and compassion. "Of course, I'd go as far as to say that Agnes was not well prepared by her parents for reality—for the choices she'd have to make in the moment. A lot of the time young ladies aren't talked to the way I wish they could be! If they only knew what to expect, they might better guard themselves. Which makes me think—I don't suppose you ladies might appreciate some knowledge on the subject? For the sake of avoiding future compromising situations becoming even more compromising, I mean."

"Yes!" Violet exclaimed, eyes alight with that somewhat evil glint that always appeared whenever she stood to make someone very uncomfortable. In this case, that was Ivy.

Ivy kicked Violet as hard as she could. That was quite enough of that.

"But perhaps some other time." Violet cleared her throat and rubbed at her shin. "I do think I'd like to hear your perspective, though."

Aunt Daphne cast a somewhat confused look over her shoulder, then nodded and continued pulling grass.

Ivy turned all her attention to Duncan, who alternated between babbling, grasping handfuls of Ivy's hair, some of which had managed to escape from her carefully-tied ribbon, and feeble attempts at walking, which inevitably ended with him sitting down hard, a shocked expression on his face.

There was nothing so precious as a baby this age—except, perhaps, a baby of any age. Children in general were delightful, really. Ivy could never countenance the opinion that they were nuisances or meant to be 'seen and not heard.' Children were, to Ivy, a window into her own soul through which she could see the best of humanity—and, at times, the worst. Children were an excellent example of the highs and lows of human nature, for even if loved and coddled and taught to follow all the rules and regulations, they rebelled. Ivy had always loved the Bible verses that compared people to children not because it made her feel safe, though it did, but because it made her feel understood—if there was grace and understanding for a toddler having a tantrum, there was grace and understanding for Ivy.

Of course, if she wasn't careful, her mind would start wandering down a much more difficult path when it came to children—one of longing and then despair. The longing because it would be nice to be a mother herself, or at least to have the ability to watch children on more of a daily basis. And then the despair, for to be a mother, she would need a husband, and to have a husband, she could certainly not be Ivy.

It always sent her down a sad path that could only lead to more sadness, and she tried not to think about it. But it just didn't make sense that she'd have such a drive to mother *something* if there was never anyone to mother. Except her siblings, of course, and she wasn't even with them right now. She winced at this thought, wondering why she'd come up here when some of the things, and certainly most of the people, that made her happy were located at Pearlbelle Park.

God, what are You doing with me here?

There was no answer, and Ivy sat still and continued to think. She should, truly, reject the notion that God could never work marriage and a family into Ivy's life if He wanted to. However, she doubted that He would. Furthermore, something in her soul suggested that to narrow one's entire existence down to just a family circle would severely reject several other commandments. She knew she must reach out, for there was so much suffering and so much she could do to aid with it ...

But again she circled back to, "But I'm Ivy." She always would be Ivy, after all, and what could she do against all the cries of pain in all the countries in all the world? Nothing.

Still, there could be one small thing—one baby to cuddle, one Agnes to love, one Aunt Daphne to humor, one Violet to speak truth to. She sighed and pulled Duncan onto her lap, cooing nonsensical things and reminding herself with his solid, chunky warmness that there was something right here and right now to be done, always. Even if that was just resting in God's glory on a blustery October day.

Aunt Daphne was rambling about Venice now, and Ivy put the rest of her brain power into listening to that. It was interesting, after all —Ivy didn't really want to travel, but if she ever had the courage, or perhaps the right person to travel with, she'd like to go to Venice. And Florence and possibly Rome, but Venice was high on the list.

"You've traveled a great many places," Violet commented. She sat now with her knees clutched to her chest and her eyes somewhat distant, but she'd managed more 'in the moment' action than Ivy had, certainly.

"I have, with Roger, my husband. We had a lot of adventures. As a young girl, I didn't think I'd travel, but by the time I got married, I was ready to be done with London and society, so it seemed the best choice." She again leaned back on her heels. "It was a very enjoyable experience, and I learned a lot."

Ivy wondered if this was a sore subject still, as she always struggled to decide when it was appropriate to start talking about dead loved ones—for Ivy it was simultaneously *always* and *never.*

"Roger and I never wanted to stay in London for long, so I was glad when our finances finally allowed us to leave it all behind. After that, it was a fairly simple matter of traveling from place to place and doing what good we could." She sighed. "On one hand, I miss it. On the other, I'm too old for that life anymore. Not that I'd precisely call myself *old*, but that I really ought to be settling. People have been saying that to me since I was eighteen years old, but now it really is true. I do hope that I'll find ways to be useful."

"Mm ..." That was almost exactly Ivy's struggle. She didn't feel she could live a life of constant adventure, constant change, yet what was there to do? She wanted to be useful, but she felt so stagnant at home ... and so frightened when there was change. Those two quarreled in her head. She both wanted and feared a challenge. What was she to do?

"That's why I wanted Violet to come here. I felt that this would be a safe place for my dear, insane niece." Aunt Daphne let loose a small chuckle. "Of course, my sister was never any kinder to me than she is to Violet, so I don't believe a word of it. If I'd been a different person, I might have taken Violet along with me to the Continent ... but I didn't get the whole story until recently. Dorothea is so dreadfully nonsensical at times, and that husband of hers is a brute. I said so from the beginning." She harrumphed. "Pardon me speaking about your parents that way, but it's just true."

Violet shrugged and cast Ivy a sidelong glance. She probably agreed with Aunt Daphne for the most part, but she tended to withdraw her opinions around members of her family. It appeared that even her plainly kind-hearted aunt was no different.

"Simply put." Aunt Daphne paused and cleared her throat. "Simply put, I want Violet to have the love, support, and safety that I never did when I was her age. Heavens, why am I talking in third person? You're right here—I'm turning into your mother, perhaps, after all. I mean, of course, that I want *you*, Violet, to have the love, support, and safety that I never did when I was your age. Not that you have to stay with me, but that I like that it's a choice now. I never had any options until I got married, and even then it was hit or miss for the first few years while Roger and I worked a few things out and figured out who we really were."

Warmth filled Ivy's chest. If Aunt Daphne wasn't exaggerating her commitment to her niece's safety, it would appear that Violet could potentially benefit greatly from her aunt. Now, would Violet let herself? That remained to be seen. All the same, it was so lovely to have the option of being benefited. Ivy knew that from experience.

Of course, right now that was the central issue in Ivy's life—who or what was her Aunt Daphne?

Violet, meanwhile, seemed unsure what to say. She sat still, clutching her knees, eyes distant. "Thank you," she murmured at last, a quiet, confused mutter. "I don't know what the next step is for me. I don't want to be a burden to the McCales, but ... my parents' home is just not ... That is, if I want to have any form of pleasant reality, my parents' home is not an option. But I'd be a burden to you, too, in time."

"That's not true!" Ivy exclaimed, before realizing that perhaps she couldn't be the one to determine whether or not Violet would become a burden to Aunt Daphne. Her ears burning, she pushed forward nonetheless. "It's not true that you're a burden to the McCales. Besides, Violet, you're not the only one that feels lost." There. She'd admitted it. "I don't have much of a purpose these days, either, you know. And that's hard on me. But I know God will help us both find it ... and, Violet, think how glorious it will be when we do!"

Violet hummed noncommittally.

"I was confused for many years about my position in this world." Aunt Daphne turned to her little piles of weeds and began combining them together, preparing it all to be carried away. "For a good half of my life thus far, I had no idea where I belonged and how I ought to serve God. But I found that my lack of confidence was simply a stumbling block. The best way to serve God was to dive into every day as if it were my last ... and do all I could to further the Kingdom! There can be no hesitance. Better a wrong step than none, I say."

Now, Ivy liked that. Much as she'd hate to fail at anything, she did feel her own cowardice—or anxiety, if she wanted to use the term Dr. McCale did—got in the way. Intriguing but scary.

"Well, it's about time for lunch." Aunt Daphne pushed herself to her feet and dusted off her skirts. "We're going to go in now. Get Duncan, Ivy—he's got dirt in his mouth, so do try to spoon some out before we go into the house. Though I don't suppose it'll hurt him terribly." She turned toward the door then paused, hands fisted in her skirts, looking very much like Violet when she was forcing emotion to the back in order to get something done. "Thank you, girls. For coming here and keeping me company. You'll both make my life a little brighter, and a little more purposeful, while you're here, however long or short that time is. It's been ... it's been difficult since Roger died. Or when not difficult, at least *different*. And I thank you for the part you're playing in this ... this rebuilding of my life."

Then, without waiting for a response, Aunt Daphne stormed forward like an eager thundercloud, her next task being luncheon.

CHAPTER TEN

Jordy woke the next morning to the sounds of cows lowing and milk pinging against metal buckets, along with the smells of manure from below and wet moss from the roof. It was still dark save for the glow of the lanterns from below him, and he blinked, his memory grasping for a foothold of his actual location.

Then it came back to him, and he slowly sat up, swung his legs over the side of his pallet, and rested his bare feet on the straw-covered floor of the loft where Mick, Ben, and he had all slept together when they were lads. Here they were again.

He admitted he was a bit annoyed to be back where he'd started, especially since no one here understood that he was capable of anything serious. But he was, and he'd prove it to the folks of Keefmore as he had to the professors and then doctors in London.

He quickly pulled on his trousers, stockings, and boots then tucked his nightshirt into his belt, deciding not to bother with getting dressed all the way before chores. He also left the bedclothes scattered about the floor—it was rare that Mrs. McAllen entered the loft, and they'd rather get scolded once every few months than keep it tidy all the time. It wasn't worth it.

He half-stumbled down the ladder and found his brothers already busy milking their six cows.

"Good morn," Jordy said. "Sorry for bein' late. Must've overslept."

"Ach, it's a'right ... on th' first day," Mick said, grinning over one of the cow's back. "Ye'll have tae take some jobs from us, ye ken—we canna do them all, an' 'if any wouldna work, neither should he eat,' as th' sayin' goes."

Jordy laughed. "I'll earn me keep. But I've never known ye tae milk th' coos. I thought tha' was Edi's job."

"Aye, usually." Mick shrugged. "She's been crabbit these last few months, an' never more so than when Tris is gone up tae pasture. She's always flichterin' about, clipin' on us, makin' everyone run fair mad. Canna wait until this December—she'll wed then an' be oot o' our hair."

Jordy grinned and stretched. He could understand why Mick would be unsympathetic to the plight of his lovelorn sister, especially since she appeared to be taking her grief over Tris's absence out on the lads. "Have ye already run th' sheep out?" he asked without addressing Edith's nonsense.

"Nae time for tha' yet. We're runnin' late today, on account o' such a long night, talkin' wi' ye as we did. But," Mick reflected, "we dinna mind much, seein' as ye're here noo. We missed ye, Jordy."

And it was always nice how much they loved him, too. But they didn't really know him, so that was to be expected. "Thank ye. I'll mind th' sheep—we still runnin' them out through th' barn?"

"Changed what we were doin' twice while ye were gone." Mick pushed himself up to give Jordy a saucy grin. "But, aye, now we get them oot o' th' barn, an' Bean takes them the rest o' th' way."

Jordy's brow wrinkled. "Bean?"

"Aye. Wee collie pup. I forget ye werena properly introduced, though ye probably saw him runnin' about yesterday. Only," Mick added, "he isna such a wee thing anymore. Edith brought him home nigh on two years ago, wet an' bedraggled, long-legged thing. Didna know who he belonged tae, an' we never found anyone who did, so we kept him an' named him Bean McBean." Mick grinned. "He's th' best collie dog we've had. Aye, Sean an' Gypsy are good, but they dinna have a way wi' th' sheep tha' Bean does."

As if offended, big Sean raised his black head in the corner and whined. Jordy and Mick laughed—even Ben smiled.

"Ach, Sean, I didna mean it!" Mick placed a hand on his chest in apology. "Just ye are better for other things. Ye're a good guard dog, and ye used tae be good with th' sheep, but ye're gettin' tae old to run th' fields day an' night. It's time tae take a rest, old chum. Ye an' Gypsy both."

Sean thumped his tail in agreement. He was a great dog with all sorts of breeds in him, from what Jordy could tell, and he'd been around the farm since Jordy was a small boy—Sean was at least fifteen years old now. Jordy was surprised he'd lived that long. Yet he seemed almost as young as ever, if a little slower to move. In Jordy's way of thinking, Sean was ageless.

Their other dog, Gypsy, a mid-sized yellow mutt, had to be almost ten by now. She'd been a young dog when Jordy had left, and now she was showing her age. Aye, it was time for another dog. He only hoped Bean could live up to Sean's and Gypsy's reputations.

"I'll go meet Bean, then. Is he a friendly dog?"

Ben made a coughing sound.

Mick laughed. "Aye, Jordy. Tha' dog has never met a stranger. He's no guard dog, tha's for certain. He may look at ye odd at first, but he'll never growl or bite ye ... no' unless ye're a truly suspicious character, I suppose. It's on account o' Edith spoiling him, I think. He slept in her room at first, an' even noo she brings him scraps an' pampers him like she never did Sean or Gyp."

Jordy grinned. "I'll go run out th' sheep now an' see ye at breakfast. Should be soon, eh?"

"Probably about half an hour." Mick shrugged and returned to his task. "Any rate, we're almost done here. On our last coos."

"Good." Jordy picked his coat up from where he'd tossed it on a hay bale last night and shrugged it on, flopping his hat on top of his head. Then he ventured into the crispy unknown.

The cold bit at his face as soon as he stepped out of the barn. He closed the door quickly and hunched his shoulders against the chill.

He hurried up the path to the sheep shed, running to beat the shivers. After all, he did have to get the sheep out quickly. Wouldn't do for them to spend the whole morning in the shed without food or water.

He opened the door and slipped through. The sheep baaed and bleated, shifting away from him and packing close to each other, but he managed to wade through.

As he reached the troughs, he was met with a medium-sized dog, about knee-height, mostly black with white paws, a white stripe down his face to his nose, and a white tip on the end of his tail—classic sheepdog markings. His ears were perked up, and he cautiously wagged his tail from side to side.

"Hullo, Bean," Jordy said. "I've come tae help ye with yer sheep for a while."

Bean seemed to think this was all right, and his tail thumped, as if glad he'd made a new friend.

"Ye're no' a bad lad, noo are ye?" Jordy asked, leaning over to pat Bean's head. "Good dog. Let's get them out an' get them water."

Jordy opened the big doors to the shed, and the sheep hurried out. He stood to the side, not wanting to get trampled. Mick was right about Bean, he observed. The dog got all the sheep out of the shed and congregated around the water troughs. Jordy made his way over and pumped water until the sheep had drunk their fill. Then Bean moved them away.

Some part of their dumb sheep heads seemed to register the pattern of walking away from the shed and troughs after drinking, but that didn't lessen Bean's job. He darted in and out, weaved about, continually fixing the sheep with an intense stare. Jordy leaned back and watched, impressed. It was rare that he saw a dog give eye that well.

Bean was really a majestic creature. Not large, as most of the truly impressive dogs were, but he moved with a grace of movement that was quite eye-catching. His dedication was apparent, and Jordy found himself respecting that even if he wasn't the kind of dog Jordy liked. Jordy wanted a big, lovable ball of fur who could go from cuddling to taking a man down and chewing his arm off in seconds. But that wasn't practical for a working dog—quick and canny was better.

After shutting the gate to the pasture, leaving Bean to make sure the sheep got well settled in for the day, Jordy jogged back to the house. Ben and Mick were leaving the barn with the milk in its big steel jugs, and Jordy hurried to help them.

"Just thought o' somethin'," he said as they walked around to the washing room at the back of the house. "Shouldna William and Tom be helpin'?"

Mick snickered. "Mum has them helpin' in th' house this morn, poor lads."

Ah. Jordy remembered the days when Mum had called them in once a week or so to clean house before work mornings. "Tha' must've made them happy."

"Aye." Mick's eyes twinkled. "Happiest I ever seen them."

Jordy chuckled. "I imagine so. I can see them doin' th' house chores with a cheerful smile on their faces."

Even Ben had to grin at this thought.

They reached the washroom door and made their way in, setting the milk on the floor in the corner and walking into the kitchen.

Mrs. McAllen turned from the stove and smiled at them. "Ah, there ye three are. Have ye done everythin'? Sheep an' cattle?"

"Aye," Mick said. "We havena finished muckin' th' stalls. But ..."

Mrs. McAllen placed her hands on her hips. "An' why do ye expect tae eat before ye've finished yer jobs?"

"It's late, Mum—I'm half-starved!" Mick protested. It was a fairly common excuse—in the McAllen household, lateness was a problem. At least Jordy came by it honestly. "Ben? Jordy? Are no' ye as starved as I am?" he added.

Jordy and Ben both nodded.

Mrs. McAllen sighed. "A'right, then. But, first thing after breakfast, ye get yer work done so ye can spend th' rest o' th' day helpin' yer father. No protests."

Mick mumbled about having to do Edith's chores as well as their own, but didn't make any further protestations as he pulled off his mucky boots and walked across the room in his stockinged feet to the table.

William and Tom dashed into the room then, William holding a broom and Tom a cloth.

"Finished yer room, Mother," Tom said in his sweet, high-pitched, little-boy voice. He was only seven years old, and Jordy had few memories of him, having only visited a few times since his birth.

William leaned his broom against the wall. "Didna really need doin'."

"Aye, but I'm doin' some o' Edi's things, so ye must do some o' mine. Say hullo tae yer brother."

William raced over to him and engulfed Jordy in a quick embrace before jerking back and tipping a grinning face up to his big brother. He was twelve now and starting to catch up to Jordy in height, so it wasn't much of a look up. He was gangly and awkward with a heavy sprinkling of freckles. Jordy supposed things would get worse before they got better. It hadn't started looking up for him until he was sixteen, and even then he'd still felt like a wee lad.

"It's good tae see ye, Liam. Ye're becomin' a young man," Jordy said. "Now, dinna ye go an' get taller than me like Ben an' Mick. 'Twould be more than me pride could take."

William grinned. "I'll try no' tae, Jordy, but I canna make any promises."

Jordy chuckled. "I suppose ye canna, can ye? Ach, well. I'll hope ye stop growin' halfway up." He turned to his youngest brother with a smile. "Hullo, Thomas."

"Tom," Tom mumbled.

"Thomas is what I named ye, an' I dinna see why one o' me lads canna keep th' good Christian name I gave him," Mrs. McAllen protested.

Mr. McAllen chuckled. "Ye ken't it was a lost cause when ye married me, Annis."

"Well, I'm no' givin' up yet," Mrs. McAllen replied. "His name is Thomas. Tha' was th' name I chose for him, an' it'll stay tha' way."

Jordy highly doubted it, but he offered his mother a sympathetic smile all the same. He enjoyed all the nicknames. It made boring, ordinary names like George, Benjamin, and Michael become more practical Jordys, Bens, and Micks.

He definitely never wanted to go by 'George.' Too stuffy. He'd been called it about a hundred too many times when he was in London—every teacher or superior he'd ever known had insisted upon calling him his full name.

He wanted to settle in and go by 'Jordy' when the more formal Dr. McAllen wasn't required.

Edith came down the stairs. She glanced about the kitchen and frowned.

"Ye lads need tae sit down; ye're all clutterin' up th' room," she complained, placing her hands on her hips like Mrs. McAllen.

Indeed, she was very like their mother save for her hair, which was a burnished auburn rather than strawberry blonde and graying, and the fact that she was younger, her body slimmer. Both had big, blue eyes; pale, smooth skin; small noses; a narrow, tapering face; and bright-red lips. Quite an attractive pair, though he was prejudiced, perhaps. He took great pride in his mother and sister.

Jordy found a seat at the table along with his brothers and father. They weren't allowed to do any cooking after Jordy once burnt five loaves of bread in two days when Mrs. McAllen was visiting relatives a county over. Since then, men were strictly off-limits as far as doing any kind of kitchen work went—which, Mick often reflected, was a champion excuse. He always followed it with a joke about how Jordy's clumsiness and forgetfulness had served them well for once.

Jordy shrugged his shoulders lightly to himself as he thought about this. It was true that he could be dreadfully clumsy or forgetful sometimes. He couldn't number the times he'd left a milk pail somewhere and had a dog drink it all before he came back or left a gate open or dropped a dozen eggs. He didn't really know how all these things happened to him—only that they did, and he might as well accept it and make allowances for it.

He'd become better about it, though. He wasn't late for everything —just some things—and he worked hard to keep himself neat and tidy, to not drop or misplace things, to make sure all his possessions were where they were supposed to be. It was somewhat difficult, though.

After all, he couldn't change all at once, and he doubted he'd ever be quite as organized as most folks. Especially most doctors. They could be particular about how their instruments were placed. Not him. As long as everything was clean—he wasn't about to allow them to be unsanitary; that would be foolish—he didn't care what order they were in on the tray.

His family sucked him back into another round of questions about being a doctor, who he could help and how, and what his practice at Keefmore might look like, and he gladly obliged them, happy to have his thoughts off more dismal subjects.

Being negative helped no one but the devil, and Jordy was well convinced of this fact. It was his responsibility to direct his thoughts in productive ways. Though he might fear his inability to be the well-informed doctor Keefmore needed, and though he might feel he never deserved a future beyond the one he had, those were just fears and feelings. Far better to march on and do his best with what he was given.

Even if he felt he'd dealt himself a loaded stack of cards.

Jordy met Violet and Ivy at Aunt Daphne's house early the next morning, and they walked together to a doctor's office building toward the outskirts of the village. Of course, it wasn't really an office building —at one point it had been a store of some sort; it had a front room with a built-in counter, according to Jordy, and two rooms in the back that would be a "general practice" room and a private office, which could also serve as a surgery room if need be.

There was also a second floor above that Jordy didn't think he'd use much, if at all, though he was debating moving a cot up there and living in the building full-time. Especially since he had paid a hefty sum for it, both of his father's and his own money.

When they arrived at the back of the building, Edith, William, and Tom unloaded cleaning supplies and various tools from the wagon. Jordy pulled a key out of his pocket and opened the door.

Ivy followed Jordy into the building. It was dark inside, so she hesitated at the door while Jordy marched in.

He struck a match, and a low flicker filled the room. "I'll use th' front as a reception area—an' see, there's a closet for supplies. Th' other room will be for anything I must keep private, or as a place for me tae sit if I need tae. It's actually larger than I expected."

Ivy smiled. "So, it will be a good place for your practice?" she asked. "Will it work, that is?" she added as he seemed to hesitate to answer.

"Aye. It's perfect." He blew out the first match, lit a second, and moved toward the front. "Th' first item o' business is tae get th' windows unboarded. It looks like all th' glass is perfect here."

Ivy walked slowly into the building. The room was dim now that her eyes had accustomed to it. It smelled musty. Dust lifted off the floor with every step she took, and there appeared to be cobwebs hanging off everything.

"I'll need an operatin' table," Jordy said. "Not tha' I will necessarily need tae cut intae anyone any time soon," he added, perhaps seeing her wince—she hated the idea of operations. "It's for any sort o' medical procedure, Vee."

"Ah," Ivy exhaled.

"Then we'll get it cleaned out, dusted, an' broomed from floor tae ceiling. Next we'll get everythin' arranged as best we can. Ach!" He dropped the match to the floor. It flickered out on the way down.

"Are you all right?" Ivy asked anxiously.

He chuckled. "I'm fine. But let's get a lantern—an' then open these windows, aye?"

"Yes." Ivy wrapped her arms around herself against the dark.

Edith stepped in with a lit candle in her hand. She raised her eyebrows. "Forgettin' somethin'?"

Jordy grinned bashfully. "At least we can get tae work now."

Ivy smiled. "How can I help, Jordy?" She was going to do the best she could.

Jordy glanced around. "Th' first step is tae get th' boards off the windows, like I said. I'll open these first and then th' ones in the front. Edith will get ye organized as far as cleanin' goes."

Ivy nodded and stepped obediently outside. In less than no time, all the boards were removed from the windows, and the cleaning began.

Neither Ivy nor Violet had cleaned before, so it was interesting work for them, to say the least. At first, Ivy felt insecure and worried. But Edith patiently showed her the correct dusting and sweeping methods. Once she overcame her fear of the cobwebs—mostly through laughing at Jordy along with his siblings for his hesitancy to go near anything that might hide a spider—she proceeded fairly easily.

Edith worked fast, and Ivy was willing. Violet got in the way until Edith became strict—even a little stricter than Ivy thought completely necessary—and Violet soon straightened up, though she was still a lackluster worker. Edith chose to ignore her then and kept on working tirelessly, with Ivy doing her honest best to keep up.

While the women were thus employed, Jordy, William, and Tom set up a cabinet and a few chairs that Mr. McAllen had donated and made a list of all the other bits of furniture—including an examination table, shelves, and perhaps a desk for the office—that he'd be needing. Jordy set all his supplies in the cabinet, and Ivy followed behind and straightened them.

He also had a medium-sized black bag, like every other doctor in the world carried, which he'd already prepared. Ivy opened it and found a crazy conglomeration of his medical possessions—and a few other items, including a watch and what appeared to be an old, smelly sock. So, with Jordy's permission, she emptied the bag, cleaned it out, and sorted it.

"Ye ken I willna keep it tha' way for long," Jordy said, plainly amused, when Ivy presented him the nice, clean, neat bag—free of random objects, which had no business being there.

"Yes," Ivy said, realizing this was probably true—knowing Jordy. "I suppose I'll have to sort it on a regular basis."

Jordy chuckled. "Aye. If by 'regular' ye mean every day o' yer life until one or th' other o' us dies, because it would be a full-time job," he said, winking at her.

Ivy shook her head. "You'll have to try. Doctors are supposed to be neat and clean."

"An' so I am. Or, I suppose, my instruments are, an' tha's wha' matters," he said. "I'd never let them get a speck o' dirt on them. I ken better than tha'. But I dinna believe rumpled clothing an' a disorderly bag will hurt me patients any. If they dinna like it, I dinna care."

Ivy sighed heavily. "Jordy, what am I going to do with you?" she said, though she sensed her voice was more tentative than she would have liked. Trying to tease Jordy back required more practice than she'd had as of yet—seeing as she wasn't really the kind of person who teased people or even knew when they did—but she was determined to do so.

It wasn't fair for him to make fun of her and she be unable to respond in kind. She had to start paying attention and figure out when he joked and when he meant things.

Jordy took a deep breath and made a gesture of despair. "I'm quite hopeless." He dropped his eyes.

Did he mean it? He seemed so serious, his expression so blank and despondent, his shoulders slumped. Ivy couldn't stand that. "No you're not, Jordy. You're anything but hopeless. Why—"

Jordy grinned. "Vee, did it ever occur tae ye that I was teasin' about tha', too?"

Ivy scowled. It seemed he read her thoughts all too well. "I don't understand you, Jordy McAllen," she said. "I really don't."

"Ach, I dinna want ye tae, Ivy Knight," Jordy said. "It'd be nae fun if ye did."

"But I want to understand," Ivy said, forcing back the frustration, needing to explain this feeling to him. "I want to be able to tell what you're thinking and feeling, and when you're teasing me and when you're not, and I want to tease you back and talk to you and—and be someone who you trust to talk to. Who will understand you." His face was blank, like he couldn't grasp what she was trying to say to him any more than she knew sometimes if he was serious or not. "Jordy, I want to stand on level ground with you—as equals. But I can't. I'm not enough."

"Nae, Vee. Ye're more than sufficient for th' life ye are livin'."

Ivy shook her head. "No. I'm not, Jordy. If I were, I could understand everything—you see? Be a normal woman like ... like Edith. In some ways, even Violet is better than me. Yes, she has her problems, but ... but ..." Her chest tightened, and tears welled.

"Ye're nothin' like Vi, thank th' Lord above," Jordy said. He put his hands on her arms and turned her to face him. "Listen tae me. Ye're somethin' special. God made ye so unique an' brilliant. I dinna say tha' just because I can."

Ivy nodded, drew back, and rubbed her sleeve across her eyes.

"Nae, dinna wipe yer face like tha'—ye're a lady, remember? Ye have a handkerchief?"

Ivy nodded and pulled it out of her sleeve. "I ... I can't do anything right."

"Canna do anythin' right?" Jordy asked incredulously. "Why, ye've been twice th' help Violet has this morn. Just ask Edith. An' ye're three times as pleasant, an' tha' would make up for it even if ye were th' worst worker in Scotland."

Ivy nodded and wiped her eyes. "I'm sorry for being such a baby." She struggled to control her voice. "I don't know why I got upset."

"It's been a busy day, an' I canna imagine ye got much sleep last night, bein' in a new place," Jordy said. "It's a'right. Really, Vee. Dinna think o' it again."

"I'll get back to work." Despite Jordy's words, she was deeply embarrassed. She hated how weak she was. How easily she cried and got upset over simple things and how quickly words and sounds and sights and simply moving confused her until she couldn't react to them anymore. Why did Jordy even want to be around her?

"Wash yer face first," he said, giving her a critical look-over. "There's a pump in th' back. No one needs tae ken about this."

Ivy beamed. How sweet of him to think of that. She'd thought that if she was going to act like a three-year-old, then everyone might as well know—it was a fair punishment. But since Jordy had offered, she supposed it wouldn't hurt to clean up a little—and she knew that cool water would feel lovely on her hot face.

CHAPTER ELEVEN

While they worked that morning, Ivy had occasionally heard children's shouts, and she'd soon realized that quite a number of small boys and girls had collected in the lot behind the building to play games. She mostly ignored their noises after the first few times until she heard high-pitched wailing followed by scared shouts.

Being nearest to the door, she darted to it and peered out. A small girl of five or six was curled up in a ball on the ground with the rest crowded about her. She felt Jordy step behind her and glanced over her shoulder.

"How do ye feel about havin' our first customer now?" he asked before stepping out of the building and jogging over to the little girl's side. Ivy raced behind him, not knowing if she could do anything but wanting to be there. She was accustomed to her younger siblings being hurt and making all sorts of noise—though she generally left any caring of them to Anna—and she did feel that she could help somehow.

Jordy knelt next to the little girl and glanced up at the faces about him. "What happened?" he asked.

"She tripped an' landed on her arm—an' now she says it hurts," explained a serious-faced little girl with dark hair and eyes. She knelt next to the now whimpering child who was just her age, resting a hand on her shoulder lightly.

"I see," Jordy said. "What's yer name, sweetheart?"

"Tha's Bridget," supplied the dark-haired girl. "Bridget Owen. I'm Mairi Blakely, her best friend."

Jordy nodded. "Bridget," he said, "I can take a look at yer arm an' see if it's broken. I promise I willna hurt you."

"Nae!" Bridget jerked back, tears streaming down her face. "Dinna touch it!"

"I'm a doctor, Bridget, so I ken wha' I'm doin'." Jordy kept his voice soft and low. "It's a'right. I must see it, though."

Bridget's eyes flicked about restlessly, but she relaxed her body enough to let Jordy lift her arm up a bit. She shuddered, and Ivy put her arms around the girl, holding her steady and murmuring words of comfort.

Jordy nodded his thanks before returning his eyes to the little girl. "Mm-hmm." Ivy watched his face carefully, but he wasn't showing any obvious emotions besides concentration. "A'right." He leaned back on his heels.

"Well?" Ivy asked.

"It'll have tae be set. Ye had a hard fall, Bridget. It'll need tae be in a cast, an' ye'll have tae rest it." He smiled. "But dinna worry. We'll heal ye up."

Bridget nodded. "A'right. Will ye do it?" She was trying her best to be brave, but her voice trembled about the edges, and Ivy could tell she was fighting tears. "Will it hurt?"

"A bit, but ye're a brave lass. Right?"

"Right," Bridget repeated, setting her jaw firmly. "I can take it."

Jordy's eyes met Ivy's then, and she saw the concern there, concern he'd kept hidden from the child. Then he turned to the other little girl. "Mairi, is't?"

"Aye, sir."

"Who are wee Bridget's mum an' da? Can they come? I'd like tae see them before we set th' bone."

"I'll run for Mrs. Owen!" one boy offered, and he took off down the road as fast as his short legs could carry him.

"Bridget's got a mum but nae da. Th' illness took him this summer," Mairi said simply.

Bridget nodded jerkily, and her fingers dug into Ivy's arm. The poor child wasn't doing well at all. "Is there anything we can do for the pain, Jordy?" she murmured.

"Dinna need it!" Bridget exclaimed boldly, but Jordy seemed to consider it.

"She'll have laudanum so we can get it set, but we should ask her mum first."

Ivy nodded. That was probably wise, but she still hated to see the child suffer so.

Not five minutes later, a woman heavy with child emerged from the crowd of children. "Bridie! Wha' in heaven's name have ye gotten yerself intae this time?" She spoke with an accent slightly different from those of the McAllens and even her own child, tainted with more of an Irish flair.

Bridget shifted her weight slightly but otherwise didn't move. "I'm sorry, Mum! I couldna help it. I wouldna have busted me arm if I could've stopped it."

"Ach, I'm for knowin' it, Bridie—I am." Mrs. Owen managed to get herself down on the ground despite her impending motherhood and took Bridget's free hand. "Ach, me babe! 'Tis just like ye tae break it outside our new doctor's office, an' nae mistakin'. Ye've th' luck o' th' Wee Folk wi' ye."

"Yer mother is right." Jordy straightened. "Mrs. Owen, we'll need tae set her arm an' put it in a cast. I've done it many times before, an' I'm no' worried—seems tae be a simple enough break. But it will hurt her, an' I'd like to give her some laudanum. We'll do it on th' front counter in th' office, since I dinna have a proper table yet—but we've just finished cleanin' everythin', so it's all ready for her. I only need yer permission."

"O' course, we'll have tae have her fixed up somehow." Mrs. Owen leaned back in a half-squatting position, regarding her daughter skeptically. Yet, despite Bridget's distress, her expression remained calm. Ivy doubted she would've been anything but hysterical in Mrs. Owen's place, but the woman's face showed nothing but affection for her daughter and a quiet contentment.

With William's help, Jordy managed to get Bridget transferred to the counter and gave her the laudanum. Mrs. Owen stayed with her until she was unconscious and then slipped to the side to give Jordy room to work.

Ivy shuddered and looked away and felt absolutely sick the entire time Jordy worked with Bridget's small arm, but at last it was done, and Jordy bound the arm and fashioned a sling across the girl's chest.

"Ye did well," he murmured to Ivy as she gently straightened Bridget's body in the aftermath. He raised his voice to reach Mrs. Owen. "She'll be out for another half an hour, an' then drowsy."

"Thank ye, doctor. Tell me what I owe ye, will ye?"

Jordy glanced at Ivy, cocked his head, and shrugged. "Hmm. Mrs. Owen, Bridget is me first customer, an' a rather surprising one at tha', so I'll offer my services for free this time. But if Bridget goes an' breaks th' other arm, I might charge ye a bit."

Mrs. Owen nodded. "I canna say I'm in a position right noo where I can turn down charity, so I'll accept tha', Dr. McAllen. My sincerest thanks. Bridget is always gettin' in one scrape or another. This willna be th' first time she's hurt one part or another o' her, though this is th' first time she's broken anything. I wouldna have known what tae do, but I ken't ye would."

Jordy smiled. "Ye're most welcome. Why dinna we bring a chair in, an' ye can sit here until Bridget awakens?"

"Tha' would be lovely."

They found a plain chair in the other room and brought it in. Mrs. Owen gratefully took the seat, and Jordy slipped out to continue his work in the waiting area.

"I never caught yer name." Mrs. Owen smiled at Ivy. "I'm grateful for yer part in this. I can tell ye're a tender nurse, Miss ...?"

"Oh, I'm Ivy Knight. I'm not really a nurse—Jordy is my friend, and I was just here helping set up the office. But I want to be of use," she added. That was her primary motivation for now. Though she wasn't sure yet how it fit into the bigger picture of her life.

"Ye still worked as a nurse for me bairn an' were fairly useful from what I can see, so I'll still say 'thank ye,'" Mrs. Owen said. "Do ye have tae get back? Or can ye sit an' talk a spell?"

Ivy hesitated. Perhaps she ought to get back, but that calmness that she'd noted before in the woman appealed to her, so she lingered. "Talking would be lovely, Mrs. Owen."

"Oh, please, call me Ena," Mrs. Owen said. "I may no' look it, lass, but I'm no' tha' much older than ye. Only about—how old are ye?"

"Nineteen," Ivy said, then added, for nineteen often seemed so young, "Twenty this January."

"We're about four years apart. Nothin' more." She smiled. "Tha's no' much in th' general scheme o' things. So call me Ena. Please."

"I will," Ivy said.

"An' I'll call ye Ivy."

Ivy smiled. "I'd like that."

"So wha' do ye do, Miss Ivy? If ye're no' a nurse, I mean. Ye talk like an Englishwoman, so I suppose ye're wi' tha' new lady—Mrs. Wright, isna it?"

Ivy nodded. "She's my friend Violet's aunt. We both came here with Jordy—Dr. McAllen, that is—and are visiting for a time. I don't do much, I'm afraid—I play the piano, and I read, and that's about it." Nothing really important. Which was why this work with Jordy felt vital now. She'd seen him heal now, and it appealed to her in a way very little else in this world had. Though a calling wasn't, perhaps, a part of it, there was certainly a magnetism.

"Ach! Now tha' I ken tha' ye read books, I willna give ye a moment's peace, I'm afraid. I love readin', but books are expensive, an' it's always been hard for me tae find them. Bob—" She paused for a moment, then continued on. "Me man would bring me books as gifts, sometimes. No' often, o' course, but when he could. So I have some, but never enough, I'm afraid. I imagine ye've read plenty o' books."

"Yes." Ivy couldn't imagine not having access to dozens of novels. How horrible that must be! "I've read quite a few books. There's a nice library at Pearlbelle Park—that's my father's estate—and I can always go there if I want something new to read. People bring me books as gifts, too. Especially my father. He brings me books almost every time he comes home from London."

Ena leaned forward on her seat. "Tha' sounds wonderful, Ivy. I canna imagine it." She sighed. "I wish I had a whole library o' books. So many tha' I could read an' read an' never stop." Ena's soft, brown eyes glowed as she spoke. "Bob brought me a book by Emily Brontë—*Wuthering Heights*—an' I loved it. An' three by Charles Dickens—*A Tale of Two Cities*, *Oliver Twist*, an' *Our Mutual Friend*. They were lovely; my favorite was *A Tale of Two Cities*. But me favorite o' all was a novel by Jane Austen that me brother brought me many years ago from Edinburgh—it's called *Pride and Prejudice*. Have ye read it?"

Ivy's heart smiled at the mention of so many good books. "I have. I liked it very much, though my favorite of Miss Austen's novels is, by far, *Sense and Sensibility*. I enjoyed *Persuasion* as well."

Ena's eyes widened. "Have ye read all her books, then?"

Ivy nodded. "Yes, I have. I didn't like *Mansfield Park* as much, and I'm not sure I understand *Northanger Abbey* or *Emma*. At least, that's what my brother-in-law, Peter, said. He thinks I missed the whole point of the novel when, really, I didn't much like Emma—the character, I mean—and I didn't see why Mr. Tilney would like Catherine, even though he says that's just because I'm so like her."

Ena smiled. "Tell me more about them, will ye, Ivy? It's good for me soul."

Ivy nodded and obliged, eager to finally have someone to discuss her favorites—and even her least favorites—with. It seemed like so long since Alice and Peter had left—the two people whom she'd talked with most about novels.

She told Ena about the rakish Willoughby, the dependable

Colonel Brandon, the noble Edward Ferrars. Of Marianne's dreamlike spirit and Elinor's sensible outlook and how their different approaches to life gave them very different outcomes.

Of silly Emma Woodhouse, who thought she could control everyone's life for their better good—who only wanted to help—but who failed miserably to do so. Of persuadable Harriet Smith and chatterbox Miss Bates and perfect Jane Fairfax and dashing, dishonorable Frank Churchill.

She told of Anne Elliot's lost chance at happiness—of Captain Wentworth returning—apparently a little too late. Of the fateful letter—the line, "I am half agony, half hope."

She then talked about sweet, little, plain Fanny Price, who held to her morals to the bitter end. Of her cousin Edmund—easily distracted but ultimately the kindest, best man in the book. Incomparably.

And—at last—innocent, naïve Catherine Moreland and her teasing, intelligent suitor, Mr. Tilney.

"They sound wondrous," Ena sighed when Ivy was finished. "Ach, someday I hope tae meet them all. But I dinna know if tha' will ever happen."

Then, in a flash, Ivy remembered. "Why, I have several books with me—and so does Violet. I'd love to loan mine to you, and I'm sure Violet wouldn't care. She can't read them all at once—I know she brought at least eight, with the assumption that she would bother the McCales to send her more."

Ivy's heart twisted to see Ena's eyes light up like stars. "Ivy, if ye did tha', I could never thank ye enough. It ... it's almost tae much for me. It's overwhelmin'." She paused to wipe her eyes with her sleeve. "I'm sorry," she said, catching her breath. "I'm no' used tae folks offerin' me things anymore."

Ivy smiled, reaching her hand out and taking Ena's. "I'm glad to do it. I don't mind."

Ena sniffed one last time and leaned back on the chair, resting her hands on her abdomen. "Few have talked tae me these last several months," Ena said. "Ye see, last summer th' illness struck all o'

117

Keefmore hard. Especially th' children. But it was mine tha' caught it first. Me wee ones, Bobby and Flora. They were only four an' two. An' from them, th' rest o' th' town got it. I … I dinna ken if tha's true or no', but the folks of Keefmore believe it is. Believe it's our fault." Ena laughed a little hysterically. "An', o' course, tha' is enough tae make me guilty."

"I don't understand," Ivy said. "That doesn't make sense. Why, you didn't purposefully allow your family to get sick and then spread the illness to the rest of the town. You couldn't have helped that."

"Nae, when ye're grievin', ye dinna ken that. Ye dinna ken anythin' except ye've lost a loved one, and ye need someone tae blame or ye'll explode. They blamed me. After all, hasna the illness struck me hardest? Took two o' me bairns as well as me husband? It must mean tha' I was cursed—bewitched—tha' some ill magic was at work in me house. Ach, it doesna keep them from comin' tae me shop, thank th' Lord—they're no' that superstitious. But it does keep them from friendship. An' tha's a'right. I ken. It hurts tae lose someone, especially a wean ye brought tae this world."

Ivy sat there, shocked by the fact that anyone could be so cruel to a poor widow with one child only six years old and another on the way. How could they be so mean after Ena had lost so much? Didn't they know that Ena would have prevented this all—same as any woman would have—if she'd had the choice? She couldn't comprehend how anyone could be so stupid.

"Dinna worry about it, Ivy," Ena said. "I dinna. It's their choice tae be tha' way. An' I dinna care wha' they do. It's me choice tae accept it with grace and dignity. An' I dinna mind so terribly—really. I have Bridget, th' new babe, th' shop, an' everythin' I could ever need. God is good."

Ivy nodded. She didn't fully understand how Ena could be so accepting of the terrible things that had happened to her, but it impressed Ivy. That kind of grace under terrible grief, under unbearable pressure … it was like nothing Ivy had ever seen before. She didn't believe she'd be as strong as Ena, if given the chance.

Ena smiled at Ivy. "Ye are special, Ivy Knight. Ye know tha'? God sent ye to me so I could have someone tae talk tae, an' no' only tha', He sent me someone who shared an interest with me. I dinna ken about ye, but I find tha' miraculous."

"Yes," Ivy said thoughtfully, "I suppose it is almost a miracle. I ... I'm glad I've found you, too. I haven't had someone to talk to about books in a while. Well," she said quickly, "at least not in over a month. Not since Alice and Peter left."

"Alice an' Peter?" Ena asked.

"Yes, my sister and brother-in-law. Alice is my twin, actually."

"Oh, ye're a twin?"

"Yes, I am. But we don't look too much like each other," she added. "Alice has dark eyes and hair—especially compared to me—and her face is shaped different. And she's taller."

Ena smiled. "I was told tha' no' all twins look alike."

"Yes, Alice and I don't. We're very different. I suppose it's unusual, but Mother says we look less like each other now that we're older than we did as children. I think," she said after a minute, "it's because I take after Mother and Alice takes after Papa."

Bridget stirred on the table and moaned, and Ena and Ivy both rushed to her side.

"Mum," Bridget mumbled. "I'm thirsty."

"Shh, love. I'm sure we can get ye some water. How do ye feel?"

"Me arm is sore."

"Mm-hmm. Dr. McAllen said it would be for some time. But it's healin'. Ye'll have tae bear a bit o' pain—an' perhaps we can make ye a special tea tae help." Ena smoothed Bridget's hair back from her head. "Are ye ready tae go home? We'll clean ye up an' tuck ye intae bed."

"A'right." Bridget yawned.

Ivy went to fetch Jordy, and he gave the patient permission to leave for home. He had William take her there and see her settled, but he told Ena that it wouldn't be long until Bridget was feeling much better. But, he said, she'd still need to keep the cast on for at least six weeks, and even after that, her arm would be delicate for some time.

"I'd just advise as much caution as ye can muster, lass," Jordy told Bridget, his brows set as he regarded her, but his eyes belied the seriousness on his face. "But dinna worry—I'm sure ye'll heal up, an' I'm sure yer mum willna let ye go tae far."

"Nor will I!" Ena exclaimed. "We'll be mighty careful with our Bridget after this." Before she left, she told Ivy she wanted to see her soon and encouraged her to stop by Owen's Mercantile as soon as she could to talk more about books.

Ivy agreed to just that, pleased to have made a new friend. It would seem that doing the next right thing in Scotland wasn't going to be as difficult as she'd feared.

CHAPTER TWELVE

According to Jordy, who didn't take long to catch up on all the Keefmore gossip, everyone in the village had been trying to make an acquaintance with Violet's Aunt Daphne for the last few months—but none had succeeded.

Which was why it took Mrs. McAllen less than a week to realize her position as a new friend of Mrs. Wright's visitors and leverage it. So now Aunt Daphne, Violet, and Ivy were riding with Jordy toward the McAllens' farm to have supper with his family.

"I think," Jordy said in an undertone, "tha' Mum has prepared a feast. She's so proud tae have been th' first woman in Keefmore tae convince this mysterious new stranger tae visit her, one way or th' other."

Ivy couldn't help but smile at the thought. She rubbed her hands together—they were always cold now, she'd found, except when at Aunt Daphne's house, where the fires were kept roaring night and day —and leaned forward on the seat. The wagon pulled around a bend, and she caught sight of the McAllens' farm in a small valley below.

"What time is it?" she asked.

"Dinna ken." He patted his trousers pockets absently with his free hand, eyes fixed ahead of them. "An' dinna have me watch."

That was because, when Ivy had asked him to check the time right as they were leaving Aunt Daphne's house, he had put it in his inside coat pocket. How had he forgotten already? Well, it was an easy problem to fix. She reached into his coat.

"Vee!" Jordy jerked back.

Ivy drew her hand away and raised her eyes to his. He was looking at her like she was a snake. She'd done something wrong, then?

"What're ye doin', lass?"

She swallowed. She hated being in the wrong, especially when it came to her friends' disapproval. "Your watch is in your left inside pocket. Remember?"

"Right." Jordy reached in and pulled it out. "Just after five." He mumbled the words rather than spoke him, and he didn't meet her eyes.

Oh dear. It must've bothered him for her to get so close. If she explained, would he understand better? "I wondered how much time it took to get from town to your house."

He grunted but looked at her—at last. "Ye could've asked me tha'." His tone wasn't reproving, at least; he'd softened his expression, too. So he didn't hate her. That was a good sign.

All the same, she ought to apologize, for apparently a boundary had been crossed. "I'm sorry, Jordy."

"Ach, dinna be sorry all th' time, Ivy. There's nae need tae be." Jordy pulled the horses to a stop in front of the house and jumped to the ground. He held his arms out, and Ivy made her way down to stand beside him.

"I really am sorry," she murmured. "Did you think—?"

"Wheesht. 'Tis a'right." Still, Jordy stepped back, and she felt the distance between them. If only she knew why. "Run on inside. I'll take care o' th' horses."

Ivy left him behind and, with Violet and Aunt Daphne, proceeded into the cottage. They were greeted by a slightly flustered Mrs. McAllen, but Aunt Daphne put a stop to the bustling almost immediately.

"Is there something we can do to help? Cleaning or cooking?"

Mrs. McAllen assured them that there wasn't, but Aunt Daphne was persistent, which was how Violet and Ivy ended up sweeping the floor and helping Mrs. McAllen with the fireplace and all manner of other chores.

They set about their work and soon finished the cleaning. Even Violet was uncustomarily careful and diligent. She took the broom without complaint and ran it somewhat awkwardly along the floor.

Just as they finished, Jordy and Edith appeared in the doorway. Ivy raced to him, eager to share her accomplishments. Perhaps *then* he would see that she'd meant no harm earlier, and they could still be friends.

"I set the table all by myself—mostly—and we finished making bread, and I helped with the stew ..."

Jordy placed his hands on her shoulders. "Slow down, Vee. Tha's all fine. Ye're becomin' quite th' little housemaid, are no' ye?"

Ivy laughed. "I don't know about that, but it's been lovely."

"She's terribly cheerful about workin', she is," Mrs. McAllen said, chuckling softly. "It's almost unnatural. Ye're sure ye havena brought us a faye—perhaps a changeling, Jordy?"

Jordy shook his head. "No' tha' I ken. I believe she's human. Only she's a braw lass."

Ivy beamed at what she assumed was a compliment. Working made her feel useful and worthy, and she enjoyed it. She'd quite honestly never felt like that before. Like someone actually might consider her worthy of praise. The kind of person who could actually do things. Helpful things. Useful things.

"Whatever she is, we're glad tae have her. Violet wasna bad help, either."

"Really?" Jordy said, turning to Violet. He smiled brilliantly at her, and even though the grin was directed at another person, it still made Ivy happy. Ivy wasn't sure why. Jordy was just like that.

Violet seemed to light up—perhaps for the first time Ivy had seen since she arrived in Scotland. "It wasn't much," she mumbled, but Ivy could tell she burst with pleasure.

Ivy didn't blame her. It must be a wonderful feeling to be praised after all she'd received was derision for the last few days. Of course, Violet thoroughly deserved every word said about her by Jordy—even

Ivy admitted that. What had caused this sudden regression?

"Speakin' o' chores, Ivy, how would ye like tae learn tae milk a coo?"

Ivy jumped at the sound of Mrs. McAllen's voice. She felt her hands grow cold as she realized what the woman had said. A *coo* was a cow, and she couldn't do that! But she didn't want to disappoint Mrs. McAllen, so she didn't say a word.

"It's a job ye'll catch on tae fast. Jordy will carry th' milk pails in, an' he can give ye any help ye need, so ye willna be alone."

Ivy glanced at Jordy, feeling slightly reassured. She knew he would be able to help her, and somehow she'd be all right. Even if cows were big and capable of trampling her into the ground.

"I'll teach ye how, Ivy; ye needna worry," Edith assured her as if reading Ivy's thoughts.

"I can help her," Jordy protested. "Nae need for ye tae help, Edi. I remember how tae milk a coo."

Edith laughed, her blue eyes twinkling almost the same way Jordy's did. Although, of course, Edith's eyes weren't near as pretty as Jordy's. "Noo, Jordy, I dinna think ye're th' person tae teach anyone about milkin', do ye?"

Jordy's face reddened all the way to his ears, but he still smiled. "Tha' was when I was a lad—all o' tha' was."

Ivy blinked. Now what were they talking about?

Edith placed her hands on her hips. "Jordy, how am I tae ken tha' ye're no' just as bad noo as ye were then? Why, ye could be just as careless as th' young boy I ken't. But, aye, I suppose we can give ye a trial run." She winked.

"I'm thankful for th' opportunity tae prove myself, Yer Highness." Jordy scowled. "Would now be a good time for me tae teach Miss Ivy th' rudimentaries, or have ye already scheduled our first session?"

Edith nodded and waved her hand towards the door. "Get on with ye. An' dinna bring back empty pails—an' if I smell a whiff o' smoke, so help me, Jordy!"

Smoke? Ivy wondered. What did smoke have to do with milking a cow?

"Ach, woman, 'twill be a'right." Something about Jordy's expression told Ivy this talk had him even grouchier than her reaching into his coat had. Was he just in a bad mood?

"Really, though, Jordy," Edith said, growing more serious. "Nae tomfoolery. Ye need tae get this job done an' then get back here for dinner. Ken?"

"Aye, I ken. No one would believe ye were me wee sister, Edi."

Edith simply shrugged and turned to walk to the kitchen.

Jordy stepped out of the cottage, gesturing for Ivy to follow. She closed the door carefully after her and scurried to catch up. She was shaking, but it wasn't from the cold. It was silly, perhaps, to be so worried about something as simple—and as tame—as a milk cow, but they really weren't small animals. Though Ivy was taller, they were considerably heavier. She knew that the cow did have the ability to hurt her if it wanted to.

Still, in her head she knew it to be an irrational fear. Most of her fears were irrational. But they weren't any less fears because they were irrational. They weren't any less real to Ivy. She thought Jordy would understand this—at least, she hoped so.

Jordy held the door of the barn open, and she stepped through. "We'll start wi' Lucy. She's th' gentlest o' th' bunch—th' oldest, tae."

Ivy nodded.

Jordy placed a hand on her shoulder. "Ivy. There's naught tae be scared of. I'm right here. Nae matter what Edi said, I can take care o' everythin'. A'right?"

Ivy attempted a smile and managed to get the corners of her lips quirked up. "All right."

"Then let's get started. An' dinna let me hear tha' ye canna. Ye're physically capable o' milkin' this coo, are no' ye?"

Ivy hesitated, then nodded. "But I've never done anything like this before, and—"

"An' ye're frightened. Naturally. I would be."

"You would not," Ivy said. "I don't think I've ever seen you scared. Even if you were, you wouldn't falter." Jordy, Ivy felt, was the bravest person she knew. He was never afraid to move forward into a new situation. That was one of the things she admired most about him.

"Perhaps, perhaps no'. I've been afraid a time or two in me life, Vee, ken. Ye have a harder time than some conquerin' yer fears, but tha' doesna mean ye canna. Aye?"

Ivy raised and lowered her chin in what she hoped seemed a positive, agreeing manner.

"A'right then. Th' first thing is tae fetch tha' milkin' stool." He grinned at her. "One step at a time, eh?"

Ivy smiled back and lifted the milking stool down from the hook where it hung. "There," she said, returning to Jordy's side.

Jordy picked up a metal bucket and turned it about in his hands. "They were wooden when I was a lad. So there's been some change in Keefmore." He shrugged. "But I suppose 'twould be a pity if anythin' had tae stay th' same forever. It's th' stuff scary fairytales are made o'. Th' princess locked in an eternal sleep ..." His voice trailed off as he approached Lucy. He stepped into her stall and patted her back and side. "Hey, there, lass. Easy, darlin'. Tha's it." He turned to Ivy. "Hand me th' stool."

She eased to the door of the stall and extended the stool to him, an arm's length back. He laughed and took it from her.

"A'right, tha's enough beatin' about th' bush. Come in here."

Ivy backed off. "What if I were to watch you the first time?"

Jordy hesitated, then nodded. "A'right, tha' sounds perfect. But ye have tae watch from inside th' stall. Ye canna see a thing I'm doin' from out there." He extended a hand to her. "Really, Ivy. I won't let anythin' get ye."

Ivy took a deep breath and stepped into the stall. She kept close to the wall, then slid behind Jordy so his body was between Lucy and her. "There! Are you satisfied?"

Jordy was shaking silently and couldn't seem to answer.

She summoned enough courage to slap his shoulder. "It's not funny. Can we get this over with?"

He wiped his eyes. "I suppose so." Jordy set the stool down, sat on it, and positioned the pail under Lucy's udder. "Did ye catch all tha'?" he asked, grinning at her over his shoulder.

"Yes," she said. "Go on."

"It's simple, Vee. There's no' much tae it. Ye grasp th' teat at th' top—here—an' then squeeze down. Be sure tae let up and let the teat refill. I ... I canna explain it." He demonstrated a few times, squirting frothy white milk into the pail with a satisfying *ping!* sound. "See? No' frightening at all."

Ivy shrugged, none too convinced. The cow was still big.

Several minutes later, Jordy finished milking the cow, then turned to Ivy. "Tha's all there is tae it. An' see, once ye learn it, ye'll never forget—though I think me arms will be sore in th' morn." He winked. "We'll continue with Sunny. A'right?"

Ivy backed out of the stall, and Jordy followed, holding the almost-full bucket with the stool tucked under his arm. "Ye're goin' tae have tae touch th' cow this time," he warned.

"I know," Ivy whispered. "I suppose we'd best get it over with."

Jordy returned with the empty pail and handed her the stool. "Ye have tae do this now," he said. "Nae gettin' around it. This is a good time tae conquer yer fear."

"Why?" Ivy asked.

"Because it's th' present."

Ivy glared at him. "I can think of a lot of better times. Like tomorrow."

"But tomorrow is always in th' future," Jordy teased. "It will never be tomorrow, Vee. It will always be today."

"Then let it be some other today," Ivy hedged.

Jordy led her toward the next stall and opened the door. Pushing her in before him, he set the pail down and took the stool from her. He placed it on the ground next to the cow and patted the seat. "Come an' sit. I'm right here. An' Sunny is sweet as a bug's ear.

Lovin' old creature."

Ivy twisted her hands together. "I didn't know a cow could be loving."

"*Noo*," Jordy said.

Ivy slowly slid onto the stool, feeling her way, eyes tightly closed. She turned her head to the side and opened her eyes to find Jordy kneeling next to her. "That wasn't so bad," she admitted.

"Pat th' cow's side. Just tae get her used tae yer bein' there."

Ivy hesitated again, and Jordy took her hand and placed it on the cow's flank. "She willna bite ye, Ivy."

"I know," Ivy whispered. "Give me a moment."

Jordy placed her hands on the cow's udder. "Start. But dinna think on it."

"How?"

"Listen tae me. I'll talk."

"Oh!" Ivy glanced up at him. "I have a question for you, actually, Jordy." She turned to him then stopped. "I ... I'm not sure ... if I ..."

A smile danced around his lips, and she knew he was amused with her stammering, but she couldn't help it. "Go on, Ivy. It's a'right."

Ivy nodded and took a deep breath. "Jordy, what was Edith talking about? Earlier, I mean. It made you embarrassed."

"Ah, right." He put his hands over hers and began guiding them. "Tae be honest, Vee, I'd almost rather no' tell ye. I'm ashamed o' it, but when I was a lad, I had a lot o' accidents. I'd almost burnt down th' barn twice when they had me stop milkin'. Kept leavin' lanterns lyin' around, an' I always let th' dogs get to the milk or left it lyin' somewhere tae spoil." He shook his head and grinned. "I was a fool, a'right. Always droppin', burnin', breakin' things. When I grew older, I moved away, but ye already ken I wasna much better at McCale House, an' ... Suffice tae say, I've overcome all tha', but there are things I still struggle wi'." He shrugged. "Most people here likely think o' me as tha' clumsy lad. Irresponsible, completely immature. Always late, always messy, a social butterfly incapable of stickin' tae a job for more than half a blink."

Ivy's chest filled with compassion and a slight trace of indignation. "You're not like that."

Jordy smirked. "Perhaps no'. At least, no' so much anymore. But th' whole town believes I am. Even me own family, I think."

"But it's not true," Ivy said. "Why, Jordy, you're the most wonderful, responsible man I know. I'd trust you to the ends of the earth."

Jordy laughed. "I should let ye be me spokeswoman. Ye're tha' good at it."

Ivy shook her head. "I only speak the truth."

"Ye're a particularly cheerful individual. I love ye for it. But it's no' necessarily realistic, much as I'd like it tae be. Ye ... ye believe folks ye love are infallible. But they're no'. I'm no'."

Ivy smiled into his eyes, needing to somehow convey to him that what he'd said wasn't true—couldn't be true—that he was wonderful, and she didn't think anyone could possibly be better than him. He was simply too good.

Jordy reached past Ivy and stripped the last of the milk. "There. Tha's it. Only four tae go. Abby next, then Eve."

Ivy rose from the stool and picked it up, gazing wonderingly at the cow. Had she really milked a cow? And nothing bad had happened? She turned to Jordy, wonderstruck.

He rose and grinned at her.

"Oh, Jordy, I did it!" she exclaimed. Blood pounded in her ears, and her legs felt weak in the aftermath, but it was done. She had done it. As Jordy rose from a kneeling position, she threw herself into his arms, almost upsetting the pail of milk.

"Thank you, Jordy," she whispered, placing her lips close to his ear. "You ... you needn't feel as if you're not good enough for anyone. You're more than enough for me."

She felt him starting to draw away from her almost before she'd finished speaking. She'd sensed he didn't want her touch ever since they'd met, but she had ignored it. Now, she let him step back, shrug his shoulders awkwardly, and turn, milk pail in hand.

"I'll take care o' this." His voice was gruff, perhaps angry, though she wasn't sure. She hadn't thought Jordy to be exactly a perfect gentleman—not in the way of following etiquette, anyway, though she otherwise thought him quite valorous—but perhaps he felt she'd shown impropriety and that was why he was mad. But Jordy was her beloved friend; surely there was nothing wrong with a brief embrace. Especially one stemming from gratitude.

"Jordy!" She followed him out of the stall. "I'm sorry if I offended you."

"Nae, no' at all," he said. "Close th' door an' fasten it, will ye?"

Ivy did as he said. "Jordy, I couldn't bear to lose your friendship. I don't make a lot of friends, and I hate being alone."

Jordy was smiling broadly when he turned to her with an empty pail in his hand, back to normal as far as she could tell. "Ye'll always be me friend, Vee."

Ivy didn't reply. She wasn't sure. She feared losing him as she feared nothing else in this life. She was confident in keeping Violet's friendship simply due to her dependency, and she knew her own family would love her no matter what. But Jordy? What if he grew tired of her? What if, someday, he found her boring and uninteresting? How could she make anything sure with Jordy? She didn't really know him that well—at least, she didn't think so.

Yes, he was a good man, and she trusted him to take care of her and anything else he was responsible for. But a relationship was another thing entirely. They might always be friends—he might always be kind, treating her as he treated everyone—but it was hard to be *close* friends with Jordy. He only seemed to share all of himself with a few people. She wanted to be one of those people, but she couldn't tell if he felt the same or not.

"Vee, come. I'm no' goin' tae let ye slack," he said, winking. She scurried over to his side and preceded him into the stall. Without even thinking about it, she set the stool down and sat on it, then reached for the bucket. Jordy looked amused. "Ye're catchin' on fast, are no' ye?"

Ivy laughed. "I suppose I am."

Jordy knelt next to her. "A'right. Remember, dinna just squeeze—an' alternate hands; gets it done faster."

Ivy nodded and obeyed. For a minute there was no sound but the somewhat delayed pinging of milk into the pan, then Ivy spoke. "Jordy."

"What?"

"Sometimes ... sometimes we feel that we're responsible for something. Or rather that it's our fault when it's not at all."

Jordy didn't reply.

Ivy struggled for words. "It's just that ... that ... when my cat died—Kitty—I'd ... I'd had her almost all my life, you see."

"I'm sorry, Vee. Are ye a'right?"

"Yes, I'm all right." Though it was sweet of him to ask. "It was several years ago now. But when she died ... I felt bad. I don't know why. There was no reason for me to feel that way. But somehow I felt if I'd done something differently, she wouldn't have died. That was untrue, but I couldn't help it; that was how I felt."

Jordy nodded, eyes fixed at a distant point as he mulled over her words. "I see what ye mean. But—"

"No, Jordy. No buts about it." There. She could be firm, just like him. "Sometimes we carry guilt for things that aren't our fault. It's a part of life—but it's no less true that I feel that way. And ... and that *you* feel that way."

Jordy leaned back on his heels. "Vee, sometimes ye're very wise."

Ivy felt her face grow warm. "You think so?"

"Aye. Wherever do ye get these things from, anyway?"

Ivy shrugged. "I don't know. They just come to my mind."

Jordy laughed and lightly touched her back. Ivy supposed when he initiated it, it was all right for there to be casual affection between them. She'd remember that. "Let's finish milkin', me wee wise woman."

CHAPTER THIRTEEN

Jordy arrived at the office quite early the next morning. He hadn't slept well the previous night, and he got up as soon as it could feasibly be called "morn." He'd gone into the loft above the sheep and scoured it before coming out with his coat wiggling and screeching, and now he placed that coat—and the small creature within—in the smaller room at the back before beginning his daily ritual of shuffling through all his equipment and making sure everything was in order.

He wanted some way to make his attitude up to Ivy. He knew he'd acted gruff yesterday, and perhaps she didn't understand that. She couldn't. She wouldn't think of it. But he would make it up to her, and, even if he couldn't explain exactly, at least she'd know he was sorry.

He'd thought it all out by now. Ivy was a beautiful woman, and it was only natural for him to be somewhat attracted to her. He was only human, of course. Therefore, it wasn't really wrong—as long as all he did was notice.

He couldn't let himself long for her—and desiring her would be a sin. Not Ivy. Why, she was a student of McCale House, and Jordy was supposed to be taking care of her. He couldn't let those kinds of feelings seep into their friendship.

It was nothing but idle attraction, because he had nothing better to occupy his mind. Well, he'd keep his mind busy and not let her near him, and the problem would be solved.

He nodded to himself, reaffirming his decision, as she entered the office through the back door, a bright smile on her face.

Good—it made it easier if she wasn't upset. How dreadful it would be to have her hate him. He really did want to be her friend ... but only friends. It would be wrong—especially since he had nothing to offer her. He didn't like blondes all that much anyway.

"Morning, Jordy." Her hair caught an early beam of light from the window and turned golden.

He grudgingly admitted that blondes were the prettiest of all women. Just an observation—nothing personal, of course. "Good morn, Vee."

"What do we have to do today?"

"Weel, I want tae see if we canna get th' rest o' th' medicines unpacked, an' I want tae keep a log." He glanced around and found the book he'd set aside specifically for that purpose. "It'll take us an hour or so, is all."

She nodded and turned to the shelves where the carefully-packed boxes had been stacked. He found himself mentally commenting that he liked the way she'd done her hair—pulled back, not tied up or braided—and then scolded himself for it.

"I-I have a present for ye."

Ivy stood still, then turned, her expression inquisitive. "A present? But why?"

"I ... Ye did such a good job wi' th' milkin' yesterday eve, an' I thought ..." He swallowed. "I thought ye deserved it."

"Oh." Then she waited.

Jordy hurried into his office and found that the wee creature had scurried under his desk. He caught it before it had a chance to run off and turned back into the main room.

"Here. What do ye think?" He offered forth the small tabby kitten.

Ivy gasped and reached for the creature. "Ooh, Jordy, she's gorgeous. Is it a she? I've never seen such a dear, little thing!"

Jordy grinned. So that had pleased her after all. "I'm glad ye like her."

Ivy held the kitten close—almost smothering her, Jordy thought—and smiled broadly. "Can I really keep her? Oh, what will Aunt Daphne say?" She raised those big blue eyes to his face, full of concern.

"If Aunt Daphne willna let ye keep her in th' house, she can stay here or come home wi' me until I move in." He shrugged. "'Twould be no problem, a wee thing like tha'. An' yer parents would have nae problem ...?"

"Oh, no! I just hadn't been able to get a new cat because ... I felt so bad about Kitty." Her voice grew a little thick, and Jordy became even more concerned for the amount of squeezing the kitten was currently getting. "But I'm so glad to have her, Jordy! What shall I call her?"

"It's yer choice, Vee."

"I think I'll call her Heather." Ivy didn't even look at him after that, talking softly to the kitten, having completely forgotten why she'd come over in the first place, apparently.

Which is probably for the best, he thought as he pulled the boxes down and began unpacking them. *If she keeps looking at me, God only knows what'll happen.*

The bell Edith had installed over the front door tinkled, and Jordy stepped into the front room. There stood a buxom woman wearing a large, gray apron over her brown dress, her arms folded across her chest and her dark eyes iron-hard.

Jordy smiled. "Morn. I'm Dr. McAllen. Wha' can I do for ye?"

The woman harrumphed. "I'm Mrs. Dunmore, an' I'm th' midwife here. I thought I ought tae come an' see wha' ye were all about—an' introduce meself."

"Ah." Jordy knew all about the terrifying Mrs. Dunmore. She'd been here about as long as he could remember, and she had a daughter who must be fifteen or sixteen by now—though the lady herself was long-widowed. "I ken ye noo, Mrs. Dunmore. Pleased tae

134

have ye here. Is there anythin'—"

She held up her hand. "Nae formalities, please, sir. I only wanted tae tell ye tha' I dinna intend tae associate wi' ye, but neither do I object tae ye. Th' people who want yer services will come—an' I canna do some o' wha' ye can do. But neither can ye do some o' wha' I can do. Tha's just how it is."

Jordy had to grin at that. Blunt honesty mixed with gruffness. How he'd missed that in England. It was the Scots way, after all, wasn't it? "Thank ye, Mrs. Dunmore. As for me, I'm glad ye're here tae attend tae th' women as they need ... an' glad ye dinna take issue wi' me stitchin' a few cuts an' settin' a few bones."

She made another disapproving sound at the back of her throat. "I'd hope ye can do more than tha'! But, aye, I willna object tae tha' at all." She whirled on her heels and marched back toward the door. "Good day, sir."

"Good day, Mrs. Dunmore."

He chuckled to himself as he returned to the office. "Me greatest enemy can be considered defeated, Vee," he called. "Where have ye gotten tae?"

"Your greatest enemy?" She appeared in the doorway of the office, Heather still cradled close.

"Aye. Th' midwife has given me permission tae be here." He glanced around. "Which is nice, given tha' I'm well-settled. Why dinna ye go home for th' rest o' th' day? I can manage here."

"Oh, all right," she said without even looking at him. It was quite clear that she wouldn't be paying attention to anything or anyone but that cat for the rest of the day. She walked out of the office.

"Away wi' th' fairies," he murmured as he turned back to the things he was unpacking. Still, he was glad he'd managed to please her.

Ivy was still clutching Heather close when she arrived back at Aunt Daphne's house. The little kitten had still not protested much to the enthusiasm of Ivy's first love, and she was glad because she couldn't have stood to bother the kitten ... and yet how could she help but hold her close?

Aunt Daphne and Violet were sitting in the "garden" in front of the house. Aunt Daphne looked relaxed, and Violet looked like she was about to freeze to death. Understandable, as that the day was decidedly cold.

But Aunt Daphne took great pride in spending time in her garden, and there was no force of nature yet discovered that could remove Aunt Daphne from a place she wanted to be. Of course, it hadn't snowed yet, so they would have to see how she dealt with spending time in her wondrous garden when it was covered in a blanket of white.

Aunt Daphne had again dirtied a lovely dress and was elbows deep in mud. Violet raised her eyebrows at Ivy and shook her head slowly, mouthing the word 'insane' over and over again. Ivy restrained a giggle and approached the pair.

"Good day, Aunt Daphne," she called. "Isn't it too cold for gardening?"

"Nonsense." Aunt Daphne leaned back and swiped her hair from her eyes, smudging mud across her cheeks and forehead in the process. "I've no use for a constitution, and if I did, it wouldn't be delicate, so why shouldn't I be out in this weather getting some work done? And Violet agreed to come along to keep me company."

Violet mouthed the words 'by force,' but Ivy ignored her.

"That's nice." Ivy knelt to Violet's left. "Jordy McAllen sent me home with a kitten. I hope that's all right."

Aunt Daphne dismissed Heather with a wave of her hand. "Yes, yes, that's fine. The more the merrier."

Violet held out her arms, and Ivy reluctantly allowed her to take the kitten ... though only to be nice. She couldn't wait to have Heather back.

"Little girl," Violet observed in a soft voice. Cats were about the only things that convinced Violet to show sentiment. "So sweet. What are you calling her?"

"Heather."

"Lovely."

"I never will understand why people seem to think you need sunny weather for gardening." Aunt Daphne humphed. "I've gardened in all sorts of weather all over the world. It gets you outside, in the fresh air. The type of fresh air surrounding you matters little when it comes to that, in my opinion."

Ivy smiled. It wasn't so much the sunny weather as the spring, but she supposed she could see Aunt Daphne's point, too. Some of the work could be done in the autumn, after all—and Aunt Daphne's methods seemed to have kept her strong and healthy.

"Yes, I've tended gardens all over the world," Aunt Daphne mused, clucking her tongue and almost talking to herself. "Italy, Switzerland, France, Spain. Even India, once, though that was only for a month, and I didn't have much success. I'm not quite sure I understand the climate."

Violet smothered a chuckle into Heather's fur, though Ivy was able to catch it, close to Violet as she was.

"But that life taught me a lot. About my own impatience and about how I have failed, again and again, to follow through on my promises. And it also gave me a place to rest my mind over the years, when things have been quite stressful, when my life has been quite full." She then displayed what could only be counted as a grin. "And it gave me a place to escape from Roger for a few hours, when things were difficult. He never liked gardens."

Violet raised her eyebrows. "I thought you loved Uncle Roger. I didn't realize you had difficulties in your marriage."

"Every marriage is difficult, Violet." Aunt Daphne shrugged. "And we were both strong-willed, stubborn people. We fought as much as most couples, perhaps more. But it was good for us, and we found a balance in the end. Besides, it can be important for a man and his wife to give each other a bit of space, if needed. Not always, but it can be."

"Hmm ..." Ivy was of the opinion that if she was really close to someone, she would never want them gone ... but, of course, that was not true. Ivy desperately craved time to herself, with just God and her facing the entire world of her mind, and she could never give that up, even if she, at times, caught a fascination with one of "her people" and was unable to imagine herself separated from them for a moment. For years, that had been Alice, Mother, and Nettie, sometimes interchangeably and sometimes all at once. Violet passed in and out of her life like a vapor, but that didn't mean Ivy didn't want her that way. And there was Jordy. She felt now that they were adults, she might want that kind of friendship with Jordy, even if it wouldn't be exactly appropriate for her to grasp at it.

"What I was trying to get at, though," Aunt Daphne said, "is that it's important to embrace challenges, new experiences, new friendships. They can bring us so many glorious things! Starting a garden in the Swiss Alps when you only intend to be there for a few months might seem insane, but perhaps you'll meet friends along the way. For that matter, perhaps you'll change lives along the way! I've a feeling I did. And all because I've always trusted my gardening instincts."

Ivy laughed aloud at this, though she understood Aunt Daphne's point. But she wasn't going to even try to restrain her amusement now. "Aunt Daphne, I wish I could have a life like yours! You have such adventures, and I can tell you've helped people."

"Only after a great many struggles with my character! After all, I wasn't quite born with a servant's heart." Aunt Daphne winked. "I was thirty or so before I even began trying to cultivate one. Before it was all about Daphne. Daphne, Daphne, Daphne. Oh, and Roger, sometimes, but usually, for many years, only if it benefited Daphne. But there's a great deal to be said for how following God refines you— once you begin that praying and Bible-reading, your heart changes, and then you change. And for the best! So don't doubt, Miss Ivy, that you won't have adventures—and that you won't help people. Because you will."

"She already has," Violet commented. "Ivy always helps me, even if neither of us knows it in the moment."

Ivy flushed at the praise. "That's not true. I'm sure sometimes I'm not helpful! I'm only human, after all. But, Violet, I do love you so—there's not much I wouldn't do to help you. And I think it's easy for me to try to reach out to you, my dearest friend. But to others?" She shrugged. "You know how shy I am. How can I help?"

"In so many ways!" Aunt Daphne exclaimed. "It all comes down to letting go of yourself and holding on to Christ. However, I would add that you needn't be pressuring yourself to take on the world. Nor will your calling be mine, Ivy. Don't try to do what I did, not exactly. God has a different purpose for each of us, and sometimes what might be a selfish act from one person can be the best possible next step for another. Listen to Him, and He'll make sure your path is clear as it needs to be."

A different kind of warmth, a cuddly, cozy warmth, filled Ivy's chest. Truth always did that for her—gave her a sudden burst of delight. Well, not always, for at times it would sear into her heart like a brand, and that hurt like anything. But, in general, it caused that pleasant warmth, for she tried to make sure her heart was open enough to receive such truths. And these last few months had perhaps been the most open time in her life.

"Thank you for that wisdom," she murmured, not sure she had more to offer as her mind was still processing some of the harried thoughts running about it.

"Oh, wisdom, is it?" Aunt Daphne shook her head. "I can't believe I have any to give, but if you think it is, well, thank you, dear! I'm glad I have something to offer." She rose to her feet. "We ought to go inside now. I suppose that's enough for today."

Enough for today? Indeed, everything Aunt Daphne had said could now be counted as enough, and more, for it had filled Ivy. But Aunt Daphne was referring to the torn-up garden. Ivy, too, rose and followed Aunt Daphne and Violet into the house, looking for the next opportunity to take Heather back for more snuggling.

CHAPTER FOURTEEN

I vy didn't know much about etiquette—people scared her, so she avoided society—but she had been told that it wasn't polite to visit someone soon after visiting them the first time. Technically, Ena was supposed to visit her before Ivy could visit again, but Ivy supposed that part wouldn't apply in Scotland.

The main thing to think about, then, was bothering Ena any more than was strictly necessary. Or, rather, waiting as long as Ivy could wait —she wanted to see Ena again. She somehow felt that Ena was going to be her special friend. Instinct was her primary guide here, but her instincts were often right, and she'd learned to listen to them.

Three days after her original visit—it was a Saturday afternoon—Ivy couldn't stand it any longer. She told Jordy where she was going, put on her coat, and marched up the street to Ena's shop.

There were a few people milling about—one standing at the counter paying for items, another browsing.

Ivy skirted around them and came to stand off to the side of the counter. Ena threw her a sideways smile and returned her full attention back to her customer—a gruff, old farmer. When he'd finished paying and turned to leave, Ena faced Ivy.

"I didna know if I'd see ye again or no'. How are ye, Ivy?"

"I'm well. How are you?" Ivy asked.

"I'm fine. A wee bit tired, but tha's tae be expected." She gestured towards her stomach. Ivy blushed, not used to that kind of frankness, causing Ena to grin. "Sit down on th' other stool here, Ivy, an' we can talk. I need tae keep tae th' counter today—hope ye dinna mind."

"Not at all," Ivy said. She stepped around the counter and took the offered seat.

"I'm glad ye came," Ena said. "Ye're a sweet lass, an' it was a pleasure tae talk tae ye. As I said, no' many talk tae me anymore, an' I missed tha' more than anything. An' havin' someone tae discuss books with is lovely an' all."

Ivy's eyes widened. "Oh! I forgot. I do have a few books I'd love to give you. Actually, I have two novels by Jane Austen with me— *Persuasion* and *Sense and Sensibility*—as well as several by others. One by my brother-in-law, in fact, though I don't know if you'll like that or not."

"I'll like about any book, Ivy." Ena laughed. "But dinna worry about it. If ye really want tae do me tha' kindness, then I'd appreciate it, but it is a grand favor, so if ye dinna get tae it, I dinna mind."

"Will you be at church tomorrow?" Ivy asked.

"Aye. At least, I always try tae go. Some days it's hard ..." Her face jerked slightly, and Ivy's heart squeezed in sympathy for whatever pain, physical or emotional, kept Ena from attending. "But I'll try since I ken ye'll be there."

"Then I'll bring a few of the books," Ivy said. "You can give them back to me whenever you get the chance—you're welcome to keep them however long you want. Months, if that be the case; I won't read them. I'm busier than I thought I'd be here."

"We canna all be idlers like me," Ena said. "I read while I watch th' counter oftentimes. Most o' the farmers buy in bulk, so I only see them once a month or so. It brings in a tidy sum but no' much work. Least, none I can do just now. Later, when I'm feelin' better, there will be repairs an' sorting an' arranging o' the back rooms. Tha' kind o' thing. Me Bob always kept himself busy with th' books an' fixin' th' outside an' odd jobs around town an' such, but I canna do tha' th' same as him. No' yet, at any rate—perhaps after th' bairn comes. It's only a month or so tae go now."

Ivy nodded. "I see what you mean. I'm not doing much. I help with meals and around the house at Aunt Daphne's. Then I mostly take care of children when I'm with Jordy, it seems. He says it's great help, but it doesn't feel like much. I fetch and carry things for him. Still," she reasoned, "I could do more."

Ena nodded, her eyes focused on some distant point toward the front of the shop. "Aye. Ye might. But it might be tha' ye're doin' exactly what th' Lord wants ye tae do. Do ye feel content with what ye're doin'?"

Ivy wrinkled her nose. "Yes, well, most of the time. But couldn't that be my own laziness?"

"Perhaps with some, Ivy, but no' with ye. At least, I dinna think so. Ye're not th' kind tae be lazy, are ye? I dinna ken ye verra well, but I dinna think so."

Ivy shook her head. "I don't know."

Ena was quiet for a minute, thinking, before she spoke again. "Let's see if I canna put my thoughts intae words—a struggle most days an' never more so than noo, but I'll attempt it, willna I? Noo, God wants everyone tae do somethin', right?"

"Yes, but some more than others." Alice had made that more than clear. "Me less than anyone else."

"Why is tha'?"

"Because of who I am."

Ena's brow furrowed for a moment. "Ach. Ye'd made me forget tha', even though I've been hearin' th' gossip. They said ye're simple, mindless—no' because they ken ye but because ye came from tha' place—McCale House, wasna it? But, Ivy, I've never seen ye act in a way tha' would make me believe tha'. Aye, we havena ken't each other long, but I feel as if I've ken't ye for years. An' I'm no' afraid tae vouch for ye. Ye're a canny young lass. Ye have a mind. Ye have a soul. Ye're perhaps a little different. More than anythin', I think ye're shy. Perhaps ye dinna understand some things. But tha' doesna make ye any less deservin' o' God's love, His thoughts, or His calling."

Ivy nodded, though she wasn't sure. After all, Alice said that not everyone necessarily had something big and great to serve God—and that must be true. Alice never lied.

"But, Ivy, it could be tha' this is what ye're meant tae do. I dinna ken. I canna say. It's up tae ye ... or, rather, up tae God. He'll show ye what He wants ye tae do. I promise." Ena smiled. "He's always guided me if I only take th' time tae listen."

Ivy sat still for a minute, considering this. "I always try to listen to God," she said at last, "but sometimes I feel that there's nothing to hear. That He isn't saying anything to me."

Ena nodded. "I ken it feels tha' way sometimes, Ivy, but it's no' true. God always guides us as we need it. He always cares for us. Ye have tae have faith. Have faith—an' really listen. Pray. Read His Word."

Ivy bit her lip, unsure what to say to that. She read the Bible every night, prayed almost constantly, and she believed she listened. She had known it was Him who pushed her to go to Scotland—and then Keefmore. To help Jordy. But what else was there for her? She certainly enjoyed helping Jordy, felt fulfilled by it—but she didn't know whether she was really being useful.

Perhaps Jordy was making work for her. He seemed to sometimes, and he was the kind of person who loved to include everyone—especially everyone amongst his friends.

Was it because he wanted her to feel better that he kept her around, or did he truly need her? Did he even enjoy her company? There seemed to be so many things to doubt.

But, if God approved, if He had truly asked her to go to Keefmore, then what had she to doubt, really?

"God wanted me to come to Keefmore," she whispered, "so it's all right. No matter what, it's all right. His hand was in this from the start."

Ena chuckled. "Tha's certainly a pleasant thing, isna it? Tae ken tha'? I always love it when His will is clear. It simplifies things." She paused to help a customer, and Ivy stared at her hands, considering their conversation and her new thought process. Yes, God was moving in her life, all right. There was no mistaking it.

After the customer had left, Ena turned to Ivy again. "I'll hear if someone else comes in. Would ye like tae go back? Let me see." She reached under the counter, pulled out a large gold watch, and flicked the lid open. "Just after four. I believe Bridget an' Mairi are playin' upstairs. They'd both love tae see ye. Bridget's talked o' nothin' else."

Ivy smiled. "I'd love to see them."

"Good! Let's go back. I'd like tae sit down on somethin' a wee bit more comfortable. Me back aches." She rose slowly. "Run along ahead o' me an' call th' girls down."

Ivy scurried through the door into the parlor and then to the bottom of the stairway. "Bridget, Mairi," she said.

Ena came up behind her, laughing. "Ye're gonna have tae speak a wee bit louder than tha'. Bridget! Mairi!" she shouted. "Come down. Miss Ivy is here."

The two girls soon appeared at the top of the stairs and ran down. Bridget threw her good arm around Ivy and gave her a rambunctious, if awkward, hug while Mairi stood off to the side.

Ivy wondered how these two girls, so different, could be friends. Bridget was clearly a wild tomboy, while Mairi was the perfect little lady. But, Ivy supposed, she herself tended to be closest friends with people who were bold and bright, perfectly confident with social interactions, and she was anything but. There was something to the saying 'opposites attract.' She liked Jordy, after all, and they couldn't be more dissimilar.

"I'm so glad ye've come back!" Bridget drew away from Ivy after one last squeeze. "Ye're a wonderful person."

"Why, thank you, Bridget," Ivy said after a slight pause. How did one respond to compliments? She had little experience.

Bridget turned to her mother. "May I give Ivy one o' me biscuits?"

Ena, who had lowered herself onto a seat behind Ivy, nodded, almost laughing again. "Aye, Bridget, ye may."

Bridget darted off to the kitchen and soon dashed back in with a plate. Ivy wondered vaguely if Bridget was following any of Jordy's instructions to 'be careful' at all. "Here they are, Miss Ivy." She held out the plate, and Ivy selected one of the biscuits and took a bite. Bridget watched raptly while Ivy chewed.

"It's quite delicious," Ivy said after she swallowed.

Bridget grinned. "Thank ye, Miss Ivy. I worked verra hard on it."

"An' left yer mother tae do all th' cleaning up," Ena added. "Now, run along, both o' ye. Miss Ivy an' me are goin' tae have a chat, a'right?"

Bridget and Mairi nodded and ran up the stairs.

"She's active, isn't she?" Ivy said.

"Aye, always has been. Even when she was a wee one," Ena said, smiling fondly. "She can be trouble, but she's normally a good lass, an' I love her."

"But of course," Ivy said. "She was—is—your eldest?"

Ena nodded. "Aye. Me firstborn. We put value on th' first child, ye ken. Bob and I both were. But then, every child is precious. Still, people are always more excited about their firstborn."

Ivy cocked her head. "Excuse me if it's prying, but ..." Could she ask? It couldn't have even been that long ago. Still, curiosity was an emotion Ivy experienced often in her calmest times, and right now it pried gently at the back of her mind, asking all sorts of questions she wouldn't dare to speak aloud.

"Ye'd like tae know about me family? It's a'right, Ivy. I dinna mind talking about them. In fact, I love tha' ye're givin' me an opportunity tae do so. I'd like nothin' more." Ena smiled. "Ye see, they meant so much tae me, an' losin' them was ... was th' hardest thing tha' has ever happened tae me. But tha' doesna mean I dinna want tae talk about them. In fact, just th' opposite. I want tae remember every precious moment, tae save it. Tae never lose them, no' within me. Rememberin' is easier than forgettin', ye ken."

Ivy nodded, smiling sympathetically. Ena's song was definitely a sad one. "It must be so difficult."

"Oh, aye, at first. But later on, after th' pain eased somewhat, I could think clearly, an' I ken't I never could stop thinkin' about them —an' I didna want tae. Until ye have yer own bairns, yer own man, Ivy, ye will never quite understand what it's like. But anyone can understand family an' love. At least, I know you can." She paused for a minute.

"Two babes gone," she said, "an' me darlin' husband. Me first an' only love, ye ken. Married at sixteen an' never regretted it. Thought it was th' hardest thing in th' world tae wait a wee bit over a year tae learn tha' Bridget was comin'." Ena shook her head in amusement. "Impatience an' youth go hand in hand, me mother used tae say. Passed on, ye ken. She was Irish, an' never happy here, but she loved Da—after he died, it didna take her long tae pass o' a broken heart. I'll tell ye their story sometime, perhaps. Bob's folks live in Edinburgh now, but I dinna like them." She rolled her eyes toward Heaven and heaved a great sigh. "They think they ken how tae raise Bridget, but they dinna. She's me child, an' I'll raise her as I please tae. Dinna need their ideas or their suggestions. An', aye, she's a rascal sometimes, but she's six, an' she canna be expected tae be patient just yet. Perhaps when she's older."

Ivy nodded. "I've four younger siblings. I can understand that."

"Four? An' then ye an' yer sister? Tha's a nice-sized family. I would've had more, ye ken." Her eyes darkened for a minute, then she forced herself to smile. "Nae use cryin' over somethin' tha' will never be." She paused again, brow furrowing. "An' I willna say I'll never remarry. It's ... it's tae soon. I dinna ken. If God asked it o' me, I'd have an open mind on th' subject. But right now I canna imagine it. Bob ... Bob was me only love." She sighed. "Nae use thinkin' on it. I think I'd need at least a few years, an' I know God willna ask it o' me unless I'm ready."

Ivy offered a weak smile. "You're right. But, Ena, I don't understand something."

"What would tha' be, Ivy?" Ena asked, brightening up, though Ivy couldn't tell whether it was natural or simply something she did by rote.

"You ... you lost everything. Yet you're so cheerful. I'd almost say it hadn't happened if I didn't know it had. How can you be so happy when such tragedy has struck you? How can you not rebel?"

Ena leaned back on her chair and stared off into the distance, seeming to see beyond Ivy into a place far away. "I havena lost everythin' exactly. Aye, I lost Bob an' Bobby an' Flora. An', aye, I loved them more than life itself. I would've given anythin' tae preserve them. Tae save them. But God is still there. He's still watchin' over me. He gave me Bridget an' this wean." She placed a hand on her abdomen. "He gave me this shop, steady customers, an' th' ability tae support meself in spite o' it all. He gave me His Son, tae die on th' cross for me sins—an', Ivy, they have been many, an' they would have dragged me down tae Hell if it were no' for Him. So, nae, I havena lost everything. I've lost three lovely people who God gave me. An' I relished every moment o' my time with Bob, Bobby, an' Flora. I loved them with all me heart. I wouldna give up those years for th' world. But they were th' Lord's before they were mine. An' I know tha' in me heart. An' I am at peace, knowin' tha' they are all safe in paradise. I will see them again, Ivy."

For a moment, her face glowed before a shadow passed over. "But I did no' always accept so readily. In tha' first dreadful month, I rebelled. I asked God, 'Why? Why me? Why me family and no' any o' these others'?' I wanted tae kill myself, I think, an' I would've if I didna care about me babe an' Bridget—I ken I thought about it. I certainly didna want a thing tae do with God.

"But then, when I was at me worst, I heard His voice, as clearly as if He was standin' in th' room with me. He said, 'Ena, why did I send Me own Child tae die for ye, if I do not love ye, do no' love yer babes an' yer husband?' An' I saw His glory an' His love." She paused and smiled. "It has no' been easy, ken. I'm no' perfect. But I have His joy. I trust Him. I will be faithful, even unto death."

Ivy sniffed and ran a hand across her face to find it wet with tears. "Oh, Ena. If only I could have your faith."

Ena cocked her head to the side. "An' why canna ye? Faith is no' just for th' strongest. It's for us all."

"I know," Ivy said, "but if I were given such an incredible trial, I wouldn't stand firm as you have done. I would crumble."

"How do ye know?" Ena asked. "Ye never do until ye're put tae th' test. Dinna worry. God only gives us what we can carry. An' ... an' I do believe ye have a stronger faith than ye think, Miss Ivy." She ran her sleeve over her eyes and laughed a little hysterically. "Sorry. I shouldna have put tha' all on ye. I just felt tha' I could tell ye. No one else has wanted tae listen."

Ivy felt her jaw set and her vision narrow. "Oh, how could they be so cruel? How could they abandon you in your hour of need?"

"Wait a minna, there, Ivy! It's a'right. I understand. I dinna ken tha' I wouldna have acted th' same if I were in their place. Like I said, we all need someone tae blame when we're hurtin'."

"That's no excuse," Ivy said, filled with fiery indignation. It wasn't fair for them to blame Ena for something so far from her control—and something that had caused her such suffering, too.

"It's a'right, Ivy," Ena assured her. "An' it hasna been so bad, really. They still come tae me shop, but they're superstitious. I admit I'm a wee bit meself. Heard tae many fairy tales, I imagine. If ye ever have some time on yer hands, sit down an' listen tae some old man. They have enough stories tae keep ye busy for months on end. Elves an' dragons an' witches an' wizards—all sorts o' excitin', meaningless stuff."

Ivy's eyes widened. "Those sound fascinating."

"Ach, they are. Scots have th' best imagination. At least, I've been told," she added with a wink. "We're tae proud tae admit it if there are better storytellers out there. Me mum would have said th' Irish were better, but anyway, there's no one like th' Scots for passin' tales down. No' tha' I'm prejudiced or anythin'." She laughed, and all sad thoughts seemed put away from her now.

Ivy was truly in awe. Ena was perhaps the strongest woman she knew—perhaps even more so than her mother or sister, it seemed. Though that was probably a matter of what trials had been presented, she decided, not wanting to downplay her beloved mama and Alice.

"Will ye stay for supper?" Ena asked.

"Oh, no, I couldn't!" Ivy said. "In fact, I'd best be going. But I'll come visit again soon—and, remember, I'll bring those books to church tomorrow."

Ena's face lit up. "I can hardly wait for tha'. But," she added, "only if it's no trouble. I wouldna put ye out o' yer way."

"No, not at all. Like I said, I don't need them, and I'm glad to share them with someone. I feel as if giving them to you to read means that they're not quite so useless. I'll bring the three to start you off."

Ena outright grinned now. "Thank ye, Ivy. Thank ye. It will bring a light tae me world tha' ye canna even begin tae understand."

The two women embraced, and Ivy left the shop to head back to Jordy's office.

CHAPTER FIFTEEN

Ivy felt gawked at when she entered the little church building the next day. She placed her body deliberately behind Jordy's and in front of Mick's for the best protection from curious eyes, but still she felt violated. Oh, how she hated being looked at and wondered about.

"Dinna worry, Vee. They'll tire o' ye soon. Ye're just a novelty." Jordy tossed a grin over his shoulder as they filed into one of the pews.

When she was settled between Jordy and Mick, her Bible clutched on her lap until her fingers turned white, she let herself breathe a bit more easily. She sat like everyone else, she wore a simple dress and a boring hat, and she came with the McAllens. Nothing to make her stand out or feel different.

Yet she did. She felt very, very English. She wasn't even sure what a Scottish church service would be like. This day she'd learned two new things already—first, that 'church' was 'kirk,' and second, that Jordy thought it very funny that 'Kirk' was their overseer's name.

"Now, what kind o' name is tha'?"

"Well, it's his name," Ivy had said. Then, suddenly feeling quite brave and quite clever, she'd asked, "What kind of name is McAllen?"

Jordy had roared at that, and Ivy had blushed so hard she felt her face would burn off.

"Dinna worry."

Ivy glanced at Mick. He winked at her.

"We're no' a bad bunch. Ye just have tae be patient an' let our good side shine through." He patted her shoulder, unexpectedly tender for such a big, broad boy, then turned his eyes to the front of the church.

Jordy tugged her sleeve, and she turned to face him. "I think me wee brother has taken a fancy tae ye," he said in a voice that, though it was low enough, could still plainly be heard by Mick.

Ivy's eyes widened.

"Havena!" Mick protested, cheeks paling until a fresh set of freckles stood out like spots on a Dalmatian. "I ... I was just tryin' tae be nice! I mean, she's a nice lass an' all, but I dinna even ken her! Really, Jordy!"

Jordy grinned. "I was just teasin', Mick, though I suppose I can see how Miss Ivy's looks could go tae yer head." He reached up and tugged at a loose lock of her hair. Ivy cast him a scolding look but couldn't keep back a smile. Jordy was so much fun to be around.

After a bit of friendly joking about the low likelihood of either actually attracting a woman at any point in the next fifty years, the two brothers settled in to wait for the service to begin.

Soon they were singing hymns. Ivy was glad the tunes were familiar, as puzzling over words and rhythm generally took one out of worship and into confusion. She needed an acceptable way to sing until her lungs stretched and her mind cleared. Nothing could possibly be better.

She did notice the pianist, an elderly woman who squinted quizzically at the open hymnbook in front of her, wasn't quite up to the task, but despite a few sour notes and the overall slowness of the progress, Ivy still liked singing the hymns.

The rest of the service was uneventful. It truly wasn't so different from the little church she attended at Creling, the village near to her father's estate.

Ivy did find it challenging to understand everything the minister, who spoke with a heavy accent, was saying, and sometimes she found herself asking Jordy for a translation. However, she was starting to learn the differing language that was Scottish brogue, and the preacher's words rang clear and true in her heart, which was the principle of the thing.

After church she spoke briefly with Ena and gave her the novels.

"Now, see if these dinna keep me up until three in the morn readin'!" Ena exclaimed. Then she laughed. "If I can keep me eyes open, tha' is. Even th' book may not be enough just now." She patted her stomach. "Bairn likes me tae sleep half th' day, ye ken."

Ivy smiled, not sure how to respond.

"I'll see ye in th' morn, I believe," Ena went on. "I'm bringin' Bridget tae Jordy's office tae let him look at her cast."

"Of course! I'm sure that will be wonderful," Ivy said. "I look forward to seeing you then!"

That night, Ivy jerked awake and glanced around the room. All was quiet, and she couldn't think what had woken her up. There were no sounds, and her spine wasn't shivering, so she wasn't afraid. She found Heather's small, furry body next to her on the pillow, fast asleep.

What was it? She whispered a prayer into the dark, and though no response was heard, she still rose and put on her dressing gown and slippers.

In the hallway, she detected a dim light coming from under Violet's door. Hesitating at first, she no less crossed the hall and rapped lightly on the door.

"Violet?" she whispered.

There was no response. Ivy rapped again.

Still no response.

At last, she tried the doorknob, feeling she couldn't leave. Not with the way her throat tightened, the way her fingers trembled, urging her to do something, anything. The dynamics of these demands were fortissimo, and at last she couldn't resist. The door opened, and she stepped in.

Violet propped herself up, wiping a hand over her eye and slipping what appeared to be a folded paper under her pillow. "Go away, Ivy."

"Vi? What's wrong?" Ivy whispered. "Are you crying?"

Violet's eyes were hard and cold. "Leave me be."

"I can't. Not when you're hurting." She crossed the room and took a seat, gingerly, on the edge of the bed.

"Trifle, I can't promise I'll be kind," Violet warned. "I need some time alone. Please, just leave. I don't want *you* to be the one hurting. Not because of me."

"But ..." Ivy swallowed. "I'd rather hurt with you than leave you to hurt alone. Tell me what's wrong. Or promise me you'll tell someone else, if you can't confide in me. Jordy, perhaps? Please don't suffer alone—tell one of us. He'd be able to help." Though Ivy never had solutions to Violet's problems, Jordy, the assistant of Dr. McCale himself, might have one.

Violet laughed hoarsely, a sound that made Ivy's bones shake. "You still think he can make everything right, don't you? Still think he can do anything? Oh, God help me; I think so, too." She dropped her face in her hands. "Don't you see that nothing can ever make my life easier, Trifle? Nothing ever will. Nothing can make this stop."

"No, Vi, I don't see." Ivy squeezed her friend's shoulder. It seemed that Violet was having another of her nightmares; nothing she said made sense. "I don't understand what you want—what you need. What can I do?"

"Nothing ... nothing. It's all so hopeless."

Ivy pulled Violet's head onto her lap and stroked her hair. "It's all right, my dearest. Don't worry. I'm here. Tell me. What's hopeless?"

"My life."

"Oh, Violet," Ivy crooned. "You're anything but hopeless. You just need to give it to God. Give *yourself* to God. Know that He loves you no matter what. Know that your worth is not based on what you do, what you are."

Violet didn't reply.

"Please, tell me what you're thinking," Ivy whispered. "I need to know."

"I'm thinking that I ... I'm unworthy of love. I hate myself."

"Don't. Don't hate yourself. Stop thinking. I know it's hard. I understand; I can never stop thinking about things, either." Ivy took a deep breath. "But when you stop thinking about yourself—about your own thoughts and emotions—you'll feel better. Calm down. Breathe. I've got you."

"What should I think about, then?" Violet struggled to sit up, and Ivy let her.

"God," Ivy said without hesitation. "Think about God. He loves you, remember?"

Violet nodded. "I do think about Him. But whenever I do, all I long for is to be with Him *now*. Out of this world—in Heaven, where I can stop living. I want it to stop. I want to ... I want to die. I want it to be over. Why am I still here? There is no use for me. If God truly loves me, He would take me now."

"That's not true, because He loves you enough to make you live out your purpose here." Ivy pressed a kiss to Violet's forehead and adjusted her position to be slightly more comfortable. "He created you for a reason. Please don't say He didn't, dearest, or you'll make me think the same—and I'm just coming out of that battle."

Violet didn't reply for a long moment. "I'm not sure God cares about ... about a person like me. Why would He? I've never done anything right. I ... I treat everyone terribly. I haven't served Him in any way, and I'm ... I'm insane. I might as well be an animal."

"You're not an animal." Ivy gave Violet a fierce hug. "You're a human, same as me. Yes, you can be somewhat ... You can struggle to be kind to people, but no matter who you are or what you do, God still loves you. He'll always love you." Violet *must* believe that. Sometimes it was all either of them had left, and they both must believe it. "Settle down. Breathe ... breathe ... breathe."

Violet's breathing slowed, and Ivy lowered her back down onto the pillow. "I ... I can't ... be a good person." The hiccups were there but steadily easing. "I can't. I'm so wrapped up in the darkness."

"It's all right. Go to sleep. It will all be fine in the morning."

"So scared," Violet whispered. "I don't know anything anymore. I don't know what I'm supposed to be doing with my life or if there's anything I can do."

"We'll work on it together," Ivy whispered. "Don't worry, dearest. There's nothing we can do about this now. I'll pray for you—and you must pray, too. God will help you. Promise me to be more pleasant, though?"

Violet nodded. "I'll try, Ivy. But I can't promise anything. You know I'm not a good person ..."

"Shush. Let's pray before you go to sleep." Ivy dropped her face into Violet's hair and closed her eyes. "Dear Lord," she whispered, "my friend Violet is feeling badly about herself. You know her heart. You know, in the depth of her soul, she wants to serve You." Ivy took a deep breath and continued. "Lord, please give Violet Your peace, cover her with Your grace, make her feel Your glory. She needs You. We're not looking for a quick solution or an easy answer. We know we won't, either of us, receive one on this earth, probably. Nevertheless, we seek Your love and comfort confidently, knowing that You will be with us in all we face—every challenge, every fear, every moment of agony and grief. We know we were not promised perfection here on earth, but, Lord, if You could ease our burdens in any way, please bless us, heal us, help us. In Jesus' name I pray, amen."

"Amen," Violet murmured.

"Shall I stay until you fall asleep?"

"Yes."

Ivy laid her head on the pillow next to Violet's and closed her own eyes, her silent prayers increasing in depth as she drifted off to sleep.

Violet didn't want to come down to breakfast the following morning, saying she was too tired and would prefer to sleep in. When Ivy explained this to Aunt Daphne, the woman looked troubled.

"I'd wondered if Violet wasn't feeling well." Aunt Daphne fidgeted with her napkin and then took a sip of her tea with a somewhat harried air. "She seemed offish last night. Ever since church, she's been prickly, in fact, but I'm starting to realize that Violet has a normal prickliness level and then an extreme prickliness level."

Ivy almost giggled, but it was more serious than that. The things Violet had said last night had been concerning, and Ivy's natural instinct was to smother her friend with love and reassurances ... and to internally go through her every interaction with her and try to figure out how she could have acted differently to prevent this state of depression. Of course, there was rarely, if ever, anything Ivy could have done differently, but she thought so all the same, her mind running over every word and small gesture over and over, searching for something broken that she could fix. But the brokenness was never quite within her reach.

Aunt Daphne's fingers drummed against the table in a restlessly changing pattern. "I know there's nothing I can do. When I was young, and even sometimes still, I had dark times. I was often caught in fits of despondency, but nothing compared to what Violet has gone through."

Ivy nodded. She often felt much the same—that she couldn't hope to understand what Violet was going through, although she did have her own small experiences to draw from. "Violet definitely does struggle, and she struggles hard. But I'm so glad she's struggling rather than just giving in to everything as she used to! Though, of course, some of that is just striving for the will to live, whether she knows it or not."

Aunt Daphne frowned. "That's what I'm worried about. When you have no will to fight for life, what do you have? Nothing. That's the first issue—wanting to live. It's been a long time since I haven't wanted that, but I remember well. I'm sure it affects everyone differently, this type of depressive thought process, but, for me, it was like a dark cloud hanging over everything. I didn't want to think, let alone act."

Ivy felt like that from time to time, too. Though, for the most part, it wasn't even as bad for her as Aunt Daphne was describing. No, Ivy suffered from something different—the easiest way to put it being that she was afraid always, and if she didn't address it almost immediately, it seemed to go beyond a simple fear and into the territory of an unstoppable physical battle. Or perhaps it was more spiritual. She wasn't sure. All she knew was that she did suffer, and that, at times, the terrors were great.

But it had gotten better. Little by little, at least understanding herself had allowed a kind of control, a tenuous control. And Christ comforted her, always. What would she ever do without Him?

"I wonder if there's anything I can do to help Violet." Aunt Daphne tapped her chin twice, then proceeded to dive into her eggs with enthusiasm. She swallowed and raised her eyes to Ivy's again. "What do you think? You know her best, I'm starting to realize. What can I do to make my niece know that she is loved and wanted here?"

"I think offering her this place as her home has gone a long way in that direction." Ivy took a sip of her tea and mulled Violet's reactions to Aunt Daphne over in her mind. "I think she likes you. I even think she enjoys your presence. Violet just needs a lot of patience ... She really does! It was a long time before I was sure of her friendship. But I do love her, and I'm confident she loves me ... even if she isn't always sure how to show it." Ivy was almost always sure of Violet. Sometimes her friend could act absolutely horrible, and when Violet struck out, she never failed to hit all the soft places in Ivy. And that hurt so badly.

"You're probably right, there. Building a relationship takes time, but I want to rush into things. I feel that way about everything. I'm looking for God's opportunities for me in Keefmore, but they haven't come yet ... With the exception of Agnes and Duncan, of course, whom I was able to help greatly, I think. But I'm so impatient for the next thing. I have so much time on my hands these days!"

That was a strange thought to Ivy, for she disliked busyness in general. It was so much nicer to take life at a relaxed pace, every moment flowing into the next in a gorgeous harmony. However, that wasn't always possible in the modern world, and she understood that. Even if, at times, it was frightening.

"I used to always have something to do," Aunt Daphne bemoaned. "There aren't really charitable institutions to visit in Keefmore. But, I suppose, that means I ought to start my own." She tapped her chin. "There must be a need for something."

In such a small village? Ivy wasn't sure. It wasn't as if there were beggars roaming the streets. "Perhaps. But if there are needs in Keefmore, I'd say they are more personal or at least spiritual ... rather than your typical asylum for the poor or orphanage." That was her guess. She didn't know the village very well, perhaps.

"You're absolutely right." Aunt Daphne jerked to her feet and tossed her napkin on the table. "But what could I do? Who here has a need? And how would I know? I imagine it must be hard getting past all the Scot pride and privacy. I've already had several run-ins with those two beasts."

"Well ..." There was Ena, of course. "I know Mrs. Owen could use some love and encouragement. She lost her husband and has been alone ever since. The people of Keefmore haven't really been supporting her as they ought. Or maybe they don't know." Honestly, according to Jordy, there seemed to be a number of gaping holes in the community's communications. "I wonder if there's a way to help Keefmore help Keefmore," she murmured.

"Ivy, that's just it!" Aunt Daphne practically shrieked. "We need to build a community! And we'll start with the women. Agnes! Agnes!"

The young woman came running, eyes wild. "Aye, mum?"

"A pen and paper, at once!"

Agnes scurried to her task, though Ivy thought she caught the girl's eyes roll slightly before she ran off. Ivy didn't blame her, though she very much liked Aunt Daphne. She suspected Agnes did, too, even though they both acknowledged that there was definitely something of the ridiculous about her.

Agnes soon returned and passed Aunt Daphne her writing utensils, and, once again, the woman was seated and began scratching away at the piece of paper.

"A tea!" she half-shouted. "That's the way to go about these things. Tea. Tea is a grand connector of people. Think how much the British Empire owes to it!"

Ivy squinted. From what she understood, the movement of tea throughout history had caused a lot of its troubles, but she supposed Aunt Daphne might not care for tea so much as hyperbole.

Aunt Daphne looked up with a marvelously wide grin. "Thank you for this idea, Ivy. We're going to host a tea for a few women in the town. I'll make a list, but we'll definitely have your Ena Owen. We'll use it to create a community—*community*! That's what they need. We'll pray for each other, delve into Scriptures, and find ways to support each other ... and then the rest of the town. If anyone knows where Keefmore needs special help, it's these ladies."

"That sounds nice!" Ivy said. Skepticism invaded her soul, but, at the same time, it did make sense. If anyone could pull off something so unusual, it was Aunt Daphne.

CHAPTER SIXTEEN

I vy received her first letter from her family since arriving at Keefmore that following Tuesday. She'd hoped to hear back from Alice—her last few letters had been concerning, and she'd asked for further details—but it was from Peter instead.

All the same, she was pleased to hear from her dear brother.

> *Dear Little Sister,*
>
> *I've been making Alice write once a week, even though she's been rather off lately and hasn't wanted to—I think it's woman's troubles. I've asked her if she wants to see a doctor, but she seems to think this is natural. My mama is concerned, too, but we've decided to let it be for the time being, since she mostly just wants to be alone. Please pray she'll recover quickly from whatever this is.*
>
> *But all this to say, she says she's going to send you a lot of letters all at once rather than individually, and I'm letting her. I hope you won't scold me. That's part of the reason why I'm writing this to you, because I want you to know she's not neglecting you.*
>
> *We're all very well here. I'm taking good care of Alice and giving her plenty of time to rest. Again, I want to clarify that you shouldn't worry. Alice tells*

me she sometimes experiences periods of malaise after a difficult month, and I shouldn't be concerned. I'll keep you updated, but I imagine we'll know more soon. I'd hoped we were expecting, actually, but that's not the case. Pray for that, too—I know we've only been married a few months, but it is such a dearly held wish. We very much want to be parents, and I can't seem to pray without asking God to bless us soon. Perhaps that would help Alice settle more quickly, too. I ought to ask you to pray for your dear brother to have some patience! But how I loathe to develop patience rather than to get my way. How human of me!

We both miss you, and we both wish you the best. I know you're capable of anything you put your mind to, little sister, and I think you ought to set your goals higher. But perhaps that's just—what does Alice call it? "Americanishness."

I'll leave you now. Busy days here. Book comes out in February! I'll send you a copy as soon as I get one.

With all my love, all of Alice's, and all the Americanishness I have to offer.

Peter

Peter was such a good letter writer, even when this particular one was a great deal shorter than his usual five-page epistles. *Alice ought to take lessons,* Ivy thought with a smile.

Americanishness. She supposed that might be something to try for. It was one thing to be content and quite another to be stagnant.

She rose and left the office, leaving Violet buried in a book—though she didn't believe that Violet was reading so much as brooding. Her friend had been so dreary these last few days. Ivy knew it would pass with time, as it always did, but she never knew quite how to manage Violet's dark moods.

Ivy decided to go for a walk through the streets. She didn't want to bother Ena, as she'd seen her yesterday, and she couldn't think of anyone else whom she would want to visit with.

Ivy came to a stop outside the church. It was a small building with only the slightest bit of a steeple, no stained-glass windows, nothing grand or pretentious. But that didn't make the worshiping of the small Presbyterian congregation any less sincere. It impressed her, honestly. It hadn't been an especially dignified ceremony, but there had been something clean and honest about it that appealed to her.

She felt herself drawn into the church, though she tried to resist it. She knew why—she longed to play the piano that stood at the front of the sanctuary.

At last, she gave in. She pushed open the door, marched down the aisle, and soon found herself seated on the piano bench. She closed her eyes and let her hands rest on the ivory keys for a moment. Two weeks was simply too long to not be playing music.

At first, Ivy played Mozart, but she soon moved on to hymns, knowing them to be right for the setting.

She didn't know how long she'd been playing when she heard a shuffling sound from the pews and looked up to find the pastor of the congregation sitting there, watching her. She started, and her fingers slid from the keys.

"Ach, I'm sorry! Did I startle ye?"

Ivy wanted to sink through the boards beneath her feet and disappear into nothingness. "I-I'm sorry. I shouldn't be here." She rose from the bench, almost knocking it over and only managing to tilt it back upright at the last second. "I'll leave. I'm so sorry."

"Dinna apologize. Tha' was quite beautiful." He was an elderly man with a long, gray beard and large, blue eyes that seemed to take up the majority of his face. "I'd love tae hear ye play again, in fact ... Miss Ivy, isna it?"

"Yes," Ivy said cautiously. Even though he was a pastor, she still wasn't sure if she could trust him. New people were hard to judge.

"I'm Ivy Knight."

"Weel, Ivy Knight, how would ye like tae play here every Sunday? At least, for as long as ye're stayin' in Scotland."

"Wh-what?" Ivy stuttered. "You mean ... at church?" She couldn't.

"Aye, when else would I need a pianist? Ye see, Miss Knight, I dinna ken if ye noticed or no', but we havena anyone but me wife tae play th' piano, an' even she admits tae havin' no talent. We'd love tae have ye do it. A few simple hymns at th' beginnin' an' one at th' end. I've already heard enough tae ken tha' ye can do it—do it better than anyone in this town can. I was beginnin' tae despair o' tha' piano ever goin' tae any good use."

Ivy sat in silence for a moment. She loved playing the piano, and she was completely capable of doing what he asked. She didn't normally like being watched while she played, but she had performed in front of her family—even in front of close friends—and she knew she could do it. And the joy she could bring both to herself and perhaps even to others ... Yes. It was definitely worth it. Even if it might kill her.

"I'll do it, sir," said Ivy, before her mind had time to make up a million excuses.

Heaven help her.

Ivy's nerves skittered up and down her spine, and she hunched her shoulders to try to end the constant scurrying, but nothing happened. She stood close to Jordy for comfort as they entered the church—or the *kirk*, she supposed—and tried to eke confidence out of his presence.

But it wasn't working.

Violet took her hand from the other side, squeezed it, then dropped it. She knew her friend understood how difficult this would be. How her stomach roiled, her head spun.

Performing in public in front of a great crowd of people, the majority of whom she didn't know at all, was so far from her comfort zone, and she wanted to run. She wanted to run and run until there was no one at all around her for miles, and then she wanted to sit down and cry.

This was foolishness. Why had she agreed to this? She couldn't do it. She wasn't brave enough, wasn't strong enough. Certainly wasn't good enough. Her playing was *emotional*. When her emotions were everywhere, so were the notes, and getting them in their proper places was almost impossible.

The service would start soon. Jordy nudged her toward the front, and she walked, like a woman to her executioner, to the piano and took a seat at the bench. She spent an inordinate amount of time adjusting her skirt, despite the fact that the simple pastel dress didn't have a terribly full skirt—or, really, no more than was proper.

Her eyes flickered out over the congregation then, but she quickly turned them to the hymn book. The pastor had told her what he'd like to have played, and they were simple. They'd require barely any effort on her part. All she had to do was make herself play. That was all. There wasn't anything more to it.

Don't think. Don't think. Don't think.

But she was thinking. Her mind was spiraling, and she felt ill. There were too many eyes on her, and this wasn't any good. How could this be something she was meant to do? Her focus was everywhere but where it ought to be. She should be thinking about how to please God and bless these people, but instead, she was worried and afraid—and she wasn't even sure what about.

Oh, God, help me. Help me.

Her throat felt tight and full, and she couldn't breathe. Her vision blurred ...

The pastor was giving her a look. She ought to start. She must, she should, and yet, with blackness rapidly taking over what was left of her eyesight, fear kicked in, and she jerked to her feet. The piano bench clattered to the ground.

Breathing heavily, she stepped back, tangled in her skirt, defenseless under the prying eyes. Oh, they must despise her now! How could they not? She was weak, helpless, and she couldn't even do one simple task ...

Helpless. Worthless. Hopeless.

"Ivy." It was Jordy. How had he gotten to her so quickly? His arm went around her waist, keeping her upright. "There noo. Shush. Dizzy?"

She nodded and steadied herself with a hand on his shoulder.

"A'right. Dinna fash yerself. Breathe."

She dropped her head on his shoulder and tried to breathe. She felt another hand on her shoulder and caught Violet in her peripheral vision. The piano bench was righted and her skirt straightened without her having to move at all.

She heard the pastor saying something in the background. What was it? That it was the first time she'd played in front of a crowd, and they could have grace for that, couldn't they?

She forced the buzzing in her ears to quiet to the point where she could hear the pastor's voice.

"I remember a time," said he, "when I was nae more than twenty years old. I was in Edinburgh then, in trainin' under Pastor Keith, a renowned preacher o' th' Word. I was tae train tae be his replacement at th' time, long before I ken't where Keefmore was or what 'twas all about." He chuckled. "I was a green lad, I was. But one week, Pastor Keith came down with th' influenza, an' I was asked tae step up an' give the sermon. Will ye guess what happened? I'd been workin' wi' Pastor Keith all th' last week, an' I started growin' feverish an' coughin' an' me stomach was ready tae leave me body—thank th' Lord th' choirmaster had th' sense tae pull me away from th' pulpit before I decorated it wi' me breakfast!"

The congregation laughed, and even Ivy was able to sigh out a small smile. Jordy squeezed her shoulder.

"Better?" he whispered.

She nodded and swiped at her eyes. "Thank you."

Violet's hand moved to her lower back. "Don't let it beat you, Trifle. You wouldn't let me give up, now would you?"

She certainly would not. Taking a deep breath, she seated herself on the piano bench again, this time with Jordy and Violet flanking her, and began the opening bars to the hymn.

Though she knew it wasn't exactly fitting, they applauded her after the first song, and after that, it got easier and easier, and her spirit found a place where it could rest—and see the beauty of the music and the words and the voices raised heartily to praise God.

And, in her heart, Ivy praised Him, too, for without Him, and without the good friends He'd sent to keep her safe and loved, she never would have been able to play.

The lad gripped Ivy's hand with a force that took her breath away, but she could never pull back from him. He was trying so hard to be brave, but it was clear the big-city doctor with his stethoscope and cabinets of medicine and various frightening tools were scaring him. Of course, it didn't help that he had one arm curled about his stomach—she wasn't sure if his physical pain or his apprehensions about Jordy's treatment was bothering him more.

"Noo, Rabbie." Jordy leaned one hip against the examination table. "This isna goin' tae be so bad. All ye've got is an upset stomach —which is wha' comes o' eatin' a half a pound o' grain tha's meant for yer plow horse."

Ivy covered a smile by glancing toward the window, then turned her head back to Rabbie McDowell's face. He was a dear boy with big, blue eyes, his cheeks pale enough to show every freckle individually.

His mother had remained in the waiting room, a somewhat exhausted-looking woman with a hat drooping over her eyes and three small children clustered around her. It appeared that Rabbie gave her a daily run for her money.

"Were ye really tha' hungry, Rabbie?" Jordy quirked his eyebrows. "Couldna ye ask yer mum for a heartier breakfast?"

Rabbie scowled. "I just wanted tae ken why Bessie loves it so. Tha's all. I didna ken it'd make me sick." He hiccuped. "An' I didna think, even if it did, Mum would get worried an' take me down here." He sent another glance around the office. Yes, the location was definitely more frightening than the actual ailment for this young boy.

"Hmm ..." Jordy tapped his chin, eyes twinkling at Ivy over his patient's head. "If ye havena cast up yer accounts yet, I doubt ye will. But ye're goin' tae be in for some stomach pains for th' next day or so. Rabbie, ye canna eat horse grains. Ye ken they have th' chaff still in there?"

"I didna eat tha' part! Weel, mostly, exceptin' as I thought it might be better for me." Rabbie folded his arms across his stomach and moaned woefully. "I thought Mum wanted me tae eat more o' me oatmeal, an' this is like tae th' same thing."

Jordy did chuckle aloud that time. "Aye, weel, 'tis different, lad. But all's well tha' ends well. Ye could've tried a lot worse things, couldna ye have?"

Rabbie nodded. "So I'm a'right?"

"Ye're a'right." Jordy turned to the medicine cabinet. "Yer mum, on th' other hand, is fit tae burst wi' her fears. See wha' ye did tae her? Ye'd best watch yerself, worryin' yer mother. 'Tis no' a game a real man plays. Noo, I'm givin' ye somethin' tae ease yer stomach, but, in general, this is just a waitin' game. Ken?"

Rabbie swallowed. "Aye."

Still smiling, Jordy lifted the boy off the table and let him out of the room to give instructions to his worried mother, and Ivy picked up a damp cloth to wipe down the table.

Jordy seemed to enjoy this type of work, and, frankly, Ivy did, too. She loved seeing little boys and girls most of all, but it was always nice to help Jordy in the little ways she could. Of course, she didn't know much about medicine, and she was sure she wasn't brave enough to do most things, but she did her best, even when her stomach roiled and vision faded. She'd yet to actually faint, though once or twice Jordy had sent her outside or told her to take a deep breath and sit down.

Jordy was good at knowing Ivy's limits and when to push them, so she'd helped with just about everything now. As of yet, Jordy had been very successful in helping everyone who came to him, and Ivy had been moderately successful in aiding him in doing that. She was proud of her friend, quite proud. She knew he had some doubts hidden deep, in the dark places he didn't share with many people. Nonetheless, he was brave and confident in his actions, and that was what counted.

Every day she saw more and more of how Jordy would build a life here. She was only grateful she was allowed to join him in it, even if it was just for this short time.

Jordy returned to the examination room ten minutes later. "Rabbie was th' last o' them for noo, Vee. Why dinna ye head home? I ken ye've tha' tea tae prepare for, an' I might make a call oot tae th' Keiths, if I've th' time."

"All right." Ivy turned to the basin at the back of the room and set about washing her hands. "Thank you for letting me help again today, Jordy."

"Thank ye for helpin'." There was a note of amusement in his voice. He still hadn't quite managed to understand what doing something like this, something useful, meant to Ivy. However, she forgave him readily for his ignorance. How could a person like Jordy know the uselessness of everyday life? Everything he did was so grand.

She caught up her shawl and walked out the back door. As always, there was a sizable crowd of children gathered in the empty lot behind Jordy's office.

They appeared to be playing some kind of tag. Ivy had never really played with children when she was small. More recently, she'd started playing with her brothers and sisters, and that had been fun.

Not that she could ever outrun them, and they seemed to have an endless store of energy. But it had been quite entertaining—and, she thought, a good way to spend time with them. However, they were overwhelming, for Ivy more so than anyone. Children raced about like a piece by Mozart—actually, like the trilling, lighthearted, but quick Piano Sonata No. 16 in C Major, or at least the first movement. That was about as perfect a description as she could get, though others might choose a less peaceful and beautiful piece. However, they were wrong. There was plenty of drama in that sonata, at any rate.

Ivy wasn't quite sure about the rules of the game these Scottish children were at. There was much running and tagging and sitting and running again. They were all shouting, laughing, calling out names. Whatever the game was, it appeared to be quite amusing. At least to watch.

"Miss Ivy!" Bridget left the group and came to her side, arm swinging with only some restriction in a loosened arm sling. Heaven help Ena. "Would ye like tae play with us?"

Ivy hesitated. "I don't know how to play, Bridget. I'm not very good at games."

"Ach, I'll teach ye," Bridget assured her. "We all want ye tae play. Please? It's a real easy game. Ye try tae tag everyone ye can, an' then when someone tags ye, ye sit down, an' when they get tagged, ye can stand up again. It goes on an' on."

"Sounds like it does," Ivy said, eyebrows raised. "How does it end?"

"When everyone is sittin' down but one, but tha' almost never happens. We almost always get called in first."

A boy came up behind Bridget, scuffing his bare toes on the ground impatiently. "Wha' did she say?"

"I'm still convincin' her, Angus. Dinna be so impatient!" Bridget exclaimed. "What do ye think, Miss Ivy?"

"All right, I'll play," Ivy said. "You have to be patient with me. It looks like a hard game. You have to keep track of who tagged you, right?"

Bridget nodded. "But it's not tha' hard once ye get started." She took Ivy by the hand, led her into the middle of the lot, and introduced her. Then the game commenced, and Ivy found herself whirling, trying to keep up.

Ivy lost track of the times she was tagged then got up and was tagged almost immediately again. But it was great fun, and she found herself laughing almost to tears, panting and struggling for breath but perfectly content.

It really was a wild game, and more enjoyable than she'd imagined any game could be. There was much yelling—"I tagged ye!" "Nae, ye didna! Ye're blind!" "Aye, I did, too, ye bletherin' idiot!" But it was all in good sport, and none of the children really meant a single one of the derogatory comments they threw at each other.

Ivy remained seated after a time, even though she could have risen, laughing too hard to keep running.

Just watching these children was an absolute joy. They had so much energy, so much joy for life. She sometimes wondered, when one of her siblings was trying to make her life miserable in every possible way, why she liked children so much. Then she'd remember. It was these types of moments, when the inhibitions were clearly absent and the happiness uniquely there. Ivy tried to be this carefree— longed to become childlike again in her joy, her freedom, her bravery.

Sitting on the edge of that empty lot, it then occurred to her that she felt quite joyful, quite free, and quite brave. What was this? Could she already feel at home in this place so far away from her normal reality? Or, rather, was this reality becoming her new one?

Ivy could see herself here in Keefmore. Helping Jordy, spending time with Aunt Daphne and Violet, going to church here, playing the piano, and getting to know these children. They were dear children, too, around their rough edges. But there were needs, as Aunt Daphne had mentioned. For instance, someone ought to start a Sunday school.

Of course, she'd need the pastor's permission. And Keefmore did have a somewhat newly-established, struggling grammar school, too. The teacher, Miss Locke, would be attending the tea—

Oh! She jumped to her feet. She had no idea of the hour, and she would hate to be late to an event she'd helped plan. Though no master at etiquette, Ivy did know arriving after the set time for something you had invited people to wasn't polite at all.

She raced back to Aunt Daphne's home to hear the clock toll the half hour as she arrived. Good. She still had time to tidy up and help with any last-minute preparations. Aunt Daphne, who was already fidgeting in the front parlor, gestured for Ivy to hurry, and Ivy did just that.

Precisely at four, perhaps driven more by their curiosity than their punctuality, the guests arrived. There was Miss Locke, the aforementioned schoolteacher, who looked exactly as a schoolteacher ought to look—which was exhausted but kind. Then there was Ena, of course. Ivy could never have stood for Ena to be left out. The pastor's wife, Mrs. Abernathy, was also in attendance—and Mrs. Grear and Mrs. McDermid. Mrs. Dunmore, the midwife, had been invited, but Ivy had been fairly certain she wouldn't attend ... and she'd been right. According to just about everyone she'd talked to, Mrs. Dunmore kept to herself. Usually only her daughter came down for church and sat alone. Perhaps Ivy ought to have invited that daughter, but she was young and, everyone said, shy.

However, Ivy knew better than to worry about what she ought to have done when she had guests in front of her at the moment. Aunt Daphne greeted everyone with a smile and a great deal more fidgeting, while Violet looked like she wanted to be anywhere but there. Ivy didn't feel much more at ease than they probably did; however, neither did their guests, for that matter.

"Thank ye for th' invitation." Ena Owen lowered herself onto a chair at the first opportunity.

There was a murmured round of agreement, though Mrs. Grear, at least, was looking at Ena quite skeptically. Soon everyone was seated, some appearing more at ease than others. They all glanced about the room, somewhere between amazement and amusement as they took in the grand decor.

Aunt Daphne cleared her throat. "Ladies, we've called you all here today because it struck me recently that there is not much of this sort of thing in Keefmore. What I mean is that there is not much in terms of social clubs. Now, you may scoff"-indeed, a few of the ladies did look like they were scoffing!—"but regardless of what you do or do not have time for, what does or does not seem frivolous, and what is and is not normal in this village, you can't deny that there is a great need in all of our hearts for the chatter and companionship of other women. Not only that ... the help, when needed. Now, this isn't about charity. This is about supporting each other, which is quite a biblical pursuit indeed. Any objections thus far?"

The women shuffled but said nothing. A few of them, Ena included, grinned, while a few others scowled.

Mrs. Abernathy was the first to actually speak. "I think this is a good idea, Mrs. Wright." She smiled encouragingly at her parishioners. "We dinna have anythin' like this in Keefmore, but I've always hoped we would. It's just hard for me tae add tha' ontae me days, wha' wi' th' children. But, ma'am, since ye've th' time, I willna be objectin'. In fact, I'm glad ye thought o' it!"

Once the pastor's wife had approved, Mrs. Grear and the schoolteacher both echoed, softly, their approval.

"I'm no' sure I'll have time for this on th' regular," said Mrs. McDermid.

"Ach, ye can make time, canna ye?" Ena adjusted her position on the chair and regarded each of the women individually with a cheerful expression. "I ken I can, even though I've about as much tae do as any o' ye. We've all lives, but wha' will those lives be wi'oot friendship an' love from our neighbors?"

Mrs. Grear's eyes were instantly cast down. Ivy wondered if the woman knew the way the village's treatment of Ena had affected her. They likely all knew. Would they change or would they stick to the rejection Ena had faced in recent months?

But, even if there were still some hard feelings to be worked through, the ladies did settle down after Ena spoke. Aunt Daphne asked everyone to introduce themselves, and tell the group one thing about themselves that they might not know, and, after some bashfulness, it went as well as could be expected.

Afterwards, Aunt Daphne leaned back on her chair, seeming much more at ease, and asked questions of each lady, while Ivy poured tea and passed around cakes and biscuits, Agnes hovering in and out of the background. Thankfully, the ladies barely seemed to acknowledge their server, which was another thing Ivy had been concerned about.

As the talk buzzed around her, Ivy enjoyed soaking in the information about these women and their lives. She found it interesting how each of them had different experiences even though, supposedly, their lives should all be very routine and similar. That's what people seemed to believe about practically poor people in small villages far away from "civilization." However, Ivy just wasn't finding it to be true.

They each had their personalities, their likes and dislikes, their heartbreaks, and their joys. They each responded to Aunt Daphne's questions differently.

It would be interesting to be one of these women ... truly one of them. Living in Keefmore, socializing with them daily, knowing that she had time, plenty of time, to grow a relationship with each of them. Again, the daydream of running a Sunday school popped to the surface, for she did see a need, and of playing the piano before church every Sunday. She could be with these women all the time as one of them. She could do it.

A part of her included Jordy in that daydream, though she wasn't sure how to place him. She knew the part she would cast him if she were a little girl who still believed in fairy tales—or, rather, what she thought of him as in those moments. He had always been somewhat dashing in her mind's eye, a hero and a vanquisher of dragons. She tried not to think of him too much as the prince to her princess, but, at times, it was virtually impossible.

Ivy imagined the intimacy between them was the cause of that. Though not romantic, she was only human. How could she not think of Jordy that way? Even if he didn't want her. Even if he never wanted anything more than friendship. There was always her imagination, and, anymore, it was jumping to all the places it shouldn't.

It was time to stop the daydreaming and live in the real world. Ivy knew she was capable of becoming attached to Jordy, and, if she did that, she would end up with a broken heart and no idea how to nurse it. She'd have to leave in a few, short months, and it would only be more difficult if she let herself think up impossible scenarios.

If only Jordy weren't so perfect—or if only Ivy were. As it was, he was unreachable. Not that any man would be particularly reachable to Ivy, but Jordy, more so than any, was a man of true quality. She couldn't imagine anyone who could possibly be better ... which was one of the many reasons why he would never take an interest in her.

CHAPTER SEVENTEEN

All Hallow's Eve

Jordy felt Ivy lean into him slightly as they stood in the town square, watching the great bonfire roar and dance in the moonlight. He smiled down at her and squeezed her shoulder before stepping back.

He knew she was a little frightened—he imagined it was the first party of this sort she had ever seen—but he couldn't offer physical comfort. No, indeed. His attraction to her was too willing to betray him and make him think about things he really shouldn't.

"Jordy?" Ivy smiled up at him. "Why do they call it 'All Hallow's Eve'?"

He squinted as he thought. "'Hallow' means 'holy.' Since in th' morn it'll be All Hallow's Day, 'twas believed tha' all th' ghosts came oot tae harm good Christian men th' night before." He leaned close to her and whispered in her ear, "An' some still believe it."

Ivy shuddered. "I don't believe in ghosts." She stuck her chin out in that adorable, almost stubborn way that was at odds with her lenient personality. *The darling lass!*

He shook his head to rid himself of the thought. "Aye, most dinna anymore. But ye ken there are Wee Folk in these hills."

"Wee Folk?" Ivy's blue eyes widened.

"Aye," Jordy replied, grinning. He loved teasing this imp. "Aye. Wee Folk. Mischievous folk. Almost wee demons, exceptin' they can

176

do good, if they have a mind tae. But," he added, "they'd rather pull tricks."

"What kind of tricks?" Ivy looked almost frightened, though she still seemed doubtful, so Jordy felt able to tease on.

"Ach, ye ken—any kind o' trick. They'll let yer calves in wi' yer cows so they're dry in th' morn. They'll open gates an' make meat rot an' all sorts o' things." Jordy shrugged. "Just any kind o' mischief."

Despite his assurances, Ivy's eyebrows inched up. "Oh, I don't believe any of that," she said. "Wee Folk up in the hills? Ghosts coming out one night a year? Wasn't it supposed to be demons—not ghosts?"

Jordy fake-scowled. She was smarter than she looked sometimes, and it ruined all his best jokes. At the same time, he was impressed with her insight. "Aye, tha's too frightenin' even for me. Tha's real evil. Ghosts, though? Faye? I can handle tha'."

Ivy giggled. "It can't be that scary, Jordy, if the night is limited to what you can handle."

It took him a moment to register the words. What? Was she teasing him? It made him laugh, and he couldn't think of a good response when he'd finished. The moment had passed, leaving Ivy looking self-satisfied. Oh well.

"Jordy ..." Ivy said, brow furrowed again. She'd already thought of something more to wonder about? He sometimes thought her brain never stopped working. Funny how some folks thought she didn't have a brain at all when she was truly the most curious lass he knew. "Jordy," she repeated, "do you really believe in fairies?"

Jordy shrugged. "I dinna ken if I believe or if I want tae believe. I dinna care, either. It's fun tae imagine all sorts o' frightenin' things one night o' th' year an' tae have a good time an' tae see me friends."

"Do you think it's wrong? Rather like consorting with demons?" Ivy asked.

"Ach, nae, Vee. No' at all. I dinna believe such things, an' even if I did, we would be fightin' them by gettin' together—all good Christians, ye ken—an' startin' this great fire."

"And drinking." Ivy nodded towards the tables, which, amongst many other foods, held alcoholic beverages.

Jordy grinned. "Didna ken ye were a temperance advocate."

Ivy blushed but continued on. "No, I don't believe in drinking—at least not in excess—and I would never drink."

"Ye are a lady. No' tha' tha' would stop most in Keefmore. An' I dinna blame them—at least no' too much."

Ivy's face pinched. Apparently she didn't like that one bit. "I don't want you to drink, Jordy. You shouldn't."

"Tha's no' really any o' yer concern, Vee." She was his friend not his keeper. "Dinna fash yerself over me. I can take care o' meself."

This seemed to bring more worry to her eyes, so he resolved to change the subject. "Wha' do ye think o' Keefmore's celebration otherwise?"

She sighed but allowed him to stop talking on something they would clearly not agree upon. "We've only just gotten here."

Behind him, Edith and Mrs. McAllen were handing pies and other baked goods down to his brothers, who carried them over to the tables. Mr. McAllen had already wandered over to a group of men talking a ways away, and Violet stood to Jordy's left, arms wrapped around her middle.

He cocked his head. "Are ye a'right, Vi?"

"What?" she said, startling.

"Are ye a'right?"

"Yes. Why do you ask?"

"Ye're holdin' yer stomach."

Violet rolled her eyes. "Every time I wrap my arms about myself doesn't mean I have a stomachache." Her tone said he deserved to be abandoned in the hills during a snowstorm and left to die.

Jordy shrugged. Though Violet's mood had improved over the past few days, he wasn't surprised that it was fading again. Violet, like everyone, went through good times and bad times, but she couldn't usually help it. Jordy had learned to grin and bear it when she acted up and not to take insults personally. Despite the fact that he longed, more than anything else in the world, to chuck her in the nearest loch or at least give her a severe dressing down.

Ivy, however, was his ray of sunshine. Every day he grew to admire her more. She was so intent upon being cheerful and kind, and she was sweeter than sugar. Perhaps almost too good, in his opinion—she could let Violet treat her terribly. Thankfully, he was around to step in, and he'd been encouraging her to stand up for herself.

Edith came to his side, bumping past Violet with typical Edith-ness. After all, she considered herself the rightful owner of the place at his side. He loved Edith, but she was dreadfully presumptuous sometimes.

"Have ye seen Tris?"

"Sorry, Edi, I havena," Jordy offered his best sympathetic smile. Tristan Kendrick had been with the large flock of a farmer he worked for, earning a little extra money while finding greener pastures for the sheep. He'd been gone since before Jordy arrived but had promised to return by All Hallow's Eve.

Edith was dying to see him. Jordy understood. He was eager to see Tris, too—and to give him a hard time over courting his sister.

Not that he wasn't pleased. In fact, he was extremely pleased. It was honestly a dream come true for him. Now his best friend would truly be his brother. Could anything be more perfect?

"He'd better be here soon, so help me, or I'll track him down an' strangle him!" Edith exclaimed. "Whatever could be keeping th' man? I'm his *promised*. He has nae reason tae be gallivanting about th' hills, an' no' a word from him in over two weeks." She was practically imploding with frustration.

Jordy threw an arm about her shoulders and hugged her. "Easy, there, Edi. It'll be a'right. I'm sure he's fine. An' it wouldna do either o' ye any good for him tae be strangled, now would it?"

Edith blew out a big breath. "I dinna ken. It might do me a lot o' good."

"Aye, but then ye'd have lost him," Jordy pointed out.

"Tha' might no' be such a bad idea," Edith mumbled before stomping off towards some of her friends. He watched her go with a grin on his lips. He understood impatience, but Edith was ridiculous. She needed everything to happen her way—and immediately. But, in some ways, she was right. Tristan hadn't shown a lot of feeling in going when he did. But then, when had Tristan ever shown feeling?

"I'm goin' tae go talk tae some old friends o' mine, a'right, Vee an' Vi?"

Violet glared at him—probably more because she disliked the nicknames he'd given them than because she wanted him to stay.

Ivy, however, looked more worried. "When ... when will you be back?"

Jordy shrugged. He didn't like how clingy she had become. Granted, it was partially his fault. It was no good for her to depend on him—first, because he couldn't handle it; second, because it would be harmful to her. "I dinna ken, Vee. Go tae Edith or me mum, a'right? Ye needna wait on me tae have a good time."

Ivy seemed to draw into herself at his words—and only then did he realize they'd come out a little harsh. But perhaps she needed a little harshness. After all, she couldn't go leaning on him like a baby. He wasn't the sort who could always be there for her like she needed. She was the kind who wanted someone dependable in her life—like a rock or a mountain. He was a vapor in the wind—and he liked it that way.

"Really," Jordy said, softening his tone, "ye'll be fine, Vee. I'm goin' tae be over there." He gestured to a group of young men that already included several he knew from boyhood as well as Ben and Mick. "Ye can call me if ye need me. But," he added, "only if ye absolutely need me. No' for any random reason or because ye're bored or because ye *think* ye need me. Ye dinna."

Ivy nodded, though he could tell she was upset. Never mind that. He'd tried, and she was being childish. Perhaps it was the excitement of the night or getting to see old friends again or the smell of the wood smoke and flicker of the fires or the promise of good food and drink, but he felt a need to throw off all shackles.

Over the past few weeks, he'd been Dr. George McAllen, for all intents and purposes. Serious and staid. The kind of dependable bloke folks could bet their money on. Always there. Always at work. So little play allowed. Certainly, he was always professional and neat and, in other words, everything a country doctor should be.

But he was tired of it. Tired of pretending to be serious when he longed to laugh and talk. Tired of focusing, ever focusing, when he wanted to take five minutes for a walk in the countryside. Tonight he would enjoy himself.

Jordy loved his job, but any job could get tiresome after too long. Even the most interesting job in the world—which he believed he had. Leaving Ivy and Violet, he walked across the square to his friends.

Jordy's head swam a little later that evening. He blamed it on the wood smoke, but in the back of his mind, he knew he was no longer used to the heavy, potent ale the men—and some of the women—of Keefmore drank. Especially not in any substantial quantity.

However, he wasn't sick, so he decided he must be all right. He had a grand time eating his fill of the delicious meal, meeting with family and old friends, playing ridiculous games, dancing, laughing, singing—he enjoyed these kinds of events most.

There was so much freedom here. No restraints. No seriousness. No 'Dr. George McAllen.' Just Jordy and the rest of Keefmore having a grand old time.

Tristan Kendrick arrived at the party about an hour in. Jordy ran up to him and greeted him, but Tristan really only had eyes for Edith. He simply slapped Jordy on the shoulder and brushed past him. Jordy rolled his eyes. He'd have to watch those two over the next few weeks. He loved Tristan, but Edith was his sister, and his loyalty was to her first.

As the night wore on, the alcohol started taking more serious effect, and, when he stood up to follow Tristan across the square, he staggered.

The ground tilted and swayed and rose up to meet him. He found himself flat on the hard-packed dirt. It took him far too long to push his face up. He felt woozy now. About ready to lose his supper, in fact.

Still, he tried to struggle to his feet. He had to. Yet, in the end, the effort was useless.

Dozens of faces gazed at him with all sorts of expressions. Worry, confusion, amusement. Contempt. Disappointment. Smugness.

He heard the whispers starting already. "Drunkard." "Canna even walk." "Tae much for him tae handle." "Wild boy." "Nae good." "Worthless, worthless, worthless ..."

Jordy gave up trying and lay still.

He felt gentle hands stroking his hair and a damp, cool cloth wiping his face. He couldn't seem to open his eyes. He couldn't remember where he was or what had happened. Or perhaps it was too hard to think over his pounding headache.

A voice, sounding overly loud, cut the silence. "I think he's going to be all right, Violet. I'll run back to the village and draw more water. I want him to drink some when he wakes up. Will you stay?"

"Yes," another voice answered. "I can mind him until you're back."

There was the scuffling sounds of someone rising and footsteps walking away. He listened to them until each one didn't spike agony through his head.

He felt a blanket under him and grass and ground beneath the blanket. He could hear water, and as the knowledge that he had been at the All Hallow's Eve festival came back to him, he surmised that he was lying on a grassy bank near a stream west of Keefmore. How he'd gotten here was beyond him.

Jordy felt a hand touch his forehead, a hand that was slightly less cool but still feminine. He lay still and let her stroke his forehead, trying to puzzle out what had happened.

He had had a wee bit too much to drink. That much was clear, but events were foggy. He remembered Tristan coming back—spending time with friends—Ivy's worried eyes watching him, always watching, looking frightened and disappointed.

"Jordy, are you awake?" Violet's voice was close to his ear.

He wanted to respond, but it was simply too much effort. His tongue felt swollen and heavy. How did one speak again? He couldn't remember.

"Jordy," she repeated.

He didn't imagine it would be anything important, so he let himself start to drift back off. But he found himself fully awake—or at least semi-aware—when he felt Violet's hand slide down his cheek, cup his chin, and gently turn his face toward what he imagined must be her.

Was he dreaming? He must be. From the buzzing in his head, he knew the effects of the alcohol hadn't quite worn off. That was the problem with drinking—he couldn't see straight for hours afterward. Hardly knew what was going on around him. It wasn't good, certainly. Probably not a state anyone should willingly enter into.

He felt Violet's breath on his forehead, then her lips brushed the tip of his nose. He opened his eyes and whispered, "Vi ... wha' ...?"

"Shh," she murmured. "You won't miss one." And with that, she lowered her lips to his.

He wasn't really sure how to respond. Instinct told him to reach for her, but that couldn't be right. It felt wrong.

After a painfully long second, she drew back. "Go to sleep, Jordy. I'll see you in the morning."

He was terribly drowsy, but he didn't know what to think of Violet's actions. What could she mean by that? Had it even happened? His head began swimming again, and he felt himself drifting off.

Ivy kept silent the morning after All Hallow's Eve when she went down to the doctor's office. Jordy seemed to be brooding or hiding from the sun. She really wasn't sure which at this point.

He hadn't said anything. At least, not more than a mumbled 'Good morn'. He hadn't smiled. He winced whenever she spoke, so she'd stopped trying to communicate and simply bustled about the office, keeping as busy as possible while Jordy sulked.

She had no idea what it would be like for him. Everyone had seemed terribly disgusted at the All Hallow's Eve celebration, and, honestly, Ivy was disgusted, too. But she felt he understood why the drinking had been an issue—could this be a lesson well learned?

"Vee?" Jordy's voice was a dry rasp, and he cleared his throat—then winced—before continuing. "Thank ye for no' talkin'."

"You're welcome," Ivy replied. "It's no problem."

He offered her a tight smile and returned to the cabinets he was methodically organizing. His brow was furrowed. She wondered if he was having a hard time remembering the events of the night—and if she could fill in the details for him. But, she supposed, there wasn't really that much to remember.

Violet was also acting strangely today. While she hadn't taken a sip of anything that could vaguely be considered alcoholic, she still acted as if she were recovering from the effects of the liquid drug. Furthermore, she seemed to be actively avoiding Jordy—which was nothing unusual for Violet, but she hadn't even made eye contact with him all morning.

And—even more strangely—Jordy seemed to be acting in a similar way toward her.

Ivy slipped into the office, where Violet had curled up with a book on the chair behind Jordy's desk. "What's wrong with you?" Ivy asked. "Are you feeling all right?"

Violet avoided Ivy's gaze. "Yes, I'm feeling well. Nothing's wrong. I'm ... I'm tired. It was a long night. We couldn't have gotten to sleep before two—perhaps later, when all was said and done."

"I know." Ivy smothered a yawn at the thought of the small amount of sleep they'd gotten. "I'm tired, too. But are you sure, Violet? You seem more than 'tired.' I know you. Please. Don't hide anything from me."

Violet shrugged. "Nothing's wrong, Ivy. I don't know what you're talking about. Perhaps you're more tired than you think—imagining things like that."

Jordy came into the office and glanced at Violet, his brow creased and his eyes dark, then he turned to Ivy. His expression instantly lightened—or, at least, she thought so.

"Vee, I'm goin' tae do a wee bit o' cleanin' around th' examination room. Would ye mind helpin' me?"

Ivy nodded. "What can I do?"

"Sweep. I'll be wipin' down th' rest o' th' room."

Ivy set to work. At first, Jordy didn't say a word, just worked silently, obviously in pain. Ivy had no idea what he was going through, but she pitied him.

At last, he spoke. "Vee, I'm so sorry," he said. "I'm so, so sorry. I've failed ye."

"No you haven't!" Ivy hurried to say. First, because he hadn't failed *her* specifically, and second, because she hated to hear anyone talking badly about themselves. "We all make mistakes."

"Aye, but tha' was a terrible mistake. I'm irresponsible, aye, but I'm no' often drunk. No' even in me college days." He sighed and shook his head.

Ivy cocked her head and thought for a moment. "God forgives us no matter what, and I can do no less than He would. Jordy, I don't think you're a bad person. You made one mistake." She hadn't honestly felt that he was that deserving of grace before she began

185

speaking, but now she couldn't stop. "You haven't failed me. Yes, you showed your humanity rather obviously—don't we all, almost every day? It says in the Bible not to drink to excess—and, even so, it's foolish. But it's a sin like any other. Since you plainly regret it, God has forgiven you—because of Jesus—and so will I."

Jordy smiled for the first time this morning. "Thank ye, Vee," he said. "Sometimes I need ye tae tell me simple things, now dinna I?"

Ivy placed a hand on his arm for a brief moment. "You're my friend. You mean everything to me. You ... you're one of the best men I know, Jordy McAllen. I'd trust you with my life. Yes, you made a mistake, but I still think you're worthy of my ... my respect and admiration. And you always will be." She emphasized her words with a firm nod of her head.

Jordy was silent for a long moment. "Ivy," he said at last, "I woke up this morn about ready tae quit. I thought, 'Who would want someone as hopelessly flawed as me? I'm everythin' I promised meself I wouldna be.' But ye have given me hope. Ye're right. God's in charge, an' He forgives without inhibitions those who want tae be forgiven. Who am I tae say tha' I am hopeless when God says no one is?"

Ivy beamed. If he could see himself through God's eyes rather than the fatally reversed view he must get every morning in the mirror, Jordy would understand that what he'd just said was a simple truth. "See, Jordy? You ... you're wonderful, really," she said before blushing furiously. She probably shouldn't have said that. Oh well. The words were out of her mouth, and she couldn't unsay them.

Jordy didn't seem to notice, however. "I'll have tae earn th' trust o' th' people o' Keefmore back. It'll be long, hard work. It may take years. We Scots hold grudges," he added with a wink. Then he grew serious again. "Ivy, will ye stand by me?"

Ivy smiled. Of course she would. For however long he needed her to.

In some ways, Ivy now felt as if she were on a slightly more equal footing with Jordy. He was fallible, and that had never been more apparent. Since he also didn't use his brain, and probably to a slightly bigger degree than Ivy, she felt a special kinship to him. But there was also the fact that, beneath it all, he was still Jordy.

She wanted to see him through this rough patch. However, she was confident that they could find ways to win back the good opinions of the people of Keefmore, as well as move forward in an even more positive manner.

How were they going to accomplish that? She wasn't quite sure ... yet. There was more praying and more thinking to be done before she could arrive at a plan. Though she didn't really like plans much, so it was more like she would take this whole adventure one step at a time.

For it was an adventure, wasn't it? Another step to take, another path to explore. For the first time, Ivy was starting to find and enjoy these opportunities. She thought it was Jordy that allowed her to do that, with his own in-the-moment approach to life, his own bravery, and his own initiative.

She found an old cloth and started running it over the shelves, carefully removing bottles and equipment to dust around them before meticulously replacing them. This was the last thing she did every day before leaving—and today she had promised to pay a visit to Ena.

However, it was nice to have this last task, and it was nice, for once, that Jordy was choosing not to talk to her during this time. She appreciated the time to think. She had every intention of bringing Jordy's drunkenness up with Ena, but she wasn't sure exactly how to phrase her request for advice ...

Much less how Ena would respond.

However, Ena was a gracious woman, and she knew Keefmore well despite the fact that the village had never really seemed to accept her as one of their own and had rejected her in recent months even more so than usual. She would probably be aware of how Keefmore would react.

As Ivy dusted, it occurred to her that perhaps the damage wasn't as great as they thought. After all, it wasn't beyond most people in the village to drink. They did have a well-patronized tavern, after all. And, though drunkenness was frowned on in religious circles, it never seemed to be considered the worst sin by most people Ivy had met. That was why she loved Peter, after all—they saw eye to eye on the importance of temperance, but he also saw the importance of grace.

Grace was vital to every action and thought toward fellow human beings, and every year, Ivy learned another lesson in what judgement was and wasn't.

The last of the dusting finished, Ivy said good-bye to Jordy for the day and started down the street to Ena's shop. She kept her steps determined; she would not allow herself to be a coward about this, though she'd much rather talk about books than Jordy's moral failings. But, if she really cared about Jordy's moral failings, she would have this chat with Ena.

As soon as she entered the shop door and caught Ena's eye across the counter, her friend smiled, but it looked more like a smirk. "I'd wondered when ye'd be comin'. I wasna there, but I heard wha' happened. Th' village is buzzin' wi' it, Ivy."

Ivy sighed. "I was afraid that would be the case. Have you any idea how bad the damage is, Ena? He's so sorry. I haven't ever seen a man so contrite! And, really, there was no harm done."

Ena raised her eyebrows. "Hmm." And then she fidgeted with various items on the counter, refusing to meet Ivy's gaze.

Ivy cocked her head. Whatever did Ena mean by that? "Do you think I ...? Am I being too easy on him?" She'd hate for Ena to think she wasn't addressing the situation with the seriousness it deserved.

"Ach, nae." Ena did raise her eyes then, smiling once more. "Nae, but I'm surprised ye've arrived at this position o' grace so quickly. I'd thought ye'd come in here all mournful, lookin' for comfort, no' lookin' tae save Jordy McAllen from th' horrors o' gossip. Yet here ye are."

Ivy supposed that was fair, but she couldn't stay mad at Jordy long, if at all. And he truly had felt sorry, so who was she to hold a grudge? She'd never known him to drink before. "I just don't see the point of holding on to it. You know how I feel about it. Though most of

Keefmore might just see foolishness, I feel the full weight of it, even if Jordy doesn't—but, again, I think he does. He was quick to ask for forgiveness, but I don't think this has ever happened before. I mean, I've certainly never seen him drink." There was an inkling of doubt in her heart, of course, that said she didn't really know Jordy well anymore, not now that they were both adults, but she held on to the Jordy of her imagination fiercely, and it would take more than a few doubts to rip that away.

"Ye're right, most likely. I'd say, if ye've a mind tae, ye might go deeper tae th' root o' th' issue wi' him, perhaps even encourage him tae spend some time in th' Bible an' in prayer with ye ... or separately, if ye'd rather. That is, if ye'd like tae keep up this friendship." Ena shrugged. Her eyes remained glued to Ivy's face. Ivy wondered if there was some significance to this that she was missing. "I think ye could do th' man a great service, if he's willin' tae listen."

"Oh, I'm sure he would be!" Ivy had great faith in her ability to get Jordy to listen to her, if nothing else. They were such good friends, after all. At least, she wanted to believe they were good friends, even if at first it seemed unlikely that the friendship would last long. Still, she could treasure these days she had. Nothing had made her surer that she must treasure him than feeling, for an instant or perhaps for the whole night, that she might lose him to his own folly.

In Ivy's mind, death and distance were nothing as compared to a friendship ending due to the fault of the other. She could even bear her own guilt better than the pain of watching someone deliberately stand against what she believed in, and what she believed would best benefit them. It was what she most feared for Violet—and it was what had terrified her in the events of the All Hallow's Eve celebration.

All the same, he was her Jordy, unchanged and perhaps the better for his failure. There was a lesson to be learned in every misstep, even sin, and Ivy knew those lessons had to be a part of God's plan, though of course God would never be exactly wanting someone to sin. It was more like He anticipated their every action, but that was a realm where it got complicated. She didn't like to think about that as much, for it was better to focus on His love and grace.

"Another thing we can do," Ena said, "is bring our good doctor's drinkin' up tae th' ladies at our next teatime meetin'. We'll ken then how bad th' damage is."

"Oh, you're right!" If there was anyone who would have a good handle on these things, it was the tea ladies. Ivy settled on a stool behind the counter and smiled. "Thank you, Ena. You've made me feel so much better. Now I know what to do next."

Ena laughed. "Aye, an' isna tha' th' nicest feelin'? Noo, let's talk about somethin' lighter for a bit, a'right? Tell me wha' ye've been readin' ..."

Jordy waited until Ivy left to visit with her friend Ena to approach Violet. He didn't exactly know how he was going to have this conversation with her, but he was going to. It had to be done.

Even though it was probably more his fault than Violet's.

He pulled a chair into the small room Violet sat in and lowered himself onto it.

She regarded him skeptically over her book. "Do you want something?"

"Aye. I want tae talk about tha' kiss."

"What kiss? Oh, you mean the kiss you forced upon me in a drunken state last night?" Her eyebrows arched. "*That* kiss?"

Jordy swallowed and glanced down at his hands, which he kept clenched on his knees. "I didna ken ye felt ... forced. I thought, actually, tha' ye had initiated. I certainly didna *intend* tae kiss ye."

"Well, you did." She set the book down on the desk with a slam. "Jordy, I know your past. You can lie to Ivy, can pretend you're a man of honor, but not to me. Don't even try. I know what you've done—I heard it from your own lips."

"But ... tha's me past." He raised his eyes to her face. "It isna me present, Vi."

"Isna it?" She taunted him, imitating his lilt, her eyes angry. "Jordy, you didn't force that kiss on me, no, but I knew you wouldn't mind. It was an impulse, but have you a word of reproach to say to me? I wouldn't think you'd be such a hypocrite. I see how you look at Ivy—sweet, innocent Ivy! How could you come here and take such a posture when you're threatening the innocence of my dearest friend?"

Pain seared through Jordy's chest, and he winced. "I ... I havena touched Ivy, an' I never will." He'd keep both their honors pure. He would, God help him. His attraction to her *was* honorable, because he would never act upon it—*never.*

"But you want to. Don't tell me she's not the subject of your fantasies. If you can honestly say she's not—"

"She is *not,*" he ground out. "I wouldna do her th' dishonor." No woman deserved to become a dream in a man's head—let alone Ivy. Never Ivy. "I've kept me thoughts o' her pure. I have. An', in fact, I've kept *all* me associations with women pure ever since—ever since I told ye."

"I don't believe you." Violet stood and scooped up her book. "Moralize to me all you want, Jordy McAllen, but you're still the boy you were at eighteen. Our sins don't leave us; don't deceive yourself. You have no right to judge me for a simple, stolen kiss. You're not saving them for anyone else, certainly."

Jordy bowed his head. She wasn't all wrong. Some things never left a person. In some ways, he would always carry his past sins with him. They couldn't be undone. They had been forgiven, but they still existed, and he bore the consequences still.

But what about grace? his soul cried out. *God, God, I need a little grace! Let me have a future.*

Yet he didn't deserve it. Violet left the room, and he bowed into his hands and fought back tears, for he knew that at the end of the day, he didn't deserve anything at all.

CHAPTER EIGHTEEN

Over the next few days, clients at the office slowed noticeably, and, to be completely honest, Jordy didn't blame them one bit. He'd made a terrible mess of things, and he didn't expect any business for some time to come. Still, a small trickle of patrons continued.

Ivy's treatment toward him, of course, was nothing but tender. He was surprised by how accepting she was, as he'd believed judgement would show through after his actions. Instead, she gently encouraged him and shared Bible verses and asked him questions, making him somehow feel thoroughly shamed and thoroughly comforted. She wasn't precisely a teetotaler, either, given that her family drank in small amounts, but she was also firm and clear on her boundaries—and Jordy liked that.

He'd been feeling more and more fondly toward Ivy lately. He was amazed by the woman she'd become, by her faith and strength, and by the way she stepped into a role in his life that he hadn't thought her capable of filling. Added to that, they were now spending time in prayer and God's Word together. It was no wonder he was feeling some tricky feelings when it came to her. However, thus far, he'd managed to avoid acting upon these rampant feelings. And he never would. She was too good for the likes of him.

A week later, Jordy tended to a young man who'd somehow managed to cut a huge gash in his leg with a sickle. It was a cut in his calf, and Jordy had washed it out and was now stitching it up. Ivy, who had an aversion to blood, sat in the corner with her eyes turned away. If he asked, she would come over and help him, but he wasn't that cruel, no matter how fun it was to see her squirm.

"Well, tha's it, Ian. I'll get ye bandaged up, an' then we're done. Be more careful when ye're harvestin'. Neither o' us can afford this on a regular basis." That was a joke because Jordy truly couldn't afford people *not* making these sorts of mistakes, but he wouldn't tell Ian that.

Ian, who had been wincing and gritting his teeth but not moaning—a small mark to the big lug's credit—turned to Jordy and grinned. "Ach, it's over? Nae more stitches?"

"Ye've had plenty." Jordy grinned. "Be careful tha' ye dinna let it happen again. Ivy, will ye bring me a roll o' bandages?"

Ivy scurried to the cupboard and did as he'd asked.

"Thank ye," he said. He made short work of wrapping the man's leg. "Now, keep this dry an' clean, an' try tae stay off it. Mind?"

"Aye," Ian agreed. "I'll do me best. But there's th' rest o' th' harvest tae get in."

"Yer da will have tae hire help or wait. I'm sorry."

Ian shrugged. "No' ye're fault. I'm th' lad tae blame. Me da will be angry, though—what *can* I do?"

"Ach, let me think. Chores around th' farm. Anythin' tha' ye can do without tearin' th' stitches. Maybe ye can get a head start on th' threshin'."

"Aye, but then what will we do in th' winter?" Ian mourned.

Jordy sighed. "I dinna ken, Ian. Ye'll have tae figure somethin' oot."

"Da's been drivin' me like I'm his slave, so maybe it willna be so bad."

"Aye. Maybe no'." Jordy began cleaning and putting away his instruments, while Ian chattered on about how cruel his father was, making him work so hard—a grown lad like him, who should be starting his own farm by now.

"Can I ask ye somethin'?" Ian said after he'd finished giving his disgruntled young man speech.

"Aye, o' course," Jordy replied.

"Weel," Ian said. "I dinna ken if I should ..."

"What is it, Ian?" Jordy asked, turning to face him.

Ian's eyes shifted back and forth, then he leaned forward. "Is tha' lass o' yers really mindless?" His whisper was overloud as he nodded towards Ivy.

Jordy stiffened. The lad had better watch his next words.

"Because everyone's talkin' about it," Ian said, allowing his voice to return to normal. "Comes from McCale House—tha's th' crazy hospital where ye worked, isna it?"

"It wasna a 'crazy hospital,' as ye call it," Jordy said. His throat felt tight, and his vision narrowed. "But, nae. Ivy is no' an' never will be 'crazy' or 'mindless.' In fact, I wouldna be surprised tae find tha' she's far more intelligent than ye ever will be! Noo, will ye get out o' me place o' business? There's nae room for ye here."

"Ach, noo, nae need tae get sore, McAllen. I—"

"Get oot."

Ian rose from the examination table and exited the room. Jordy turned to Ivy. "I'm sorry. You shouldna have heard tha'. I hope ye ken he wasna right. Ye are no' anythin' like tha'. Ye are so much more."

Ivy's eyes shone with tears. Jordy supposed she was more upset than he had thought, though he didn't know why. After all, he'd taken care of it. There was nothing to be upset about now. Unless the wounds of those cruel words had bitten deep enough to scar. Jordy briefly considered chasing Ian down and beating the stuffing out of him. However, that probably wasn't the most productive use of his time, and that might leave Ivy feeling even more abandoned.

"Vee, are ye a'right?" he asked. "I ken he was bein' a fool, but it's all over now. Nothin' tae worry about. Noo, really, Vee. Dinna cry. He's no' worth it."

Ivy wiped her eyes. "You're right, Jordy. He doesn't deserve my tears. But that's not why I'm crying. I'm crying because ... because you stood up for me."

Jordy stared at her incredulously. What? Crying because he'd stood up for her? How ridiculous. As if he wouldn't stand up for her no matter what.

"I know you think I'm being silly"—she glanced down—"but, Jordy, most would have shrugged their shoulders and mumbled something and ... and never talked back to him. Never over me. *You* stood up to him, and you weren't afraid to speak what you believe to be the truth."

"It is th' truth," Jordy assured her.

Ivy shrugged. "I don't know if it is or not. But it makes me so happy that you would take my cause like that. It makes me so ... so happy."

Jordy shook his head. "I'm glad, Ivy," he said at last. He wasn't going to even try to understand her female emotions. Support them, yes. Understand them, no. He'd finish cleaning up the office and get on to the next patient—assuming another patient came, of course.

"Jordy." Ivy came to stand at his side, a soft smile on her face. "I ... I know you think I'm ridiculous, but you know not many people feel as you do about me."

"Wha' does it matter wha' other folks think?" Jordy mumbled. The last thing he needed was his only temptation since his first year of university offering him scores of unnecessary gratitude. She was already appealing enough to drive him mad, after all.

Ivy's brow furrowed. "It doesn't. But their comments aren't any less cutting, and I'm so proud of you for—"

He grunted. Time to put on a rough exterior, like Dr. McCale always did, and pretend she wasn't petting his masculine pride. "If ye say 'standin' up for me' one more time, Vee, I'm goin' tae have tae leave th' room. Dinna think o' it again."

Ivy nodded. "I won't, then. But ..."

"Nae. No' another word o' gratefulness, Vee. It's embarrassin'."

"All right," Ivy said. "But I am grateful."

"Shush, lass." There was no need to reward a man for some common kindness.

Ivy smiled and stepped closer to Jordy. She cupped his chin with both hands—seemed to be something that was happening fairly often recently—and drew his face down to her level before kissing him on the lips.

What she offered was featherlight, pure, almost sisterly. Unfortunately, as often happened in situations that involved Ivy these days, Jordy found his humanity wouldn't let her draw away. He was only a man, so he kissed her back. She'd started it. It wasn't his fault that it was feasibly the best thing he had ever experienced. Or that he was the one who put his arms about her and pulled her close.

But he came to his senses as quickly as he'd wandered away from them. He put his hands on her shoulders and held her back. "Ivy Knight, wha' in heaven's name were ye thinkin'?"

Ivy had a very surprised look on her face, but didn't seem inclined to answer. Her eyes were still half-closed, and from the expression in them, Jordy knew that she was looking for another kiss. That would *not* be happening.

"Ivy! What was tha' about? Dinna ye ken better? Didna yer mother ever tell ye no' tae kiss strangers?"

"You're not a stranger, Jordy," Ivy whispered.

Nae. No whispering. He stepped back so she'd have to talk in a normal voice to be heard. "Tha' makes nae difference. Yer mother would never forgive me if I didna keep care o' ye, preserve yer honor. I made a promise tae do just tha'."

Ivy cocked her head and narrowed her eyes slightly. "I don't see why kissing you doesn't preserve my honor. Though I didn't mean for it to be—" Then a flush did come, as he'd expected it to, and spread across her cheeks. "I just mean—I didn't think ... That wasn't what I'd intended at all, Jordy. You must believe me."

Jordy swallowed. Here she was apologizing to the man who'd treated her like an inanimate object and was now blaming her for a kiss he'd taken places she hadn't intended. "Ye should slap me, then.

But ye canna go around kissin' lads—especially no' like tha'." Not like it was all she'd ever wanted, like she was offering her heart for the taking, like he was hers forever.

All that aside, this was his fault, for she was an innocent. He opened his mouth to tell her this, but she spoke first.

"I needed to thank you somehow." Ivy looked down, wringing her hands together, obviously distraught that she'd unconsciously done something he considered wrong. How he wished now that she'd slapped him! Never had a man deserved it more.

"I told ye no' tae thank me," was all that came out after extensive scrambling for words.

Ivy shrugged. "I thought that was with words."

"Nae! An' ... an' what would yer mother think?"

Ivy's eyes were wide. "Why, I think she'd want to thank you, too."

"But," Jordy said, "would she thank me with a kiss?"

Ivy examined her feet, her face red as a beet. "No. She wouldn't. She ... she'd thank you by saying it. But you wouldn't let me, and I couldn't think of any other way! If I wanted to thank my father for something, I would kiss him."

"Aye, but I'm hardly yer father." And Jordy doubted that was the type of kiss a lass gave her da. Though, again, that portion of the kiss was his fault.

"No, you're not. And I ... I might not ..." Ivy's cheeks were bright red now. "I'm sorry, Jordy. It won't happen again."

Say something, you fool. If you let her believe that every time she kisses a man, that's the experience she should expect without commitment, it could cause some uncontrollable damage. "Dinna ye apologize one more time." Jordy squirmed but pushed through. "Th' way I ... *reciprocated* ... was wrong. As long as it doesna happen again, I think we're safe, but I was the one who kissed you *back*. It was a base impulse, and it willna happen again. Ye deserve a man who will wait for tha' kind o' kissin'." *She deserves more than a degenerate like you.*

Apparently Ivy was just as wretchedly uncomfortable with this conversation as he was, for she'd managed to back herself all the way up almost out of the room and was now fiddling with the doorknob, her eyes speaking of a desire to escape. The blush hadn't left her cheeks, either. "It's all right, Jordy. I don't think it's hurt me any. I think I ought to go now, though."

He cleared his throat. "A'right. I'll see ye later."

She made her escape, and Jordy spent the rest of the day kicking himself.

Ivy slipped into Violet's bedroom at Aunt Daphne's house, closed the door, and leaned against it. A few deep breaths, and she spoke. "Violet, did you ever think of Jordy as particularly handsome?"

Violet was lying on the bed with Heather curled up in the crook of one arm and a book in the other. "Really, Trifle, why would I think about that?"

"Oh, I don't know why you would." Ivy crossed the room and flopped onto the bed. Perhaps because he'd kissed her, and the longing she'd felt in him and for him had caused her to wonder if it was personal or simply the normal reaction. But she couldn't say that to Violet without risking it being repeated to Jordy. Violet could be vindictive like that at times, especially when she considered Ivy's innocent ramblings to be silly. "I thought, perhaps, in passing."

"Well, yes." Violet's voice held a trace of guilt that Ivy wished she had more mental capacity to examine. "In passing, I've noticed that he's fairly handsome. He has a strong, honest face, and his eyes are a pleasant color. Not to mention he's a nice height and seems fairly fit. Which are all good traits in a man, I think."

Ivy thought that was a lot of noticing in passing, but there was too much on her mind to address it. "Yes, indeed."

"I don't particularly like red hair on men, though," Violet said.

"No, I don't either, but Jordy's hair is more auburn. Or

highlighted brown, rather. Not really red." Ivy cocked her head. Briefly, her fingers had slid up and captured a somewhat wavy lock, and she had to flex her hand to shake the memory. Somehow knowing the way his hair *felt* was just too intimate, more intimate that even knowing how his lips felt. *What on earth happened? And how do I feel about it? And how ought I to feel about it, anyway?* "It goes well with him."

"It does," Violet said, her voice soft. "It does."

There was a few minutes of silence interrupted only by Heather pouncing on Ivy's hair only to be extricated and offered a tangled up ball of yarn that had been her favorite toy for the last few weeks.

"Jordy is rather dashing, wouldn't you say? Like nobility of some sort." That was the best way Ivy could describe the feeling she had for him—he was her hero, the man she compared all others to. These days, she found all others wanting. Besides, if she thought of him as nobility, and unreachable nobility at that, it became a smaller thing that she'd had such a serious lapse of judgment.

Violet moaned. "I'm not going to dignify that with a response, Trifle."

"He is. I ... I think he's almost princelike." Violet could be as negative as she wanted. She wasn't going to spoil Ivy's thoughts about Jordy's heroism. Even Jordy himself couldn't ruin those. Which she doubted he would. "He's a wonderful man. He's so cheerful and positive, and he has good sense, too. Not everyone sees it, but I do. He knows how to do practical things and think practical thoughts." Ivy paused for a minute, trying to sort her fragmented thoughts into words. "He cares about people, but not more than one ought to. He'd never let anyone boss him around unless it was absolutely necessary."

"I don't know what you see in him, honestly. I see a brash, arrogant, careless boy who exists only to plague me." She sniffed. "He's a terrible man. I don't like him one bit."

"I think you like him more than you admit," Ivy said. "Don't be so harsh, Violet. You shouldn't judge people lest you be judged."

Violet muttered something under her breath.

"Really, Violet," Ivy said, turning to her friend. "Can I be frank?"

"Please do, Trifle. Even your most frank will be like being hit by a pillow."

"Well," Ivy said, "you're terribly caustic and negative sometimes."

"See? Pillow." Violet shrugged and scooped Heather up in her arms to rub her belly. "Why don't you say I am possibly the most hateful person on the planet and have done?"

"Violet—"

"No, I don't need your pity, your explanations, or any of your preaching. You've had your say. This is something I need to work through by myself. I don't really want to talk about this, in fact. Now, what were you saying about Jordy?"

"Oh yes!" Ivy's heart lightened at the thought. "I was saying he's everything a man should be." She knew her face was red again, but oh well. She didn't mind sharing that much with Violet. She couldn't share about the kiss, so perhaps her emotions were safer.

"Sounds like you're half in love with him." Violet's eyes were fastened on the ceiling. "I'm not generally opposed to the idea of falling in love, but you wear it sappily."

Ivy glared at Violet. "I do not."

"Yes you do. You're always staring out the window and making stupid comments and such." Violet scoffed. "It's sickening."

"It's not sickening. I thought you said you were going to stop being so negative?"

"I'm not being negative; I'm stating a fact. Your ridiculously overdone falling-in-love is nauseating. Honestly, can't you at least keep your feelings to yourself?"

"Why would I want to? When I'm feeling something that is wonderful, I want to share it. I don't see why you can't be happy for me and not fuss so much."

Violet rolled her eyes. "Hmm. Well, I don't think you should slather your own joy all over me—maybe I don't want to be joy-slathered."

Ivy laughed. "You're mad, Vi. Everyone should want to be 'joy-slathered.'"

"I don't want to be," Violet said.

"Not even a little?" Ivy asked, grinning.

"Well ..." A smile perked up at the corner of her lips. "Yes. I want to be a little joy-slathered."

"See?" Ivy said. Then something like worry invaded her soul, cast an iron prison around her joy and dragged it down. Clarity came, and she hated it. "Violet, I ... I'm not in love with Jordy. We're good friends, yes, but I can't be in love with him. I ... I can't. I don't want to ... to ..." She took a deep breath and closed her eyes for a minute before continuing. "Even though I'd love nothing more, I can't let myself feel more than friendship. It would be wrong."

Violet's fingers grasped a handful of the quilt and clenched it until her knuckles turned white. "What makes you think you wouldn't be the perfect wife for him?"

Ivy flopped onto her stomach and dropped her head onto her arms. She couldn't think that way or she'd go mad. "Because of who I am and who he is." Because she did stupid things like offer a kiss to an unrelated man in gratitude. Then, no matter where Jordy placed the blame, she'd ended up taking it too far, because she had no idea what she was doing or why. This was her fault. If she'd known better, she never would've made what now seemed like an infantile, silly mistake that could've had disastrous consequences if Jordy hadn't been a gentleman about it. "You know, Violet, better than anyone, who we both are. I wouldn't place that burden on his shoulders."

"Why? Because you love him too much to hurt him?" Violet rose and began pacing, hands fluttering nervously. "That doesn't make any sense, Trifle."

Ivy sighed. "I know, Violet. I'm sacrificing something I want for something he wants. Not that I could make him want me, but that I know, even if he did, it wouldn't ever work out between us. He needs independence, and a wife like me would drag him down."

"Then you admit it?"

"Admit what?"

"That you love him."

Ivy nibbled at her bottom lip. If she said that aloud, in so many words, that would be it. The end. She wasn't ready for the end yet—rather, she wasn't ready to have her heart broken yet. Once her heart truly opened enough to be broken, she'd have to heal ... and to heal would mean to stop feeling the things she felt when she was with Jordy McAllen. And why would she ever want those feelings to stop? "I've always loved Jordy."

Violet cast her hands up in exasperation. "No, romantically. You know, like in all those novels you spend half your life buried in."

Ivy attempted a smile, bolstering it up with thoughts of kittens and warm fires and loved ones so it wouldn't tremble and betray her. She kept her voice bouncy, too—chipper, happy, lighthearted—despite the growing ache in her chest. "I've always felt like that about him. Almost always, anyway. These past few weeks—but then, I knew today, and for a moment I thought ..." Here her voice did falter, betraying her as she'd almost known it would. "But I was wrong. I wouldn't do that to him. It would be like clipping a bird's wings."

Violet took a seat on the edge of the bed. "Are you sure?"

"As sure as I can be." Unless Jordy's needs drastically changed—unless his feelings for her drastically changed, for that matter—there could be nothing between them but friendship.

All Ivy had to do was accept that and move on.

Another teatime, and Ivy felt quite morose, but she was determined to put on a show for the ladies' benefits. Not that it was really a show, for she was glad to see them and she did enjoy the meetings.

But her heart was so heavy. More and more, her feelings toward Jordy were pressing in on her, forcing her to admit things to herself that she'd never expected to. Shame always arrived on the tails of her dreams. She shouldn't even think of Jordy as anything but a friend, but here she was, with half-written fairy tales surrounding her, and the prince wasn't a willing participant. She shouldn't be planning out his entrance, on a white horse and everything, unless he wanted to enter. He didn't want to participate in her silly daydreams, so she shouldn't be having them.

Yet they were there. What was most frustrating was she could probably take command of her thoughts if she really wanted to and make herself forget that she felt something very much like love, if not the real thing entirely, and just be Jordy's friend, as she had always done. Certainly she was strong enough even now, she thought, not to let her moodiness affect others—at least, that was what she was experimenting with today. She glanced around the table. No one had mentioned if she seemed glum or even introspective. Had she succeeded?

But it didn't matter what her outward appearance was or was not betraying, for God looked at her heart. And what did He see? A lack of contentment. That's what He saw. Ivy writhed with the shame of it.

However, it was time to get her thoughts off herself and onto a better subject. Namely, anything that wasn't self-pity. There was nothing worse than that, and Ivy seemed so truly prone to it. She was always turning inward, and, at times, that brought forth wondrous fruit. At other times, it served as another way for Satan to gain a foothold on her soul. She wouldn't let that happen.

So she was pressing out of herself, and in the best way possible. She cast a sidelong glance at Ena to find herself being watched. She wondered if her friend knew. Perhaps she did. Or perhaps she just thought Ivy was concerned about speaking up, even in this small group of ladies.

Did Ena know that Ivy was only planning on talking about her favorite subject in the world?

When a brief silence fell in the plans for a church event in a few weeks, Ivy cleared her throat. "I have something I'd like to say."

Aunt Daphne gave her a queenly nod. "Go on, then. Get it out quickly." Ivy had soon learned that Aunt Daphne preferred promptness in these meetings.

"It's about Jordy." She was forced to clear her throat again, for it was quite tight. "Dr. McAllen, I suppose. In these last few days, he's seen the effects of his mistake ... No, his sin, though I'm not sure how the rest of us f-feel ..." She swallowed. "I'm not sure how you all feel, but Dr. McAllen and I counted it as a sin when he was inebriated at the All Hallow's Eve celebration ... or gathering, I suppose." Was it a celebration? She wasn't sure how to define the thing. It still troubled her. "I think he deserves a second chance. I know some people felt that he oughtn't to have acted that way—and they were right. But if we can't offer him forgiveness for that, how can we ask God for forgiveness for our own sins? That would even be true if he weren't repentant, but he is." She paused, hands clenched tightly. "What I'd like to know is, how bad is the gossip? Is this village going to hold this against him for long? Or will he be forgiven?"

There were a few beats of silence before Ena cleared her throat. "I'll go ahead an' say it—me Bob's did worse, in private. It was th' fact tha' he lost control so easily in public tha' a few o' ye are holdin' against th' doctor ... But we ken it willna happen again. Nothin' like a good knock tae th' pride tae turn a man around, an' I dinna ken tha' he needed much turnin' in th' first."

A quiet hum spread around the circle. Ivy gripped the edge of the table and examined every face earnestly, looking for the softness she needed to see to confirm that Jordy would still be able to thrive in this town—that it wasn't the massacre of his reputation that he feared.

The pastor's wife was the first to speak. "O' course we'll forgive him! He's long been saved by Christ's blood. I hope I can speak for th' rest o' Keefmore tha' one day o' drunken idiocy willna take th' lad out o' our good graces forever, Scots stubborn or no'. An' Mrs. Owen isna wrong about wha' she's said—me husband runs intae th' problem o' drinkin' often in this village."

A soft murmur started again, and this time there was more softness—Ivy was sure of it.

"No' everyone will turn back tae him immediately, but they will. Why, he's our only doctor, isnae he? We canna do wi'out th' man, noo tha' we've had him! An' I'm sure we'll all pray for him."

At last, everyone seemed to agree, and Ivy relaxed. It would seem that, though there might be a few holdouts, Jordy's reputation in Keefmore was by no means permanently damaged. And she was ever so grateful for that. She'd have to tell him that at the first available chance.

After this, the conversation drifted along. Ena's baby would be born soon, and most of the women proved willing to help her out during this time. Ena flushed and almost seemed to bloom before Ivy's eyes at the attention—Ena had been so alone, and Ivy was so grateful that that was changing.

Yes, people would be all right here ... even without Ivy. It was probably a good thing ... No, it was certainly a good thing she wouldn't be around forever to get in everyone's way. They all had a rhythm here, a way of being, and she probably wouldn't ever find a way to match the rhythm, even if she deluded herself in thinking she would be able to.

But that was just a daydream and a fairy tale. Fairy tales were fine for bedtime stories, but Ivy wasn't sure she ought to try, as much as she did, to fit them into real life.

Yes, she must stop, as least where it concerned other people. Far better to keep the dreams interior than to face the harshness she feared lay outside her mind.

CHAPTER NINETEEN

Ivy considered herself blessed to be one of the only girls of her acquaintance who enjoyed the love, counsel, and occasional correction of not one but two mothers. Now, with Ena and Aunt Daphne and Mrs. McAllen, her life was full of so much maternal influence that she didn't know what to do with it.

Yet it was the woman who had given birth to her and thereby bequeathed her with her eyes, hair, and general form who Ivy called her 'dearest mummy,' though she whispered those words secretly, as they were too childish.

She felt someday, when her mother was gone and Ivy herself was old and gray, she would long for the days of 'dearest mummy' again. However, with even her youngest siblings turning to an unceremonious 'Mum,' an affectionate but mature 'Mama,' or even a formal 'Mother,' as Alice long had, Ivy didn't want to be the only one with an unusual form of address.

Besides, lately some of the old intimacy was gone. Perhaps it had left in her mother's constant distraction or as the pulls of new babies took more of her time. More likely, Ivy simply suffered more from adulthood than from any real neglect. And she was the one who had chosen to leave.

Still, when Aunt Daphne handed Ivy yet another stack of letters, many of which were from her mother, none of the usual overly-excited music played. There was a routine to it now. It was nice—but hardly special.

The first letter she opened was from her mother.

Pearlbelle Park
Creling, Kent
November 1881

Dearest girl,
Whenever I write you these days, I say, 'I miss you! We miss you!' first. I must sound rather repetitive, but it's how all of us feel. You're our ray of sunshine!
Today I hadn't intended to send you a letter. You'll doubtless get half-a-dozen others from members of our family, and from me, about the same time you get this one. I'm not usually so unorganized in my postal planning.
However, in this case, I experienced this constant pressing on my heart that could not be ignored.

Ivy's attention sharpened, and the music that hadn't whispered to her earlier began to play soft, hesitant notes, unsure if they should burst into joy or sink back in horror. That line could mean all sorts of things.

She smuggled the letter up to her room at that point and sat down on the bed to read it more thoroughly.

The letter continued:

Of course, it could be nothing, but sometimes God does ask us to do certain things. For years, I thought that was reserved for people like Nettie. Now I'm realizing that every day we are to listen to Him. I could tell you stories, dearest, of times this has happened to me in the last year or so. I hadn't realized there were places unexplored in my heart, but I won't detract from my purpose by rambling about that.

Ivy, today I felt the distinct impression that you needed encouragement. Specifically, that I ought to write you and tell you about the type of woman you have become.

I think I've missed things. Before you left for Scotland this last time, I was afraid. My little girl, my baby, my Ivy was leaving me! And where to? Some distant place, and she declared her belief that God had called her there. I didn't believe you. I'm sorry I didn't believe you—what is a mother for if not to believe before her child even has a chance to?

Yet you began to write. Thank you for your faithful letters, Ivy. You have always been my most thoughtful and open daughter, and I appreciate this more than you know. We hear so little of Alice. But through your letters, every time I read them, God reveals more and more about my daughter.

He shows me that my daughter is a brave and strong woman who does not give up when faced with an obstacle some would say is beyond her. When you told me about playing piano at the church, I could see you in my mind's eye, from the acceptance of the task, which must have given you untold anxiety, to the first week and the second and the third. Being your mother and knowing you so well, I experienced in an instant everything you suffered. But you did it. Ivy, you did it.

He shows me that my daughter has empathy. That she truly heeds Him when He asks her to tend to widows and orphans. That she finds, again and again, the weakest and the most broken people wherever she is at—and she serves them—and she serves Christ—and even if the task is hard, she does not falter.

He shows me that my daughter has strong morals, that she has taken to heart every lesson taught to her on her mother's knee—and on Nettie's knee, perhaps more so. More than morals, you have character, Ivy. That's rarer than you know.

He shows me that my daughter relies on Him. I can tell where your strength comes from, and of course it is all due to Christ.

My dearest, I just wanted you to know today that you have my trust and my admiration as well as my love. I don't know what is happening now. Perhaps it's nothing but simply the next adventure Christ is calling you to. Perhaps it is a bit different than what you had anticipated. (I will not mention this to anyone else, even your father, but from one woman to another—the McAllen boy?)

The most important thing I wanted to communicate, however, is this: I think it's time for you to trust and admire yourself, too. I would never say this to Alice, to Ned, to Caleb, to Jackie, or to Rebecca. Honestly, I wouldn't even say it to Nettie. But to you, I say it, because I know your natural humility—more than that, your tendency to self-deprecation.

Don't believe in yourself. Believe in Christ. Trust that He has taken you to Keefmore for a reason. Trust that this calling was from Him. Admit to yourself, even for just a moment, that God's works in you are wondrous indeed. Not because of who you are, but because of Who Christ is in you, it would be an utter shame for you to waste time and energy and emotion on false humility.

Do you believe God was right in choosing you for whatever tasks He has set for you next—or was God wrong?

I'll leave you with that.

I love you so much, dear, and a better letter will follow.

Your mother,
Claire M. Knight

The letter fell on the comforter, and Ivy fell back on the pillows.

It was a lot to process, certainly. So much so that Ivy knew it would be some time before the mixed tunes and melodies quieted enough for clear, conscious thought.

Her hands came up and wiped away the tears on her cheeks, and she let out a small hiccup, as much a laugh as a sob.

To be loved by one's mother was one thing—expected, necessary. She didn't understand how some didn't love their babies, as it was such a natural part of her mother's personhood. To be known was something completely different.

And, although she could not yet tuck away all she had received, the truth did wash over her like a symphony. Her chest lightened, and the headache which had lingered at the corners of her eyes all that morning disappeared.

Perhaps there was hope after all. She couldn't have a dream future, though her mother thought so—one sad incident where her mother was wrong. But a beautiful, hard-won, helpful future? She could. She already had one, if she just kept doing what her mother believed she was now.

Following God's next step for her, as unique and carefully fitted to Ivy's abilities and opportunities as Cinderella's glass slipper.

"Much longer an' we'd have been late," Jordy complained when Ivy and Violet finally made their way down the stairs at Aunt Daphne's house, ready for Edith's wedding. "No' tha' I would mind missin' some o' th' romantic nonsense."

Ivy laughed, and Jordy tried not to notice, even though she looked quite stunning in a pink dress. It was likely a great deal simpler than the gowns she would have been expected to wear in London, but it was still quite fetching—and fancier than anything he had seen her in these last few months. "I thought you liked romantic things," she said, causing him to stop staring and start paying attention to what she was saying.

Jordy grinned. "Aye, but I dinna want anyone else tae know tha'. Men are no' supposed tae be secret romantics." He winked. "Ye look lovely. An' Violet does, too."

Violet, dressed in the color of her name, shrugged. "I look like a plucked crow. Now, let's get it over with. Honestly, whoever came up with the idea of weddings ought to be shot."

Jordy started to make a snide comment but stopped himself. He knew Violet had been having a hard time lately. He did feel sorry for her, but at the same time, he knew there was nothing he could do to help other than not cause more damage.

Violet had proven to him again and again that she didn't have his best interests at heart. Though he wished her well, certainly, he simply couldn't be anything but a distant friend to her for a while. Not until he got a better hold on himself. Come to think of it, *he'd* been having a rather challenging few weeks, too, though—he glanced sideways at Ivy—in an entirely different way.

The wedding was lovely. Edith had layered the kirk in lace, and it had actually turned out quite nice.

Once the vows were said—the plain, simple ones that were said in every village throughout Scotland—the whole wedding party convened at the McAllens' farm.

Jordy and his brothers had worked all morning to get one of the big barns cleaned and decorated to Edith's specifications. There were tables piled high with refreshments which his mother had slaved over. And, most importantly, plenty of room for dancing.

They had gone to a lot of work to get the lanterns hung so they wouldn't risk burning even a bit of hay—Jordy knew for a fact that barns could catch on fire remarkably fast at times—and the effect was lovely.

They'd built a fire out in front of the house, and it greeted the guests as they arrived. In no time, they were all gathered on the great, open floor of the barn, which had housed a couple dozen cattle that morning. The dancing soon began.

Jordy danced with his mother and Edith and a few other girls he knew fairly well but avoided any lasses who he knew to have an overly matrimonial mind. He felt that a serious doctor wouldn't flirt about—and Ivy had given him enough talking-tos before the wedding that he didn't dare take even a sip of alcohol.

"Jordy, if you take so much as a drop, so help me!" she had begun, but had been unable to think of a threat. But that was probably the most threatening he'd seen Ivy, and he wasn't going to go against her. She talked sense. No temporary thrill was worth the headache—figurative and literal. Besides, it was wrong. He knew now that she was right about that. At least in his case.

He was leaning against the wall, alternately teasing and threatening Tristan while Edith looked on and laughed, when he caught sight of Ivy. She stood in a corner by herself, perhaps a little awed by the crowd. Yet she swayed back and forth to the music, eyes filled with longing.

He understood. He loved to dance, too, but he couldn't possibly love it as much as Ivy did. Ivy was born to music. It was her life's breath. Playing it, singing it, dancing to it. He excused himself from the bride and groom and stepped over to her side.

"Vee," he murmured, "would ye like tae dance?"

She turned to him hesitantly. "Really?" There was such hope in her eyes.

He smiled. "O' course. I'd love tae dance with ye, Ivy." Instantly, a sense of foreboding gripped him, but he ignored it. He was sober as a judge and determined to maintain their boundaries. Surely this wouldn't hurt anything.

"You're not saying that because you ... you feel sorry for me? You're not just being nice?" Ivy cocked her head to the side, eyes worried. She plainly didn't want to inconvenience him, the sweet thing.

"No, Vee. I want tae dance, an' I've used up all me partners." He winked. "'Twould be selfish tae steal th' bride again. Desperate tae dance with me mother. An' I dinna ken any lasses here except those I've already danced with—an' I dinna dance with any one o' them more than once. Gets their hopes up," he said, grinning.

"Oh, you're terrible." Ivy shook her head but smiled. "Of course I'll dance with you! I'd love to, in fact."

Jordy took her hand and led her out onto the floor. "Do ye ken this one?" he asked, standing outside the ring of dancers.

"I've watched; I know," she said, obviously eager to begin.

He laughed, and they joined the dance.

She was a joy. Seemed to pick up the steps as she went, graceful and ethereal, rarely making a mistake—and not getting too off-step when she did.

Honestly, her sheer zeal for the dance was part of it. It was as if she found herself suddenly completely fulfilled—though that wasn't quite all. Music was Ivy's greatest pleasure; he knew that much. But it was also something more. It was her method of communication on some levels. He watched her closely—wanting, needing to understand her. He wasn't sure exactly how music touched her, but it was deep and thorough, and he wanted to know more about her ... more and more.

She was beautiful when she danced like this. Her eyes glowed a deep blue, her face flushed pink, her mouth curved into a broad smile. He found that he was the one missing steps—too focused on her to know what he was doing.

How could any woman in the world be as beautiful as this one was right now?

When their first dance ended, they began another—and another—and another. Before he knew it, the music ended.

They collapsed on chairs in the corner for a minute, laughing, and Ivy spoke for the first time since they'd begun dancing.

"Thank you," she said. "Thank you so much, Jordy. You don't know what you've given me today."

He held her gaze and shook his head. "Nae, Ivy. Thank ye. Tha' was th' best time I've had in years."

Ivy smiled brilliantly, and he had to admit it to himself. She was everything he'd ever wanted. But it couldn't be. He wasn't enough for her. He'd have to find some way to keep his thoughts off of her—and get on with his life.

A few hours later, Ivy wrapped her arms about herself as the chill from the outside started to seep into the barn now that the warm bodies had left.

"Jordy, can ye check on th' sheep an' lock Bean in?" Mick called as he struggled to remove lanterns from the roof. "We're almost done here, an' then we can get th' coos in an' get tae bed."

Jordy nodded. "Aye, Mick. I'll do tha'. Sure ye dinna need any help?"

"Nae! I can do it."

"Ye can break yer neck, ye mean," Jordy said, rolling his eyes but making no further protest.

"How can I help?" Ivy asked. They had seen Edith and Tristan off and now they were cleaning up everything that needed done before they could all go to bed. The hour was late—especially since they had to get up so early in the morning—and Ivy was ready to fall asleep herself.

Though Violet had crawled off to the house hours ago—they were staying in Edith's old room tonight as the hour had gotten too late for a drive back into town—Ivy determined to stick with the McAllens to the last. They had given their daughter away, and Ivy knew from watching her sister's wedding that that could be emotionally exhausting. She was ready to lend her hand in the cleanup in any way she could.

"There's no' much ye can do." Jordy grinned. "Why dinna ye come with me tae check on th' sheep?"

She smiled back. She'd never felt so close to Jordy before, and it was nothing short of thrilling. When they were dancing, it was as if some invisible connection had been formed. She was wary of it, but she supposed it wouldn't hurt to let it happen. In all likelihood, he'd have moved on to someone more interesting in the morning. Someone more like him. Bold and brash and ready to take on the world. No boundaries, all unpredictability and fun and excitement.

Oh, why couldn't she be like him? She was willing to give up her personality, her life, her very being if that was what it took. But she couldn't. She would always be Ivy. He would always be Jordy. That was the way of things.

They would always be cascading down different roads at different times and different places. These few months when they had been together—she could live off of them. There was no other choice. Not really. She was perfectly capable of living on a memory. Or she'd learn to, at least.

"What did ye think o' yer first real Scots party?" Jordy asked as they walked through a light sprinkling of snow over a layer of ice toward the sheep barn.

"Wasn't All Hallow's Eve my first real Scottish party?" Ivy asked.

"Aye, but a weddin' celebration is a party o' another sort entirely," Jordy explained. "It's a real celebration—somethin' tae be thankful for. Now they'll have their own house—bairns—an' th' circle continues. Ye see?"

"Yes, I see," Ivy murmured. She wanted to be excited and upbeat like Jordy, but it was hard. The solemn thoughts combined with the late hour made her want to lie down and weep. "I did enjoy the party," she forced herself to say, "and I enjoyed dancing with you. They were unlike any dances I'd ever seen ... and I rarely get to dance. Not with someone."

Jordy grinned mischievously. "I imagine ye dance alone a lot, then."

Ivy's face heated up. "Sometimes."

"I'd like tae see tha'."

Ivy shrugged, too embarrassed to answer.

"Aw, tha's a'right, Ivy. Ye dinna have tae dance for me," he said, nudging her. "No' if ye dinna want tae."

"Well, I dinna. Er, don't."

Jordy laughed. They stepped into the sheep barn, Bean trailing behind them. As he hopped into a trough and cuddled down for the night, Jordy waded through the sleeping sheep. "Everythin' looks a'right here," he said in a low voice. "We can head back tae th' house an' get some sleep."

Ivy nodded. She was more than ready to do that. Still, she lingered in the barn, closed her eyes, and enjoyed the warm air.

Jordy came to her side. "Ivy," he whispered close to her ear. "Are ye a'right?"

She turned to him and found his face inches from hers. It was dim in the barn already, all the light coming from the bonfire outside, but she could see his eyes darken, the pupils dilate. She closed her eyes, and, before she could draw another breath, she felt his lips on hers.

This was a different kind of kiss—*legato accelerando*. Jordy crushed her in his arms, and she tangled her fingers in his hair. He cupped her chin with one hand and drew her closer, and she let his lips caress hers, returned the touch, and relished it, until she couldn't think, couldn't breathe, couldn't feel anything but his lips on hers and his arms about her and his heart beating *vivace* against her.

And then—as suddenly as it had begun—he let her go. Pushed her away so hard she almost fell, only catching herself against the half-open barn door. Panting, she pulled herself upright and stared at him, unsure how to handle the turmoil of emotions swirling in her chest.

"Jordy," she murmured and held out a hand.

He shook his head violently and ran out the door.

She didn't see him again that night.

CHAPTER TWENTY

Jordy had never felt so guilty in his life. How could he have done such a thing? With Ivy close, he hadn't thought. He'd acted, instinctively, needing to touch her, and he'd taken it too far. But he had known it was wrong. Known she wasn't his to kiss.

He took a long, fast walk out on the moor, trying to cool off and reorganize his thoughts. But he still felt as muddled as he had before. What had he done? Could things ever be the same, or had he changed them irreversibly?

He tossed restlessly on his pallet for a few hours, then walked up to the house and told his mother not to have Ivy come down, even though they'd joked about it last night—he'd do the milking by himself after all. Since he had a full-time job that often called him away at all hours of the night, he had few chores, but he was up and needed something to keep him busy until it was time to go to town.

How would he bear the drive in? He'd have to keep talking about nonsense or something to distract her from the matter at hand—or simply not talk, though silence would be almost impossible to take.

"It's really my fault," he whispered as he milked the first cow. Jordy knew for a fact that he chose to kiss her. "It wasn't something she did, and under no strain of the imagination can I blame it on her."

He stood and went to change pails.

"It's no' as if I meant tae," Jordy said as he returned to milking. "It just happened. I dinna ken how." One minute they were standing there, the next they were kissing. "An' I dinna ken how we got from th' one point tae th' other." He squeezed down on a teat too hard, then patted the cow's side. "Sorry, Eve. But I didna mean tae lead her on. Really. It ... it was a spur o' th' moment thing. An' I dinna mean it seriously."

He didn't want to marry her. Well, he did, but he couldn't.

"It was an impulsive kiss."

Eve turned her head towards him, a stalk of hay hanging from her mouth.

"Truly. It willna happen again."

He finished with Eve and moved on to Sunny. The truth was, he was mostly worried that he'd led her on. "What if she thinks I want tae marry her? She must. There's nothin' else th' girl could be thinkin'." What else would a girl think if a man kissed her out of the blue like that?

Sunny's moo was disapproving.

He scowled at her. "I'm a coward an' a bounder. An' ... an' I do care about her. Verra much so."

Sunny seemed unconvinced.

"She's everythin' I'd want in a woman. But I canna marry her. So what will I do?"

"Why can't you marry her?"

Jordy jumped up to find Violet standing outside the barn door. He blinked. "How ... how long have ye been standin' there?"

"Oh, about as long as you've been talking to yourself. Do you do that often, or is this an irregular occurrence?"

"It's an irregular occurrence." Jordy's ears burned. He wasn't sure what to say if Violet had heard all that. He didn't want anyone to know, let alone someone as vindictive as her.

"Ah. I see. Are you worried that you're not good enough for the woman you're in love with?"

Jordy didn't know how to respond to that, so he didn't say anything.

"What? That is what's happening here, isn't it?" Violet asked, cocking her head to the side as if she were having trouble understanding. "You can tell me."

"No, I canna. Ye'll use it against me somehow."

Violet's eyes almost seemed to soften. "I might have, but last night I started to see the light and stopped wanting to hurt you for being such an idiot. Now I only want to hurt you in a way that'll rip off your scabs, per se. But is it so? That you're in love with Ivy?"

Jordy shrugged. "Maybe a little." *More than I can say.* "But ... but nothin' can ever come o' it." *I'm no' enough for her. I can never keep her safe. I canna trust meself tae be there for her, tae be responsible, tae be committed ... More than that, I canna trust her with me past.*

"Why not?" Violet asked.

"Because ..." Jordy let his voice trail off, unwilling to explain to Violet. He continued milking the cow, hoping to get done in record time. Perhaps he'd start off for Keefmore and leave Ivy here for the day. His mother could probably use some company. That was a great idea! It would solve all his problems so easily.

"Because what?" Violet said. She sure was persistent. Especially when he really didn't want to tell her something. But it was none of her business, and he wasn't afraid to tell her that.

"Violet, leave me be," Jordy said. "I have a lot o' work tae do."

"No, Jordy. Look. I ... I may be the last person you want to talk to, and I understand that." She paused. "But ... but I really do love both you and Ivy. I may act as if my sole desire is to hurt you, but that is not what I want. Not when I'm sane. I care that you both are happy, so tell me."

Jordy shook his head. "Nae, Violet. I have nae reason tae believe ye. Ye havena built any trust with me. So I'll just finish me work an' get on with me life. Please leave me alone."

Violet shrugged. "Suit yourself. Though I will say: If you really love Ivy, then what's holding you back? Why not try? Two adults can surely work out a few small differences."

Jordy scoffed. Violet had been the one to remind him of all the reasons, the many reasons, that he couldn't have Ivy. His sins, his past, the way he would hurt her. She'd been right before; he couldn't move on from the things he'd done.

"Jordy, I was wrong about you." Violet seemed to struggle with these words, but she continued speaking nonetheless. "I've been bitter and hurting. I know you understood my full meaning when I tore into you, and the point I was trying to make with the kiss. I won't insult your intelligence by saying it was anything but what it was, and I don't expect you to forgive me. But please don't take anything I've said too much to heart, for I *have* been trying to hurt you, and you didn't deserve it."

It was too late to warn him not to take anything she'd said to heart, for he'd heard the warning—and heeded it. Bring Ivy into the darkest places of his soul? Never. He couldn't besmirch her in that way.

But he already had, hadn't he?

Oh, how could he have done it? Why had he kissed her? *Again*, at that. He could never spend a moment alone with the woman, for he couldn't trust his own judgment when she was close. Granted, he could've stopped himself both times if he'd wanted to, but having *not* wanted to and having found her so willing ...

Those two factors made it feel impossible. But it wasn't. He was supposed to be a Christian. He was supposed to possess God-given self-restraint. What was he doing?

"Jordy, try this. Confess it to Ivy. Tell her the truth—the absolute truth. You shouldn't be listening to me anymore, but please hear this. Ivy is all mercy—she always has been to me, and she will be to you. Please let her make the decision as to whether she wants you in her life or not. She's an adult, isn't she? And you would never say to her face that she is incapable of making a decision on her own. So why are you saying it with your actions? Trust her. Please don't let my words be what ruins your life, Jordy."

She seemed sincere, but Jordy didn't know how to respond. He wasn't sure yet—he really wasn't. Silent prayers began to bloom in his heart—queries followed by requests for wisdom. *What do I do, Lord?*

When he didn't reply, Violet left, and Jordy quietly finished his chores.

Ivy didn't know what to think or how to manage the various emotions that played like a *basso continuo* in her heart. Here she'd figured bass was an outdated technique—and she hadn't been so thoroughly nauseated by any part of her life since leaving her mother for the first time to go to McCale House all those years ago. It was quite overwhelming.

How she hated bass clef, at least when it wasn't accompanied by something else.

Jordy didn't speak to her when she met him outside the door with Violet and climbed into the wagon. She sat in the back, curled up against Violet, saying she needed to lie down for a few minutes.

Jordy hadn't said anything. He nodded and climbed up onto the box. Not a word was spoken the whole way into Keefmore, and they silently entered the office and began setting up for the day.

Violet made a beeline for Jordy's private office and shut the door. Ivy was a little disgruntled at this. Of course, Violet couldn't know that this was one day that Ivy didn't want to be alone—or even in the same room—with Jordy.

Jordy began cleaning—something he almost never did unless there was a major sanitary issue—and Ivy went into the front room and sat at the counter, pretending she had something to do there. She'd be somewhat of a secretary for the day, she decided.

But that left her alone with her thoughts, which was even worse. Oh, how had the kiss happened? For to Ivy, it wasn't just a kiss. It was *the* kiss. It didn't matter, really, that she'd kissed Jordy once before. That had been different. Jordy hadn't initiated that one, and she could pretend she'd imagined his passion before. Now every lie she'd told herself was stripped away due to the simple fact of *The Kiss*.

She didn't know quite how it had happened. She did know that he had started it, though. That much wasn't a figment of her imagination, and based on Jordy's reactions, he had lived to regret it. Goodness, he hadn't even lived that long before he lived to regret it.

Ivy didn't know if she regretted it yet or not. It had been one of the best experiences of her life, after all, so it was hard to summon regret until worse consequences appeared—which they no doubt would, but she was too numb to feel them. Besides, if she were only going to get one kiss in her life, she wanted it to be *that* one. She couldn't say that there would be another, and she wanted to have the experience. If this was regret, she could live with it.

There was really nothing to be done about it now that it had happened. She supposed she'd have to face up to it someday. She couldn't go on and on acting like it hadn't happened.

Squaring her shoulders, she stood up and marched into the examination room. Jordy was washing down the table. She gave him credit for not washing the same thing over and over again like some might have done when angrily cleansing. He had given the entire room a thorough cleaning. Good for him.

"Jordy?" Ivy said.

He pushed himself up and faced her.

She instantly turned coward. "I ... er ... I wanted to ask ... do you need any help?"

"Nae," he said. "Ye relax."

Right. *Relax.* Not like that was nerve-wracking or anything. At least he was getting some relief from the strain. Here she was, twiddling her thumbs.

She sat down and rubbed her forehead for a minute, trying to come up with a solution. What could she say? 'You kissed me last night, and I need to make sure you understand I don't intend to marry you.' Why would she say that to the man she loved? But she had to; she wouldn't tie him down. She *wouldn't.* Not to any woman in the world—unless that woman was willing to be as adventurous as Jordy himself.

She supposed she could use those words.

She stood.

No, wait. Should she say 'you kissed me last night,' just like that? Or should she bring it up in another way? 'Remember last night?' No, too silly and cliché and needy. *Everything* was going to sound needy, though. But they had to talk. If it could be aired, if they could be serious about it and not let any emotions in—

Oh, but she needed those emotions. They kept her sane. They kept her from exploding. Was there a way to gently bring this conversation about? To give the proper nods to a wonderful friendship and a beautiful kiss and still nudge their feelings away from romance? She wasn't sure.

There was also the moral quandary of having shared something intimate, so that needed to be addressed, too. Though what could they do, unless they married to make it right? Which seemed like an overreaction. On the other hand, no one had ever told Ivy exactly how unpurified a woman—or a man, for that matter—became due to a simple kiss, or what could be termed as a 'simple kiss,' or anything that would help her decide how much she had to repent of.

What did that kiss mean, at any rate? Was it a romantic one? Why would Jordy kiss her if he wasn't interested? He wasn't the kind of man who would do that to a girl and then not pursue a serious relationship with her. At least, she didn't think so. But, after all, Jordy was an adventurous man.

No. She wouldn't think about it like that. There was some explanation. A normal explanation. Something that didn't involve romance, because goodness knew he'd never acted romantically toward her. He'd just been a good friend, and he'd certainly hated it that time she'd kissed him in the office. Perhaps it was her fault—she'd led him down this path, and now the consequences were all on her shoulders ... Oh no. How could she have? But still, his near-violent refusal of her affection before led her to believe that he would not be easily influenced unless he chose to be, so perhaps it wasn't her fault.

Had he been drinking again? Sometimes people under the influence of alcohol did strange things they never would have done any other way. Jordy *had* acted strangely, but he hadn't seemed drunk, and she was sure she would have smelled it on him, or at least tasted—no, she wouldn't think about that.

At last, she got up the courage to stand up and walk back into the examination room. Jordy was sitting on a chair in the corner with his instruments spread out on a table before him. He was polishing every one. Ivy found this amusing, but she didn't laugh. Everything felt so serious now. She couldn't even summon up a smile.

"Jordy, I ... I need to talk to you about something."

Jordy rose and offered her a wobbly grin. "Aye, an' I need tae talk tae ye." He coughed. "I dinna quite ken how tae start this, but ye shouldna be th' one who has to."

"Thank you." She blushed as soon as she said that, but she didn't know what else to say. She was quite thankful that he'd be guiding this conversation.

"Let's sit down on th' back step, where we can talk alone."

They walked through the back door, and Jordy gestured for her to take a seat. Ivy folded her knees up to her chest and waited.

"I want ye tae ken, first an' foremost, tha' this is no' yer fault." Jordy lowered himself down with a heavy sigh and looked her in the eyes. "This has nothin' tae do wi' ye. If it wasna for ... wha' I must tell ye, I would ... Things would be different, Ivy, an' nae mistakin' it. I might have some misgivin's, based on me character, but ye are perfect. Absolutely perfect."

She flushed in pleasure—but the compliment was backed by a rejection. She could feel it coming, and her chest tightened. "Jordy—" She didn't need him to tell her how dissimilar they were. She didn't need him to tell her that her dreams must and should be crushed. She didn't need him to tell her that all the fantasies that seeped their way into her thoughts every day, despite her best efforts to prevent them, were fruitless—that she'd be leaving Keefmore soon—leaving *him* soon.

He held up his hand before she could reject herself. "Nae. Let me ... let me tell ye th' story, Vee. It will change things for ye, even if ye ... even if ye havena already ... It'll change things." He swallowed.

"Please listen."

It was perhaps one of the hardest things she'd ever done, but Ivy leaned back and nodded. She didn't know what Jordy had to tell her, but it was clear it pained him, and she was willing to listen quietly despite her fears—and despite the fact that she didn't quite believe yet that his disinterest in pursuing an honorable relationship with her had nothing to do with their unsuitability.

"Simply put, Vee, I am no' a man o' honor," he said.

Ivy frowned. Nonsense. Of course he was—he was her Jordy, and a more honorable man could not be found anywhere on earth. Even if he had kissed her without being engaged to be married or even planning on being engaged to be married. She could forgive him that, couldn't she? Especially as a willing participant who hadn't even managed to bolster up the courage, let alone the desire, to give him the slap across the face he probably deserved. That was the right response, wasn't it?

Yet another thing she'd done wrong.

"Let me explain." He paused and ran a hand over his eyes. "When I went tae college, I was seventeen years old, an' I was a fool. I thought I was dedicated tae God—I thought I was a Christian. I believed all tha' me parents an' Dr. McCale had taught me, but within a few months, I cast it aside. I fell in wi' a lot o' lads in school who ... who loved tae have a good time. At first it seemed harmless—dancin', playin' about as young men do, th' occasional drink, gamblin'. I fell intae it, Ivy. I did, an' before I ken't it, I ... I'd abandoned Christ for th' pleasures o' th' world."

"Oh." That wasn't so bad, as far as tragic and now-repented pasts went. She could deal with that. She already knew about the drinking, and the gambling made sense, but during their discussions, his beliefs had aligned with her own. He was different now. Older, wiser, and plainly grounded in God's Word. They could move past that. Or at least he could, for she must stop equating her future with his. "But, Jordy—"

"I'm no' finished." He noticeably swallowed, and she was sure his eyes were traced with tears. "Ivy, I laid wi' women."

Blood rushed into her ears, and she sat still, hands clasped in her lap, and the blood kept thudding, her heart seeming to think the best thing it could possibly do in that moment was make it impossible for any other thought to exist. There was no music, not even the minor chords that usually accompanied frightening situations.

For there were no thoughts at all. Just silence, like the brief desolation before the audience clapped. Yet there was no clapping.

Perhaps not thinking was the best possible reaction, for Jordy kept speaking.

"I ... I wish there was an easier, cleaner way o' sayin' tha', a way tha' could spare ye th' harshness o' it, but there isnae. They were women whose names I didna remember in th' morn an' who meant as little tae me as I did tae them. All o' them were willin'—every one close tae me in age an' experience. But there 'tis." He stopped, and his eyes seemed to search Ivy's face for a response.

If only she had one to give him, for her entire soul felt empty. Why was it that in his sin *she* felt violated? As if she had been the one who he sullied. As if the sin was on her heart as well as his.

If this was being in love with someone—this horrible pain, this guilt, this agony, this feeling of betrayal over sins that had not been against her—she wanted none of it.

"Ivy, ye must understand ... I didna mean tae hurt anyone. Nor did they mean tae hurt me. I suppose it wouldna help a thing tae give details. Suffice tae say th' relationships ended as soon as they began and were quickly replaced by others. This went on for perhaps six months, an' then ... I came home tae McCale House, ye see, an' I ... I had tae tell Dr. McCale. I started weepin' as soon as I began tae tell him, an' since then I havena touched another woman. Tha' is, no' until ye."

She shuddered, rose, and turned from him, clenching her fists. *No.* She didn't want that clarification, because it made her feel all the dirtier. Why? Why had her knight in shining armor turned villain?

Why did he have to tell her this?

It would've been easier to live with the lie, to live with the idea that Jordy didn't want her because, simply, he didn't want *her*. Yes, it had hurt when she thought about it, but not like this. She was losing Jordy because of *Jordy* not because of herself, and that hurt more than anything she could possibly have imagined.

"Ivy, I recommitted meself tae God," he was saying. "I sought purity. I did no' associate wi' women at all, by no' leavin' th' dormitories, for an entire year. I didna go out wi' me friends—I stayed in me rooms an' studied. I didna even visit ye an' others I ken't from McCale House. An' when I was on holiday, I went straight to McCale House, an' Dr. McCale an' I would fast an' pray together ... I told Violet, an' she would write an' ask me questions about wha' I was doin', who I was seein', an' tha' helped, tae. An', oh, Ivy, I fought it mightily! Or God did for me, when I was tae weak tae do a thing but wallow in me own sin. An' God won."

But why hadn't God won a place in Jordy's heart *before* this sin? Why couldn't God have kept Jordy ... if not for Ivy, for some other woman? At least then he could've had happiness elsewhere, but as it was, she rather doubted it.

For he wasn't what Ivy had thought he was.

Oh, Lord. This hurts too much. Please tell me it's a nightmare.

But it wasn't a nightmare, and Jordy kept talking.

"Ivy, it's been four years since I have looked upon a woman wi' lust in me heart. It's been six since I have touched one—save ye, an' I suppose Violet, but tha' was ... I can explain tha'. She kissed me th' other day, but only a peck, an' I didna want tae. Ye ken how she can be—there was no desire in it. It was spite. An' I'm ramblin' noo, but I suppose wha' I'm tryin' tae get at is ye are temptin' me. Tha's why I'm runnin' scared, Ivy—I'm suddenly back tae where I canna fight, an' I dinna understand it. I mean, it's no' th' same, no' at all, because it's *ye*, an' tha's so verra different than anythin' else could be. I dinna think I'd be a man if I were no' attracted tae ye, but tha' isnae all ... Still, it doesna matter. I think I'm verra much in love wi' ye—an' since it's th' first time for me, I'm no' really sure wha' tae do wi' th' feelin'. I will fight it, an' ye will no' be disrespected any further than ye already have been, wi' th' kiss. But ..." He stopped again, and his shoulders slumped. "Tha's why we canna be together. No' tae say ye are willin', but if ye were, tha's why I canna pursue ye as ye deserve."

Ivy's shoulders shuddered with a half-controlled sob. *Oh, Jordy ...* If only she could comfort him. But the small part of her that was desperately in love—and, therefore, desperately happy that he seemed to return the feeling—was smothered completely by the larger part of her.

The part of her that had never considered that he would have such sin in his past. The part of her that recoiled at the thought of having touched a man who had been with other women in ways that remained a mystery to her.

She hadn't known how deep in she was until this moment. Before, she could deceive herself, could say friendship was all she needed even if she wanted more. Now? She knew that there was no going back. Her heart was screaming wildly that she needed to do something to make the music which had suddenly vanished return, but something small and infinitely logical had curled up in her stomach in the music's place and was keeping the beauty at bay while her mind did the hard thinking.

The hard thinking was telling Ivy that she needed to leave.

She couldn't even pray properly. Her mind spiraled in hopeless little cries as she searched for some response that would have merit, that would encourage him even as she politely extricated herself to think it over.

Ivy wanted to have grace, as she ought to have, but she couldn't because it was too fresh, and she found herself passing judgment. It wasn't her place. No sin was any worse than the other, and Ivy had sinned, too, as much as anyone—and he was redeemed. No, she should not pass judgment.

But didn't the kiss prove that he wasn't ready for this? Why would he touch her in such a way, when marriage appeared to be the furthest thing from his mind, unless he was falling again?

"'Tis a'right, Vee." His words were quiet now, a humble undertone to them that she barely registered. "I give ye permission tae leave, a'right? Walk away. Walk away an' dinna see me again. It's over. I ken tha'. Tha' kiss ... Ivy, it's changed everythin'. Dinna try tae be me savior here. I'll find me own way back—as I should."

She nodded jerkily, arms wrapped around herself, holding back the tears. At least for now. If she cried in front of him, she'd go to him for comfort, and what if that created more of an issue?

Had she made him sin? Would she be the force that drew him back to the path of destruction? No, no—she couldn't think that way. It wasn't right to blame herself; she couldn't hold that responsibility.

But she also didn't want to leave without telling him that God had grace for even the greatest of his sins.

"Jordy, I—"

He held up his hands. "It's a'right. Ye dinna have tae explain why ye need tae run. Just do it."

"But I—"

"Ivy, please."

"Oh." So it really wouldn't help? To just tell him that she would pray and that God loved him? Perhaps he was right. She needed to sort her thoughts. So she turned—and she ran.

CHAPTER TWENTY-ONE

Ivy paced up and down the length of Aunt Daphne's parlor, back and forth, over and over again. She focused on her breaths, keeping them even, not too ragged, not too upset. She couldn't cry yet—not until her mind had sorted through some of the fears and pains that tightened in her chest.

Usually Ivy didn't avoid crying, but she felt that as soon as she began today, self-sympathy would set in. This was about her, yes, but it also wasn't. It was a case where forgiveness must be employed—but whether or not that forgiveness included asking Jordy to be a part of her life was beyond her.

On the other hand, he'd made it rather clear that he didn't expect her to be a part of his life. But had he meant she wouldn't be a part of his life because he didn't really want her there in the end, or was it just guilt that made him say such things?

Was it real love he felt for her or lust?

She supposed she couldn't know any of these things without asking him, or at least without some serious knowledge about his spiritual state, but she wasn't really sure if that meant reviewing her past observations or moving forward with future observations.

If only she had someone to discuss this with! But she felt strongly that her mother wouldn't have grace for this situation anyway—she'd tell Ivy to run while she was still free. Nettie might have more grace. Regardless, Ivy didn't have access to either of them.

So she paced, tried not to cry, and felt helpless against these revelations that she had not expected—that she wasn't even sure she fully understood, for this was so far removed from her realm of experience.

In the end, she supposed, the question was simple: was his past too great to allow him to have a present with her?

"Ivy?" Aunt Daphne stood in the entryway to the parlor, removing her hat as she gave Ivy a rather skeptical side eye. "What is it now?"

Her pacing suspended, Ivy turned to face Violet's aunt, and tears flooded her vision. She hiccupped and dropped her face in her hands.

"Surely it's not as bad as all that." Aunt Daphne gestured for her to take a seat on the settee before lowering herself next to Ivy and placing a firm arm around her waist. "Tell me."

It all came out in panting sobs and half-smothered whimpers. She was in love with Jordy and he with her, but she wasn't sure. She just wasn't sure. She was Ivy, so already a relationship with him was significantly more complicated than it would have been otherwise. Adding in their obvious personality differences ... and now *this* ... how could God's will be in this relationship?

But Ivy wasn't ready to walk away. She didn't think she could, in fact. Well, perhaps she could, physically, but she'd be leaving a lot of herself behind, and she knew that.

Then there was that other part of her that knew that God had brought her to Scotland. She didn't believe He would bring her here just to experience heartbreak. Though she knew His bringing her here just to find a man was far-fetched, and perhaps not the most noble-sounding reason, stranger things had happened.

To say, however, that she had found God's plan for her in Jordy was wrong. Over the course of her time in Keefmore, she'd done things she never would have thought herself capable of. She'd played piano in front of dozens of strangers, spoken up in a group of women she knew by names only, assisted Jordy in his practice, and made new friends.

And, though she adored Jordy and though she longed to make him a permanent part of her life, she'd found so much fulfillment here at Keefmore that the calling was as much to the community as to him.

Yet she was still unsure.

"What do I do?" she finished with, body hunched over, cried out and talked out until all she wanted to do was cease existing for just a minute—or wash her face and have a cup of tea. Either way. "I love him, but what ... what do I do?"

"Well." Aunt Daphne leaned back and placed her hands, palm upwards, on her lap. "Let me tell you a story."

"All right." Stories, in Ivy's limited experience, always helped.

"When I wasn't much older than you, my sister got married, and she immediately turned my life into a personalized torture chamber," Aunt Daphne said, her tone rather void of emotion. "In her opinion, I was everything I oughtn't to be. She convinced me to move in with her and her husband—when Violet was coming, actually—and, to my eternal regret, I did it. While I was there, she introduced me to man after man, tried to convince me to put my all into making a 'good match,' and basically spent six months tormenting me. At last, I met Roger. Roger and I were kindred spirits, you know. He was a satisfactory match, but nothing like my sister had hoped for—she wanted to use my marriage to leverage her own social position, I suppose.

"But I married Roger nonetheless—and then found out he'd had past affairs that he'd neglected to tell me about. It broke my heart, loving him as I did, and then knowing that forever in his memory there'd be other women. Now, by this time, I'd managed to become a Christian—and Roger, too—which is an entirely different story, but it's why he told me the truth in the first place, because we had both dedicated our lives to Christ together, and he felt he needed to confess it. I hadn't been a Christian growing up, really, as I considered it all to be sentimental hogwash, but I'd still considered myself a good person, and I thought Roger was one, too, so I judged him very harshly. I told him I wasn't sure how I felt about that sin being a part of his life."

Ivy frowned. She could never not forgive Jordy in that case, if they were bound by marriage vows, but that was a very different situation from what she was experiencing.

"I can see from the look on your face that you're judging me for judging him, my husband." Aunt Daphne arched an eyebrow. "Let me tell you the rest. I did forgive him, and we did have a wonderful, happy marriage filled with many adventures and much contentment. We eventually ended up moving to the Continent, as you know, where we were away from the restrictions of society, and we worked in orphanages and helped people ... We made much of our lives, simply put. But all that aside, for it is yet another string of different stories, we moved beyond his past. However, I wouldn't minimize the fact that it was something we had to *move beyond*. We like to pretend, as Christians, that once we ask for forgiveness and turn to Christ, all the consequences of sin are erased. Really, the only consequence that just disappears is eternal condemnation. The rest remain—we must turn to God and seek His will in addressing them."

Ivy swallowed. She didn't want that to be true, though, because she wanted it to be over for Jordy. Still, she listened, because she must know.

"What I'm trying to say to you is that it may be very true that Jordy has progressed beyond these sins in his life. However, it is also true that nothing can erase his past. He is a saved man, a man being constantly sanctified by Christ, if he told you the truth—which, based on what I know of him, he did. He seems to be a man of honor now. But know that if you start this relationship, Jordy has already violated it before it began. He has already betrayed you, and he has already shown that a struggle with sexual immorality is a part of his life. That is a sin he will face again, one way or another, and he will have to be committed to fighting it. These things don't just go away."

"So you think he is not recovered." In which case, how could she ever trust him?

"I wouldn't say that, no. But I would say that it is a travesty to deal with the issue lightly, to just say, 'Oh well, God has covered that!' when in reality, the effects remain. He has touched other women. That's not going away. I don't care if the world makes light of it, which it sometimes does in certain circles. I don't care about the circumstances. Jordy must be responsible."

Which meant Ivy couldn't be with him, then?

Aunt Daphne cleared her throat. "But if there's healing for all other sins, there is healing for this one. If he is committed to being faithful to you and to God, and if he understands that this is going to have an effect on any future he has with you, then allowing him to pursue you wouldn't be a mistake. You just must be aware that he will have to guard his heart—and, perhaps, from time to time, you will be called upon to remind him of that." Aunt Daphne rose. "There. I think I've given you all you could need. Come to me when you decide what you want to do."

Ivy took a deep breath and let it out slowly. Though Aunt Daphne's words had been clarifying, she honestly did need some quiet time to pray and seek answers. She slipped up to her room, closed the door, and dropped facedown on her bed.

Oh, Lord, what do I do?

CHAPTER TWENTY-TWO

It was close to midnight when Jordy arrived at the McAllens' farm. He'd had a last-minute call out to a neighboring property to check on a little boy who'd come down with a mysterious illness that turned out to be "eating too many biscuits."

He was ready to collapse when he made it up to the loft. To his surprise, there was a lantern still burning. He climbed in and blinked. Ben sat on the edge of his pallet with a stick of wood and a small knife.

"Wha' are ye doin' up at this hour?" Jordy heaved himself over the side. "Mick asleep?"

Ben didn't even glance up from his carving. "Aye."

"An' ye didna answer me question."

Ben grunted. "Waitin' for ye."

Jordy dropped onto his pallet and began pulling off his boots. "Why would ye do tha', Ben?"

"Because ye need tae talk tae Miss Ivy, an' ye dinna seem tae be doin' it on yer own."

Jordy paused, then tore off his second boot. "Tha's quite interestin'. An' what would I be talkin' wi' Miss Ivy about, Ben?"

Ben didn't say a thing. Jordy raised his eyes to his brother's face. They stared at each other silently for a few moments; Jordy was the one who looked away first.

"Ye could just tell her tha' ye love her, ye ken. Why isna it her decision? I thought tha' was always what Da told us. Let th' lass have th' say."

Jordy blinked. It was unlike Ben to speak much, let alone in complete sentences. Even more so in a somewhat confrontational manner.

"I see th' way she looks at ye." Ben shook his head. "If I had a lass lookin' at me tha' way, I'd marry her on th' spot. An' dinna tell me ye havena noticed; she's no' hidin' it—an' neither are ye, for tha' matter. Why dinna ye ask her if she's willin'? It isna in us Scots tae play games and fool about."

Jordy's chest tightened. No, he didn't want to play games. He wanted to settle things; that was right. But he wasn't a consistent man on the inside. His heart was always chasing a daydream, and goodness knew he was having a hard time winning the favor of the folks of Keefmore.

Besides, given his past, it was unlikely Ivy would even want him at this point.

He struggled with the right words to express it all. Especially without revealing his past to his younger brother. "I canna offer her a forever." That was true enough.

Ben cocked his head. "Ye dinna need tae. Ye only need tae offer her yerself an' a promise tae care for her as God allows ye tae."

Jordy took a deep breath. "An' what if I'm no' enough for her? What if I stray? What if I lose me patients an' canna support her?"

"Th' Good Lord promises tae help ye be th' man ye need tae be for whatever day He brings ye." A small smile flickered over Ben's face. "Have ye even tried talkin' tae God about this? Or are ye tae afraid He'll smack ye upside th' head with somethin' like, 'marry her an' have six bairns an' let Me mind th' rest'?"

"I'm no' afraid o' what God has for me," Jordy mumbled. "I ken it's a good thing. But it isna *Ivy*. God would never—"

"As soon as we start sayin' 'God wouldna' or 'God couldna,' God shows us tha' He can an' will."

"Ye dinna ken th' whole truth." Jordy glanced at Mick's sleeping figure and then leaned toward Ben. Might as well squash his belief in

Jordy's goodness now rather than let him stumble upon it years later. "I've ... I've no' been a moral man, an' I did tell her this. I imagine noo she willna want a thing tae do wi' me. An' nae more she should! Ben, I've ... I've lain wi' women. In London, years ago, but all th' same, I ken it's still wi' me. I canna erase it from me life. God has taken th' black mark out o' me record, but He canna completely remove th' memories. Those will always be wi' me. Wha' woman wants tae enter a relationship tha' has already betrayed her before it began?"

Ben didn't say anything for a long moment, and Jordy dropped his head into his hands. Now he'd done it. Ben would never respect him again.

"A'right. Canna say I didna wonder, as I think we all saw a change in ye from tha' first year on. First, th' bad change—an' then, Jordy, th' good one." Ben's words were quiet but firm. "Mum an' Da still talk about it. 'We could see when he really accepted his faith,' they say. I dinna think they ken th' full story, nae, but they ken th' change. An' tha's wha' God sees."

Surprised, Jordy faced his brother. "I—"

"I ken ye believe this, tae, Jordy: God's forgiven ye. An', nae, ye canna expect others tae. An' I'm glad ye ken there's a consequence attached tae sin. No' everyone seems tae. Shouldna th' final decision lie wi' Ivy? I can see tha' ye've spoken tae her about th' issue, but did ye give her th' option? If ye've faced yer sins, if ye are committed, and if this is truly in th' past an' no' th' present, why canna ye have a relationship wi' her? Why canna ye accept God's grace? At th' very least, give her th' choice."

"But—"

"But ...?"

To his surprise, Jordy had no response. It was hard being hit by conviction as heavy as a grand piano. He sat staring at the wall for he didn't know how long after Ben's words. Then he bent his head and pulled his boots back on.

"Ye goin' tae pray on it?" Ben asked.

"Aye."

"Dinna make tae much noise if ye come in before morn."

•

CHAPTER TWENTY-THREE

Ivy." Agnes's soft voice was heard through the door, and Ivy set her Bible aside.

"Yes?"

"Dr. McAllen is here and asked to see you. He wondered if you would take a walk with him."

"Oh." So it was time, then. What would Jordy say to her? During a sleepless night full of tears and wordless cries, she'd come to wish she'd stayed, seen the discussion through. But it was too late for that.

Now she had a few clarifying questions to ask—if he was willing to tell her, and if he wanted to pursue her. It seemed, based on what he'd said yesterday, that he didn't. On the other hand, if he didn't, why was he here? Perhaps to try to patch up their friendship—but if there was only friendship between them, he didn't owe her explanations. She wasn't going to ask them of him.

She rose and checked her reflection in the mirror—she wasn't going to pretend for a minute, not even for her own conscience, that she didn't want to look pretty for him—before pulling a shawl over her shoulders and leaving behind the comfort of her room.

Jordy stood in the foyer, hat in hand, looking properly chastened. "Vee."

"Jordy." She smiled, because she did like seeing him and because she didn't want him to think she was angry. She was, sort of—she was angry about the sin, angry that they even had to have this discussion, for his serious face told her it would be a *discussion* and not just a *chat.* However, she was also glad—everlastingly glad, if he had told her the truth--that it was in his past and not his present, for she knew her answer to *that* immediately. He would have to be out of her life for a very long time, if not forever, if such weren't the case.

"Will ye walk wi' me a bit, Vee?"

"Yes, of course, Jordy." She made short work of the remainder of the stair steps and reached for his arm, then drew back, uncertain. Perhaps that could wait.

He gestured toward the door. "Let's go noo."

"All right."

The first few minutes were conducted in awkward, painful silence as Jordy refused to speak and Ivy bit her lips to keep herself from rushing to his defense before he got a chance to. She wasn't even sure what she needed out of this conversation. She'd come to peace with the past, but a few clarifications would be nice, and the rest lay with him. Did he want her enough to fight for her, or didn't he? Did he think she was worthy of his pursuit, or didn't he? That was up to Jordy, not to her.

"I dinna ken where tae begin." His shoulders slumped, and Ivy was hard-pressed not to take his hand. "I've told ye th' story, but Ben believes I've told it wi' verra little grace. Perhaps he's right. I do see things as verra black an' white, especially as concerns meself. It's no' like ... Have ye heard tha' one quote Vi likes so much? Wha' is it —'Life's one long ...'?"

"'Life is one long struggle in the dark.'" Ivy shook her head emphatically even as she used both hands to push misbehaving strands of hair, caught by the cold wind, behind her ears. "No, it's not like that at all. We live in a sinful world but are filled with a greater God. We can expect to suffer but not exclusively."

"Right." He sighed. "An', Vee, perhaps I'd rather suffer. Th' more I force meself tae pay for wha' God has already paid for, th' more I can justify me own savin' grace—but tha's no' th' right way o' it at all. I'm no' a Christian because I'm holy, because I did anythin' right, because I'm any different from anyone else. I'm a Christian because Jesus Christ was holy, because He did everythin' right, because He was different from everyone else. If I'm tae consider meself covered by His blood an' redeemed—if He offers me th' chance tae beg ye tae consider me, even as I am—why should I run? Why am I tryin' tae save ye from wha' God has brought us? I couldna bend yer will if I wanted tae, so all I've tae do is act wi' honesty an' courage."

At the top of a hill, Ivy paused because she couldn't walk and think and hear him all at once, so something needed to stop, and it might as well be her trembling body. There was so much to be said to him, so much she was proud of him for, so much she wanted to affirm. "Jordy—"

"Let me finish first. Then ye can reject me or no' as ye see fit. But let me tell ye wha' I've been thinkin'." He turned to face her, placed a light hand on her arm more to guide her to look at him than in restraint. "Ivy, ye ken everythin' about me sins tha' I can think ye would need tae ken. If ye need tae ken more, I think it would be better done in preparation for a deeper relationship. I promise ye I have spoken th' truth. I'm saved by grace. Christ is an' always will be me life, an' anythin' I do should reflect tha'. I willna say I'll never sin again—though I would hope I'd no' sin in tha' way again. I do ken tha' I'll always face th' same battles, but wi' God on me side, I feel confident I can win them." He straightened his shoulders then, and she felt rather than saw the life go back into him, a sort of subtle shift that told her more than words ever could about where his strength lay.

"Which, I think, brings me to *us*. Ye must ken tha' I've wanted ye for some time. Ever since I saw ye in London, tha' first time when ye were a wee thing, I've thought ye were th' loveliest woman I'd ever seen, an' me opinion has no' changed. I could ignore tha', Ivy, an' I wouldna have this discussion if tha' were all, but I feel a deeper connection tae ye than I ever have tae anyone else in me life. We'll need tae talk about all sorts o' things—homes an' children an' ... But we'd find it oot if we were tae court. Which is wha' I'm askin' o' ye— no' tae be me wife, though tha's what I want more than anythin'. I feel sure o' ye, but for yer sake, an' because o' yer parents, an' because I believe I can show ye better wi' more time how faithful I can be ..." He paused and swallowed.

"*Jordy.*" Her heart was brimming, and she wanted to say more, but she wasn't sure of the words. Ideas flew about, everything from reassurances to a few stray questions, but they didn't come.

They didn't need to come, for from down the hill, she heard, "Dr. Jordy! Dr. Jordy!"

They turned together to find Bridget barreling her way up the hill, balancing precariously with one outheld hand, the other still in a sling. Mairi was close on her heels.

"Mum's havin' her babe!" Bridget paused, one hand on her hip, and panted out the words. "Can ye come?"

Jordy shook his head and cleared his throat, his whole body shuddering. He definitely didn't appreciate the interruption, even if his reaction was subtle. "Doesna she have th' midwife an' Mrs. Abernathy?"

"Nae." Bridget's eyes were wide. "Weel, th' midwife will come soon, but Mrs. Abernathy had tae visit someone oot o' town, an' Mum doesna think th' babe will wait tae come until she's back. She says she wants two folks tae be there—dinna ken th' rest. Will ye come, Dr. Jordy?"

Jordy glanced at Ivy, a somewhat annoyed expression on his face, before facing Bridget again. "Aye, I'll come. Vee, come wi' me, an' if we have some time, ye can sit wi' Ena while I get me bag. But I want tae see tha' she's a'right first—dreadful hard tae predict babes sometimes."

Ivy nodded and followed along, trying desperately to keep up as his pace was rather quick and Bridget was running on ahead, looking about to trip and fall on her head as she cantered back through the village. Though her thoughts and feelings were jumbled Ivy wonder if it was possible Ena had only called Jordy to show her support for him, given Ivy's request, but perhaps Ena also just wanted Jordy. It was possible, after all.

They arrived at the shop and hurried through the front to the home behind. Ena was sitting in a chair by the fire with a cup of tea and a book.

"I told Bridie no' tae rush ye, but I supposed tha' was a lost cause." She smiled wryly. "Th' babe will come when it likes, an' tha' willna be for many more hours. This evenin', I think." She paused and picked up a small journal from the side table. "If ye'd like tae see, doctor, I'm a professional noo—I write down everythin'. Mostly so as I have somethin' tae do."

"Hmm ..." Jordy accepted the journal and glanced down it. "Still early labor, then? Ye dinna feel it's movin' along?"

Ena shook her head. "Nae, an' I ken Bridget dramatizes ... Here. Bridie! Mairi!"

The girls, who had been lingering in the shop, burst in. "Mum, are ye—?"

"Shush, Bridie. I'm fine. I must send ye away until th' babe comes —'tis better tha' way, so as ye can rest yer mind. I'm no' in any bad pain, really."

Even Ivy was skeptical of that. She stood to the side of the room, wishing she could run and yet not knowing where to go or how she could bear to leave. Ena seemed calm as always, but her friend had gone through a lot without a whimper. Ivy had heard that childbirth was one of the worst things in life. Her mother had certainly never spoken positively of it the few times she'd mentioned the secret and much-whispered-about event. So the dread filled Ivy like a heavy bass clef chord, and she shuddered to think what must come.

In no time, both of the girls were running off to Mairi's folks, and Jordy was chatting lightly with Ena about her plans for the rest of the day—where the bedroom was located, if she wanted the midwife to be in charge, and other things related to the birth that Ivy didn't really understand. And, overwrought as she already was, Ivy sank deeper and deeper into a panic.

"A'right. I'll leave ye tae send a message home an' collect me things. Th' midwife will like as no' beat me here, but, Vee, could ye stay wi' Ena while I'm gone? I'll be back in a quarter o' an' hour."

Never before had she been so overcome by paralyzing fear, but she forced the word out: "Yes."

"Good." And, without so much as asking if she needed any parting advice, Jordy turned and left.

Ena glanced at her husband's watch, which Ivy now saw was tucked into the blanket next to her, then scratched away at her journal for a moment. This accomplished, she turned to Ivy, looked her up and down, and grinned. "Ivy, rest easy. Here. Sit an' take a deep breath. Or go pour yerself some tea, if ye've a mind tae." She gestured toward the kitchen at the back. "Ye willna be deliverin' this babe, if tha's yer fear. Truly, it's early on. Ye can see me journal—ten minnas at th' closest. When th' pains are tha' far apart, I ken I dinna have tae worry. Ach, other women will go from early labor tae delivered faster than ye can blink, but I just dinna. No' for me first, me second, or me third, an' this is th' fourth. It's like tae be at least 'til the evenin', but if th' babe takes 'til th' middle o' th' night, I willna be surprised. Ye have nae idea how jealous I am o' women whose babes come fast! Though at least me births are easy. Nothin' has ever gone wrong—I just have tae bear up for a considerable amount o' time!"

Somehow this didn't make Ivy feel any better, but she managed to force her legs to move to the offered chair and her knees to bend and allow her to sit. She dug her fingernails into the palms of her hands and tried to appear unaffected, searching Ena's face for any sign of what was happening and how it was happening and how she might help.

"Take a breath noo! I'm glad ye're here, Ivy. It's hard waitin', especially if I've nae place tae put me mind. Ye were wi' Jordy?"

Before she could stop herself, Ivy flushed. Not that she'd ever really been able to stop her cheeks from doing just about whatever they wanted, but she still wished she'd been able to look away or tone down her reaction. "Yes ... We were ... talking."

Ena raised her eyebrows. "Dinna stop there! Yer one job right noo is tae entertain me, so ye'd better deliver. Wha' were ye an' Jordy talkin' about tha' made ye blush like a schoolgirl?"

At those words, Ivy found that the simmering heat managed to ignite into a bonfire to rival those of the All Hallow's Eve celebration. "It was ..." Complicated yet turning, through much discord, into a harmony she could follow. "He told me yesterday that he'd ..." Should she tell Ena? Sudden restraint fell over her heart. No, not without Jordy's permission. "He shared something with me about himself that frightened me, and I didn't know what to say. But he also said ..." What had he said, exactly? Not that he loved her, but it had been more than implied. "He seemed to think we might become something ... something *special* to each other." That was all the more she could commit to without him saying the rest.

"I see." Ena tapped her chin. "I wondered—ach, wait a minna." She snatched up the journal and the pocket watch again. "Hmm. No' much difference. Aye, we'll be here all day. Lovely. Wha' I was goin' tae say is, I wonder if tha' was th' way things were goin'. I see th' way he looks at ye—ach, everyone in Keefmore must. An' ye're no' exactly a closed book, either."

Ivy hadn't realized there was anything to see. However—and she took a deep breath, steadied herself, tried to calm the whirling notes colliding with each other in her head—that was how she'd imagined it would be. Heart on her sleeve, nothing to hide. In love. Truly and unashamedly in love.

Lord God, how can this be?

"After th' babe comes, for I canna quite release Dr. McAllen tae ye 'til then, ye must speak tae him. Tell him how ye feel, tae. Men are never bright enough tae see wha' is beneath their noses, an' then tae say it. Besides, nae man wants tae commit tae sharin' his heart tae a woman he's no' sure o'. Should he? Ach, aye. But ye can make it easy on him once in a while."

Make it easy on him? Oh, Ivy could do that. There was nothing that would delight her more. But should she tell him the truth that was bubbling everywhere inside her? Was this a relationship she could thrive in? The what-ifs circled about her mind again, taunting her with their unanswerability.

She heard the squeak of the door to the shop. A moment later, Jordy entered the room and set his frightening black bag down and started talking to Ena about more that Ivy purposefully chose not to listen to. She soon escaped to make sure Bridget was well settled with some friends, and then to go home, for there wasn't much she could do for Ena, unfortunately.

After a quick report to Aunt Daphne, she slipped into her room and laid on the bed, face pressed into the pillow. There were different emotions coursing through her than had existed when she'd last lain here, but they were equally as overwhelming.

Prayers felt almost irrelevant, but that was just a feeling, so she ignored it and prayed anyway. Yet, somewhere between the early hours of the morning and now, a simple confirmation had slipped into her soul, and she knew before she asked.

Yes.

It wasn't a confirmation she felt boldly, but it teased at the corners of her mind and didn't allow her to consider any other choice. *Yes.* Yes to Jordy, if he should allow her the opportunity to say the word in connection to their relationship.

But how could she give him the proper encouragement?

A kind of peace stole over her when she asked that question, and she knew she wouldn't have to encourage him. Because if a man like Jordy wanted her, really wanted her, there would be no need for her to give him the extra push.

"Trifle?"

Ivy had been too wrapped up in her thoughts to hear the door, assuming Violet hadn't just floated through the wall, and she jerked and then rolled onto her back. "Violet. I didn't hear you come in."

"Mm." Her friend drifted across the floor and flopped down on the bed. "You spoke with Jordy?"

"Yes."

"And ...?"

Ivy swallowed. "Violet, did you know ...?"

Violet nodded. "I think I know what's bothered you, and, yes, I've known since it happened. *It* being, of course, our dear doctor's sinful activities while at medical school."

Ivy frowned. Of course Violet wouldn't treat it with the seriousness it deserved. "Please don't make light of it. Surely you can see how much guilt it brings him. What kind of friends would we be if we don't take it seriously?"

Violet shrugged. "Trifle, the reason he told you is because he wants you to be more than friends. Let's not ignore that part of the conversation in favor of discussing how seriously I ought to take this. Did he tell you he loves you?"

Ivy wasn't sure if that really was so much to the point as the discussion of Violet's immediate reactions. Her tone had been concerning, after all, and Ivy hated to leave any matter unaddressed. She shook her head. "Not exactly."

"What did he say?"

"That he was sorry for what he'd done but that he believed God could have grace for even his worst failings. And that ... that I was lovely." She felt her cheeks go hot. "I think he did mean that he loved me, and I think he will ask for my hand."

Violet wrinkled her nose. "How touching. And how will you answer the dear lad?"

"I think I'll give it." She glanced sideways and caught her friend's eye. "Violet, I'm in love with him. I trust him more than anyone. But what do you think? You know us both best. Is there any reason why I shouldn't ... Why we shouldn't ... That is ..." Words faded, and she sighed. "Oh, Violet, this is such a big thing. I feel as if every other action I've ever considered has been small; this one triumphs. What shall I do?"

"I can't tell you that." Then, a small smile formed at the corner of Violet's mouth. "I would like you to be happy, actually. Regardless of what that looks like. I suppose that's not the most godly statement— though I'm sure you'd ramble on about God's love and joy and suchlike, I'm not so convinced that Christianity is the fastest path to personal contentment. But I know you'll consider the religious angles, and so will Jordy, for he's been remarkably pious all his life—and it's been real for the last half a dozen years or so, too. Much like your faith. So you've no need to worry there. But when it comes to happiness, that oh-so-human, oh-so-frail emotion, I'd like you to grasp at it, Ivy, for it is fleeting. If Jordy can give you that ..." She shrugged. "Why not?"

Ivy smothered a small laugh. Violet always had the oddest ideas, ones that Ivy must, at some point, confront. Perhaps now, however, she could be a little selfish and leave them unremarked upon. "I think I understand what you're getting at. And I wasn't asking to be happy—but he could make me happy, and more than that, he could chase joy with me, even when happiness flees. And I know it will—I'm not that naïve. I understand that pursuing this would be difficult for both of us. But he's a joy-chaser, if ever I saw one. I want to be one—and I am, at times. Chasing joy is really just pursuing Christ in everything you do. Which is what I'd like to see you do, too." Apparently she couldn't refrain from making some little nod to Violet's well-being. But her love for Violet was that of a sister, and she couldn't give up on her, ever. Not even for a moment. It'd be like giving up on a part of her own self.

"I see what you mean, Trifle." Yet Violet's expression informed her that she wouldn't probably heed Ivy's suggestion. "Yes, Jordy will pursue his joy."

"God's joy." Ivy bit her lips. How could she communicate what she meant? "I don't know if you quite understand, Violet, but that's what I'm looking for. Do you really think he's not recovered? You've made some rather dour comments."

"I think he's corruptible."

That was fair. "We're all corruptible, though, aren't we? If you only mean that to say we could sin again. But he's committed to Christ. Surely you can see that."

Violet hesitated, then nodded. "Yes ... yes, I can see that. He definitely has a fervor for his faith. You've both gotten far and away ahead of me in that area."

Ivy's heart softened, and she took her friend's hand and squeezed it. "It's not a competition, Violet. We all have a different path. But I know God will save you if you give Him the chance, so I hope for better things."

"Yes, well." Violet jerked away and stood. "Never mind that. So you're in love with Jordy, and you're convinced you ought to marry him. Then do. No hesitations. I know you. If you had doubts, they would be all-encompassing. All I'm seeing is fear, and, Trifle, there's no need to give in to that. It's clear God isn't nudging you elsewhere."

Ivy closed her eyes, then opened them and took a deep breath. "You're right. It is just fear."

"Then you'll take him?"

She flushed. "He's got to offer first, Vi."

"He will." Violet flopped back on the bed and wrapped her arms around herself, hands fidgeting nervously. "Yes, he will."

CHAPTER TWENTY-FOUR

The next morning was a repeat of the one before in some ways. The difference was that Ivy had been sleeping in the parlor, having drifted off trying to decide if she was within her rights to walk over and see how Ena was getting along—or if the little Owen babe had made an appearance yet. She'd only woken and stumbled upstairs to wash her face in the cold water on her bedside table half an hour ago when Jordy knocked on the front door—and this time she answered instead of Agnes.

"Jordy."

He grinned, though there were dark circles under his eyes. "Up most th' night, an' then I slept in me office. I'm no' tae early, am I?"

"No. I don't think anyone else is up, but I was awake. Is Ena ...?"

"Perfectly healthy, an' so is her wee lad." He rolled his shoulders. "He's a beautiful babe. She'll call him Alastair."

"Oh, how sweet!" She thought that was, perhaps, the Gaelic Alexander, if Gaelic was even the right term. She'd have to ask—but later.

"Ye can come see him, but I want tae talk tae ye first. Will ye walk with me?" He smirked. "I suppose ye'd agreed tae do tha' yesterday, an' then we were somewhat theatrically interrupted."

"Yes, of course." She flushed. "I ... I would be delighted to walk with you, Jordy."

"Verra formal. Verra ladylike." He winked and extended his arm. Despite his claims of exhaustion, his energy had apparently revived—

251

perhaps after having done the job he was best suited for, even called to. She supposed she'd noticed that: the raising moods whenever his focus was more on others. A brilliant testimonial to self-sacrifice.

She took his arm, and he led her out into Aunt Daphne's garden and then beyond.

"Where are we going?" She didn't ask because she didn't trust him but rather out of curiosity, and she felt warm with that realization. Even her father couldn't take her to an undetermined location without a scattering of questions, but Jordy was different. With Jordy, it didn't matter.

"Never ye mind."

And, again, no fear despite the mysteriousness. Hesitantly, rather *mezzo piano* in nature, the music came back. She squeezed his arm slightly, frightened by her own boldness but confident when he placed his hand over hers for a moment.

They made their way to the other side of Keefmore, which wasn't much of a walk, and then up a small hill with a path cutting through the grass.

"'Tis me family's land," he said. "Da moves some o' his ewes down here during th' height o' lambin', an' Ben an' Mick mind them. It helps tae separate some oot."

"Oh." Why show her this?

"Ye see, I'd been intendin' tae live at th' office, but tha' wouldna do if ... Let me start over." He paused and turned to face her; finding her standing close, he stepped back. "Wee bit o' space—'tisn't ideal, but I need it. There. Ivy, ye're a woman in a million, an' I brought ye oot here because ... Ach, nae." This time, he grabbed her arm and half-jogged up the path, dragging her after him.

She squeaked but managed to get her feet under her as he pulled her the last few steps up the hill and then down into a small valley.

There was a cottage sitting in the nook there, badly out of repair as far as she could tell. There was certainly a cave-in in the thatched roof, and the door was hanging at an angle.

"We dinna really use it—but it'd do. For a start, I mean."

Her breath caught. Did he mean what she thought he meant? "Jordy—"

"Nae. Dinna speak. I ken it's ugly as anythin'. But think. Use yer imagination, like ye do when ye're reading. Tear off th' thatch an' have a real, right roof an' a chimney tha' wasna fallin' off, new doors an' windows, an' o' course we'd add a fence an' ye could have yer own wee garden—tha's important, aye? I think I'd tear out th' east wall an' add a bedroom—there is one, but no' one ye'd have a lady in. It'd be a big job, almost nigh tae buildin' a new house. An' it'd only do for a few years, 'til we were more settled—but ye ken it's a start. An' if I have this tae work on, we could have time tae figure a few things out—I ken I'll be impatient if I dinna have a reason tae wait. An' we would have tae wait ..." He stopped again. "But this isna a proposal. Ach, nae. No' in so many words. I just wanted tae show ye ... show ye wha' I meant. For I could make a nice life for ye, an' I ken ye well enough tae ken tha' it'd be important tae have a nice life, though ye willna care about th' money. Ye'll just need yer own place, an' safety, an' a home. An' I ken tha'—I need ye tae ken I ken tha'."

Harsh breaths kept Ivy from replying, but she kept her eyes glued to his face. At first, his own eyes were all over the cottage—but before she knew it, he'd turned and looked at her, and she wasn't able to think—only to take him in and thank God he was here and holding her up or else she might've fallen.

His fingers tightened over hers. "I suppose I want ye tae ken tha' I've fallen for ye. I'm in love with ye, Miss Ivy Knight, an' if ye will take a risk wi' me, if ye will let me court ye properly, then I'd like ye tae ken I'm a serious suitor. I would marry ye tomorrow, but tha' wouldna be safe for either o' us, so instead, I'm askin' ye tae work toward it with me—tae tell yer parents ye have a man fightin' for ye, an' tae hear wha' they say, an' tae ... tae see where this takes us. Ivy, I love ye. Do ye think there's any chance—" Then, again, he stopped speaking and squinted at her. "It's made ye cry."

Indeed, her cheeks were wet with tears. She scrambled for a handkerchief, sniffling and hiccupping, and found one pressed into her hands. Tears, yes, but accompanied by the final movement of Bach's *Violin Sonata III in C Major*—hectic but happy. It was almost audible to her; could Jordy feel it, too?

"Thought tha' might be necessary," he mumbled. "Vee, if ye feel ye need tae say 'nae' an' ask me tae leave, I willna blame ye. This is all up tae ye. I can leave, an'—" He rambled on, nonsense words about how she was under no obligation to him, and he understood her reticence, and of course he wasn't much when it came to husband material, and on and on, the most horrid words anyone had ever said.

He thought she was crying because she didn't want this? How could he say that to her? "Jordy, no! No, no, no." She finished wiping her eyes and shoved his handkerchief into the pocket of her dress before placing a hand on his arm and meeting his eyes. "Jordy, I ... Why would I cry if I didn't feel anything for you? Really. Why would I?"

He raised his eyebrows. "Given th' things I've seen ye cry about—"

"All right, maybe I do cry easily." That was fair enough. "But, Jordy, that's not why now. I ... I just can't believe God would bless me this way. I can't." There, now she'd gotten to crying again. She drew out the handkerchief and hiccupped into it, chest heaving with the extent of the emotions she was rather inefficiently trying to contain. "Jordy, I ... I love you ... too."

Through the tears, she caught his smile, and then she was pressed against his chest, still sobbing and probably making a mess, but he held her close nonetheless. She felt his body shudder with laughter, and she wanted to push back and hit him for the insolence, but it wasn't really worth it.

"So will scarin' me out o' me wits be a daily thing or ...?" Jordy whispered the words into her hair. "I'm just tryin' tae set realistic expectations here."

She laughed then and shook her head. "No. I won't mean to scare you, at least."

"Then tha's 'yes,' isna it?" he murmured, rubbing her back. "'Yes, Jordy, I'd like ye tae come see me an' court me an' love me.' Or am I wrong again?"

"You're right." She sighed and held him as tight as she could manage. "Yes, that's exactly what I'd like."

"We're goin' tae have a lot tae explain tae yer parents."

Heavens. She wasn't even going to think about that yet—let that problem worry about itself. How would Mother and Papa feel about Jordy? No. That thought could wait. "I think they'll understand."

"A'right. So it's just ye an' me for noo." He gently disentangled her fingers and stepped back. "I canna believe I tried tae propose, sort o', an' then made ye cry instead. Tha's another thing we'll have tae work on. I canna be makin' ye cry all th' time."

Ivy shrugged. She'd tell him later, when she'd found the right rhythm for the newness, that it simply couldn't be avoided. "How long do we have to court before it can be an actual proposal?" The last five minutes had been too long already.

"See? A woman after me own heart." He chuckled and took her hand. "Let's sit an' talk tha' out a bit. I was thinkin' th' same thing, but, Vee, we canna rush this."

She agreed—and disagreed. There was a part of her that was scared out of her wits—and another part of her that just wanted Jordy, wanted a life with him, wanted to move forward quickly and carelessly. But he was right, and if Jordy—Jordy McAllen, who hardly ever looked before he leaped in all her experience with him—was committed to being cautious, it would be quite strange if Ivy were the one who objected to that.

So she sat next to him on the grassy hillside and put her head on his shoulder, and he talked about cottages and money and a lot of other things that she didn't really care about right now. Because, in her heart was the constant refrain, drowning all other thoughts and feelings—*he loves me, he loves me, he loves me.*

Inordinately blessed, Ivy leaned against Jordy and looked out over Keefmore and let herself daydream.

A Note to the Reader

Dear Reader, thank you so much for reading my novel! I had a lot of fun writing it and even more fun rewriting it. It's since become one of my favorite stories, and I am thrilled to finally be able to share it with the general public.

Ivy and Jordy's story is one close to my heart for a number of reasons. I understand feeling a lack of worth in oneself. I understand the long years of depression and anxiety this can cause. I understand being disappointed in those you love—and then coming to love them again as humans. I also understand feeling like you've disappointed yourself, like there's no turning back to the person you used to be. I understand the loss of innocence, and I understand that in the end, there is grace for even what, to our all-too-human minds, seems like the deadliest of sins.

This book wasn't originally the tale it became as I grew and matured. Originally published in October 2018, the book began as a simple tale of a girl's struggle for identity and belonging. At the time, as a somewhat younger teenaged author, I thought the title, *Beyond Her Calling*, quite fitting and clever.

I have actually since regretted the decision, but unfortunately, this book is now forever-branded as *Beyond Her Calling*—or BHC, as I call it when I'm being lazy. Now, I've realized that, as my husband puts it, "You can't go beyond your calling." A calling is there, and it's an ongoing destination, not a place you reach and move beyond.

However, I hope you readers will allow me a little leeway in this case. Though Ivy doesn't go 'beyond her calling,' literally, she finds it ... and she goes far, far beyond the expectations of her parents, sister, and other people in her life. However, 'Beyond Their Expectations' would make a clunky title.

I'm looking forward to returning to this world and these characters in book five, *A Prayer Unanswered*, which, of course, features Alice. However, there will be a book six, featuring Ivy and Jordy and Violet, *After Our Castle*.

In the meanwhile, thank you for your support, as always.

Kellyn Roth
January 2022
White Salmon, WA

Made in the USA
Columbia, SC
26 January 2022

54824091R00141